A Wreath for the Maidens

JOHN MUNONYE

HEINEMANN
London · Ibadan · Nairobi

Heinemann Educational Books
48 Charles Street, London W1X 8AH
P.M.B. 5205 Ibadan · P.O. BOX 45314 Nairobi
EDINBURGH MELBOURNE TORONTO AUCKLAND
NEW DELHI SINGAPORE HONG KONG KUALA LUMPUR
ISBN 0 435 90121 4

First published 1973

Printed in Great Britain by Cox & Wyman Ltd,
London, Reading and Fakenham

32

AFRICAN WRITERS SERIES

Founding editor · Chinua Achebe

AFRICAN WRITERS SERIES
121
A Wreath for the Maidens

To the memory of
Cy and others

Part 1

CHAPTER ONE

Hugging himself tightly and his cheeks creased, Biere focused his eyes on the ground from an angle. Then his legs began to shake. The last time he had been so upset and bitter was when Azuka died.

Biere was convinced that the boy would not have died had the doctor come over to the hospital soon after he was sent for.

Azuka had been his favourite among his brothers and sisters. Azuka would warm his meals for him, polish his shoes, prepare water for his bath, tidy his room, and follow him to places. And yet, in appearance they were very much unalike. Biere was spare in build and rather stern-looking, while Azuka was plump and of a buoyant disposition, smiling most of the time and loved by all. We were on vacation. Azuka complained of a very severe pain in the stomach, below the navel and to the right, and far worse than usual. He was taken to the hospital in a taxi. The elderly nurse on duty said it was the appendix, but that the doctor would confirm. He telephoned. Replying after the fifth call, the doctor directed that the patient's parent or relation should be advised to come and see him in his residence, which was some two miles away. By the time the doctor finally arrived at the hospital, Azuka was already unconscious. He pronounced there had been an eruption ... He would refund part of the money ... Barely four weeks had passed since then.

I was relating to him my experience in the Town Hall earlier in the day. Eduado Boga had come into the hall in full glory—resplendently white, voluminous robe edged with purple lace, and a feather fan; twenty or more stalwarts followed closely behind, most of them carrying some patently dangerous weapons. 'Eduado is our man!' the stalwarts shouted, to which he replied, waving his fan aloft like a benevolent potentate: 'You've spoken the only true word.' Then the armed escorts started bragging about their latest achievement, the gist of which was that they had despatched some younger ones, their Youth Front, to throw a bottle of acid into Kintu's face—Kintu being Eduado's most serious rival for the parliamentary seat for Oban constituency. The object was to get rid of the man before close of nominations on the following day. And although they had merely succeeded in hospitalising Kintu, it was clear they had dealt a shattering blow to his ranks. This explained the triumphant air with which they were now leading their hero into the hall. The meeting was brisk enough, right from the start. Before Eduado could walk up to the platform to address the gathering, a sizeable piece of stone went flying across, towards his face. And for the next one hour, the efficient policemen on duty were busy dispersing the assembly.

I went on to reflect: 'That's the type of thing that has come into our land! They often tell you it is an inevitable stage in the history of any nation. I can never understand what they mean by that—whether, for instance, acid-throwing is also inevitable. I may be going too far, perhaps, but our forefathers would never have done such a thing . . . This trouble started from the time the people were uprooted from their old ways of life. Not that it is wrong to modernise. My point is that they were forced to do away with the things which had bound them together for ages. And what about the substitute?'

Sensing that I was merely talking to myself, I paused; then I tried to draw him out:

'How all this is going to end I do not know!'

He looked up, at last, into my face. 'How it will end?' he repeated, a grim smile on his face. 'You should be able to guess.'

He rose with a sigh. 'See me off. . . .'

Long after he had left, I continued to reflect on his reaction to the story. He had changed of late, and radically too. Biere Ekonte! The man who had been notorious for his indifference to the affairs of the land; who would prefer to read his books and study the flowers or the sunset, uttering barely a hundred words each day. These days he was much agitated every time the issue under discussion was the inadequacies of society.

I had intended to stay in the whole of the next day. It was my Latin day; I was to revise Latin most of the day, reading perhaps some English Literature and Roman History. My plan had been to browse through the second book of Virgil's *Aeneid*. All that had to change now. I must visit Biere in the morning and try to do something about the mood in which I had put him.

When I arrived it was nearly ten o'clock. He was alone in the sitting-room, presiding over an assortment of books and magazines.

4

'What is he reading?' I asked, expansively.

'Literature,' came his reply. 'Poetry in short.'

'Latin?'

'Greek rather!' Biere had given up Latin a year ago, after the Intermediate, and was now studying for an honours degree in English. 'I bumped into Tennyson this morning.'

'Blundered would have suited me better,' I said. 'What is the theme?'

He handed the book over to me with the page still open. 'Read for yourself. Or, if you like, I can read for you.'

'Better. Go on.'

He took the book back.

He read slowly and with serious concentration:

Self-reverence, self-knowledge, self-control
These three alone lead life to sovereign power.
Yet not for power (power of herself
Would come uncall'd for) but to live by law
Acting the law we live by without fear.
And because right is right, to follow right
Were wisdom in the scorn of consequence.

He looked up again, happy, contented.

'Sounds good.' I took the book from him again. 'Tennyson has not been my poet, but I rather liked that. The inspiration of great thoughts and ideals—keep them within you. Only by so doing will you be able to face without perturbance the caprices of fortune and the inscrutable vicissitudes of life.'

'Have you heard from Edna?' I asked.

'No. But why?'

'Ruth's letter arrived soon after you had left yesterday.'

'Wherefore it follows that I should receive one?'

'Yes, since they move together and we move together, and they know our interests are more or less identical in most things.'

'To hell with the two of them!' he said seriously. 'Let's talk about more important things.'

'Like the Eduado affair of yesterday.' I watched his countenance.

5

He was quite unperturbed. 'Well, yes,' he said. 'But is there anything more to relate about it?'

'Perhaps we could go out next week to see them campaigning,' I proposed.

'Me? Go where?'

'To the town hall.'

'What for?'

'Sheer interest.'

He shook his head quickly.

'They are our countrymen, after all.'

'They are!' He managed to smile. 'As if there was a lack of countrymen here in this vicinity.'

'Anyway, I intend to go, if only for the fun of watching some of their theatricalities.'

'And listening to the putrid insincerities issuing from their lips!'

'It's said that Kanayo, the party supreme boss, will be there in person. I've always liked him for his nationalistic views.'

'I would be doing a greater service to the country by staying at home and sleeping,' was Biere's reply.

School children lined both sides of the street that led to the town hall, on one side behind the pavement and on the other behind the deep open drain. They stood chattering and jostling while their teachers, all smartly dressed, marched up and down, canes in hand. Then the sun burst out, once more, through the clouds, sending its fiery rays straight into their faces. Teachers and pupils began to murmur. Some sheltered their heads with their clasped hands, while others brushed their faces clean of sweat with crooked fingers.

Well ahead, close to the hall entrance, drums had begun to throb. There were dancers too, all fancifully attired; as yet, they were sitting on the grass lawn to the left, fanning themselves, but ready to spring to action whenever the flutist called. Behind these was another troupe, more sedate than the first in their white, cool gowns, some of them turbaned in addition. Their skin drums throbbed to a series of monosyllabic notes, weaving the beats into an uncomplicated and unrhythmic effect which rose above the noise; and their horns tooted feebly and half-heartedly. That was how it seemed to me. It was perhaps my incomprehension; I had not yet begun to appreciate the ways of all the various groups who inhabited the capital city of Oban, each group clearly distinguishable from the rest by the language they spoke and the dress they wore, as well as by the nature of their music. Fashionable people referred to them as ethnic groups.

There was yet another set of dancers, made up entirely of women, though the instrumentalists as well as the officials were men. These were already performing, rather prematurely, since the entertainment was intended primarily for the big guns who were yet to arrive. Bending down into an arc, they twisted their wrists, twirling the handkerchief in each hand; then, after some time, their waists, most conspicuous in red georgette wrappers under white blouses, began to vibrate, as if the ecstasy was confined to that region of their bodies. Finally, they started a song in praise of the great People's Independence Party, its leadership, and its ideals.

The organisers were talented producers. In the midst of the applause which followed the singing, a voice boomed through a loudspeaker:

'Who's on top?'

'P.I.P.!' came the response.

'What is P.I.P.?'

'The great party of the masses.'

'The party which will—'

'Win Independence for us.'

'And what will follow Independence?'

'We'll rule ourselves.'

'Independence means—'

'More money, more food.'

'More what?'

'More hospitals, more schools.'

'More what still? Louder!'

'More roads, more bridges.'

'Long live—'

'—People's Independence Party!'

'Vote for—'

'—People's Independence Party!'

7

A car horn blared from a distance. The notes were deep and dactylic. The crowd responded:

'P.I.P. will rule for ever!'

'Order now, everybody!' the loud-speaker sounded; there was a flurry of excitement and anxiety. The music and dancing had long stopped. The drummers and dancers now withdrew to their respective corners, from where they watched the procession which had begun to arrive.

It was a long one. First came a number of motor-cyclists, all dressed in white suits and blue berets to which were sewn the party symbol of an iroko tree, signifying both strength and wealth. They were followed by a police motorcade. Next came the local celebrities, or big corpses, as they were called, including party officials, prominent businessmen and councillors. It was difficult to see much after these had passed, for the crowd was now wild with their ovations as the core of the procession was approaching. Besides, the sun beat down furiously, and sacrilegiously, on the procession. However, I was able to identify the Mayor of Oban in his new Buick limousine with the regal identification mark, OB 1. There must have been some twelve other cars which were equally flashy and stately, each of them conveying an Honourable Minister of State. Then at the tail end of the section came the leader of the party, who was also the head of the State Government. The rear of the procession was a very mixed group which included civil servants, ministers of religion, representatives of commercial firms, both white and black, and others who had been invited to attend, or felt they ought to attend. The announcement had merely said that all other car owners should follow. Some pattern did however emerge in this group: nearly all of them rode more compact, unpretentious cars, which fact drew comments from the crowd.

'Yo—oh!' jeered the man nearest to me, who looked very needy in his torn shirt and fraying trousers.

'But why?' I wondered aloud.

'Don't you see that last one?' And he pointed at the old Minor labouring valiantly after the rest.

'Has the man committed any crime?'

'He must be a civil servant.'

8

'A teacher rather,' corrected another. 'They don't know how to take money out of their pockets. Shame on them!'

'It's possible that that is the man's taste,' I tried to preach.

'Indeed! It's possible too he prefers unsalted soup to salted. Are you a teacher yourself?'

'What if I am?' I had uttered the words before I realised I was being indiscreet.

'It looks as if you belong to the Opposition Party,' he charged, trying to convert our difference of view into a political event.

I withdrew to a considerable distance away from him.

The crowd had continued to swell, and it was out of the question now to accommodate them inside the town hall. The expert organisers, with their flair for publicity, had clearly wanted to make a demonstration of the number that attended. 'The attendance was unprecedented—so large, in fact, that the big town hall could not take even a small fraction, so that the ceremony had to be held in the open.' That was how the newspapers would carry it the next morning. And now the organisers brought the dais and amplifiers hastily out to the open yard. Twenty minutes later, the ceremony was ready to start, with the Mayor presiding.

Mayor Koko did exceptionally well today. 'I now introduce,' said he at the conclusion of his brief but inspiring opening address, 'the great guest for the occasion, the very one who has been sent to us, as it were, by the Almighty to rescue our dear fatherland from the throes of political bondage, economic strangulation and social obscurity.'

The clapping lasted some minutes.

'He is none other than our beloved. . . .'

The crowd went delirious as Kanayo rose to his feet, tall and slim, smiling and winsome, his glasses flashing over his eyes in the glare of the afternoon sun. Some stalwarts began parading up and down, as if they were trying to spot those who did not show sufficient enthusiasm about the whole thing. But what was all that stuff Mayor Koko had let out of his mouth? Empty and high-blown, it had already evaporated into the wind leaving little or no impression on the mind.

'My beloved countrymen and comrades in arms!' the party chief intoned, before gathering his white flowing gown in folds over his shoulders. 'We have all assembled here this afternoon, unmindful of the heat. I am extremely happy to see so many people, young and old, men and women, of various linguistic and ethnic origins, of various callings, but all sons and daughters of our great country. . . .'

He went off into a lively account of the struggle so far for Independence, or, as he put it, for the final emancipation. He was indeed a superb orator—that, even his opponents would concede.

'Why are we here today?' He was almost singing now. 'The answer is that we want to agree on who should be voted for in the forthcoming crucial election of the National Parliament. Crucial I say. Ask me why?'

'Why?' the crowd repeated, spellbound.

'In a few years' time we shall be independent!'

'Ye-e-e-e—!' I must have shouted louder than most.

'We shall, we must. It is our inalienable right. And to achieve that goal, we must be careful in selecting the men who will be our standard-bearers in the eyes of the world. We must ensure that we have the right men in the National Parliament. We must ensure that only the tried, tested and confirmed are sent forward to demand from the colonial master, the perennial yoke-master, that which is ours by right—that is, the right to rule ourselves.'

The ovation was almost a riot. Hands shot up into the air and voices thundered into the sky. Then Kanayo proceeded to infuse into it all an element of bitterness.

'For centuries now the black man has been kept under the yoke of servitude. He has been made a hewer of wood and drawer of water. He has been subjected to all forms of indignity—he has been branded, lynched, chastised, rejected, kicked.' He pulled out a handkerchief from one of the folds of his gown, and wiped his eyes.

A heavy silence fell. . . .

'Well, then, my countrymen,' he resumed. 'What type of persons do you want to represent you in the National Parliament? Stooges, bootlickers, lackeys, menials of the imperialist?'

'No, no, no!' sounded in thousands of places.

'You know the type.'

'Yes, we do.' And others cried out: 'Sunday Umelo.'

'We shall not speak their names, but we may mention that their party is called the People's National Democratic League. Such persons are being sponsored for Parliament by the white masters, by those who own the foreign commercial firms which tap the resources of our land. Ask me why?'

'Why?'

'I will tell you. Those business firms know that once Independence is won their days are numbered; so they try to sabotage our plans for its attainment. They want in the Parliament only people who will defend their interests, even if that means our dear motherland going to the dogs. They are full of tactics; they are full of tricks. Their commonest trick, and clearly the most deadly, is *divide et impera*.'

The applause lasted minutes.

'No stooges, my countrymen. And then, there is another set of bad eggs seeking your support. These are the ones impelled not so much by the hope of personal aggrandisement as by the stupid, corrosive ideologies with which the white educator has made them drunk. You hear them shouting moderation, gradualism and such phrases. They call themselves intellectuals. Of course you will not have them. Or would you?'

'Never! . . .'

'You know their type. They call themselves the National Independence Party—or N.I.P. All right, we had better nip them in the bud right away.'

'Nip Michael Ebo in the bud! . . .'

'Finally, we come to the third type. You of course know them already. They are your own type of citizens, candidates of the common man. For the great party, the P.I.P., which your humble servant has the honour of leading is verily the common man's party.'

At this point, Mayor Koko sprang to his feet with an alacrity which made complete nonsense of his huge form; he shot his right fist into the air and then cried out, stamping his foot on the dais.

'Long live—'

'—the P.I.P.!' they roared in a frenzy.

'Yes, long live our P.I.P.,' resumed the party chief as soon as the voices had died down. 'It's your own party. We want in it only those, like you here, who believe in economic emancipation, political vindication and social regeneration.'

And then, after another pause, the finale came: 'We have assembled here today to choose the party candidate for Oban Municipal constituency. And I've made sure I'm here in person for that. For I hear that the men of the rival parties are a veritable nuisance over here. We'll get them fully nipped today. And I want to warn Oban that we'll have one and only one candidate for the party; we must not split our ranks. I want to stress too that our great party is a national one; it is not tribal or tribalistic, not sectional or sectarian. The common man knows nothing of such vices. Wherefore, I am privileged to put up before you for election into the National Parliament none other than your illustrious, industrious, kind, tried and tested, and faithful brother and servant, no other than Mazi Eduado Boga, alias Eduado-the-Man.' He held the faithful one, grinning, mute but confident, up by one hand for everybody to see. And the whole air was filled with varying expressions of approval. The drums beat once more, and a female voice sang into the loud-speaker a newly-composed party eulogy.

CHAPTER TWO

Mr. Allen was Works Manager in the Public Works Department at Oban. People said he had served as an army officer in Burma during the Second World War; and that it was a powerful injection he received there that had spoilt his head. Among his delights in Burma was caning, publicly and personally, the delinquents in the company under him. That was mere rumour, though.

One day, I went to see Papa in the workshop. I had a message from Mamma. We were on holiday, and were playing Ludo in the house when suddenly Mamma called me and asked me to go to the workshop. I objected at first, since the game was absorbing. She resorted to flattery and promises, which won me over. I still remember the background as well as what happened in the end. Papa must not forget to buy some medicine on his way home for Dorothy, then three years old, who had whooping cough. As soon as Papa saw me approaching, he put down the tool in his hand and, ignoring my greeting, demanded in a grave tone whether anything was wrong. 'Nothing,' I said. 'Mamma sent me. . . .' Then, he ordered me to go home at once. I could not understand why.

I was still gazing when the enormous figure of a white man came charging down from the opposite building, towards the shed. A few moments later, the man was kicking Papa at the back with his solid boots, calling him a beastly, stinking, sneaky creature and other names. The passers-by, outraged on Papa's behalf, urged him to take up a hammer and smash the madman's skull with it. But Papa would not heed the incitements. It was not that he was a great believer in the doctrine of turning the other cheek; but he would not do anything which might endanger his position as head carpenter in the Department. Besides, strictly speaking, it was the law in Allen's establishment that the hours between breaks must be all work.

And that was that. I was fifteen years old at the time. I was in my third year at the secondary school.

The long vacation was over at last and we had returned to the university for the first term of our final year. Final year was the most difficult of the four years; the degree examination would be on us in nine months' time. We would have to work very hard indeed, browsing into the early hours of the morning, night after night.

The danger of failure was real enough, and the Latin lecturer would always remind us, with characteristically merciless humour, that there was a common Latin word for danger and examination. The year before, for example, in spite of their having studied with the utmost zeal and concentration, nearly two-thirds of the students in the various faculties had failed, not counting those who had been sent down earlier on as unfit. The national dailies, very much incensed at the results, charged that it was all a deliberate plan to frustrate the aspirations of the country's youth; and so on. But the writings achieved nothing in the end.

I must not fail. I must read, read, read. I must not fail. If I did—it would be terrible! Wouldn't I hang myself? Classics was not one of the most dangerous choices, since only a select few had the courage to attempt Latin or Greek. So they all missed the subject, and also missed the quiet and thorough Peter Watson who held the Classics chair and who devoured Horace like pounded yam. Why should I fail? Biere was even more confident, rightly too. He was a university scholar. This meant that the university authorities paid him for reading the numberless volumes in the library, thereby keeping the worms away. His essays on critical appreciation were a marvel to colleagues. Biere was extremely patient and painstaking as well as thorough, even when he was reading things that he did not quite agree with in his heart.

Nevertheless, one must not take chances!

We cut down on club commitments. The first to go was the Society for the Study and Cultivation of True Citizenship. We had no regrets whatsoever about this. After the first meeting, at which the members had squash, at their expense, and there was a good drove of girls (who contributed absolutely nothing except their reluctant smiles), the society had been pretty dormant. Next, we dropped lawn-tennis, retaining only table-tennis. We then resigned our offices as Treasurer and assistant secretary, respectively, of the Students' Christian Movement. Biere submitted a carefully-prepared final account, adding five shillings as a gift to the organisation he had served for so long.

We joined a new club, however. It was the Social Enlightenment Circle, membership of which was restricted to third-year and final-year students.

About six weeks after the start of the term, I received another letter from Ruth. This time, she declared, point blank, though with great regret, that she was leaving me. I must not expect to hear from her again.

I took the letter to Biere's room, which was one floor above mine. As soon as I entered, he rose from his bed and sat up erect.

'I was thinking of coming down to see you.'

'Then I am here.'

Our eyes met.

'Anything wrong, Roland?'

'Yes.' I gave him the letter.

He began to laugh, to my great discomfiture. 'I'll show you something,' he said, and took out an envelope from under his pillow. 'Read.'

I read again and again.

'She too? A conspiracy,' I said.

'Puerile, insipid, idiotic.'

'I wonder what can have got into their heads.'

'Whatever it is, it should remain there for some time.'

'Seriously, Biere, we ought to try to find out. Why should they write simultaneously? Perhaps it's what they refer to as trials of love.'

'If that would satisfy you, have it so,' said he.

'And you?'

'You may perhaps wish to let me read for my exam.' He drew my attention to the volumes of Milton and Shakespeare, and John Stuart Mill, on the table.

'Or could they have been seduced?' I persisted.

'By wealthy Lebanese traders. Or local businessmen. But that sounds a wicked thought, doesn't it?'

'What?'

'The suggestion that they have been seduced.'

'They couldn't have been. It isn't probable.'

'As for its being probable or not probable—well, that's another matter. By the way, have you read the day's issue of the *Daily Recorder*? Three lives are known to have been lost already in the heat of the campaigns at Oban. And your man Boga is sure to win.'

'Yes.'

He said tonelessly: 'Roland Medo is distressed and distraught. Just because of one silly girl! Her name is Ruth. For him, it's pangs of unrequited love. For me, it's thanks for returned dislike.'

'Silly.' I meant to be rude.

'You had better return to your room and study for your degree exam.'

The elections and their outcome dominated the next few meetings of the Circle, giving that club the much-needed new zest. For, only a year and a half old, it was still striving to find its feet after an initial crisis that had nearly paralysed it completely.

It had been formed with the ambitious aim of initiating the student members into the habit of mature thinking and tolerance. The idea had been conceived by Mr. Morrison of the Department of English. Morrison was a tall, personable young man fresh from England who, from the first week of his arrival in the university had been picked out as the university's Assistant Public Orator.

The announcement about the formation of such a club had been received with universal enthusiasm by the students. Now, at long last, they were being offered a forum for airing their views on anything, including the perversity of the university cooks, the non-cooperative attitude of certain female students, and, most essentially, the composition of the University Council. And a few hours after the notice had appeared on the notice-board, inviting interested persons to apply, there were well over one hundred signatures. Morrison had a big job pruning the list down to a select twenty. His plan was to add to the twenty some five or so university lecturers, who, as some put it, were sufficiently eccentric to embrace the Morrison fad.

It turned out, however, that Morrison did not quite see eye to eye with his colleagues on the question of method. He was for a free-for-all: every member, student or lecturer, should feel free to propose any topic and join in the discussions at any point. The rest, on the other hand, held that the thing should be smoothly regimented. 'You don't want it to degenerate into a channel for letting out barbaric neuroses?' Hughes of Medicine had wondered. But Morrison was unyielding. The others withdrew. Going further, he transferred the venue for the discussions to his quarters, which the students found extremely suitable since he was still a bachelor and had a big brand-new refrigerator. He had his series of disappointments in a matter of weeks. And then the climax came. It was during a Poetry Reading activity, and on a hot afternoon. After he had read, in his smooth and exquisite voice, portions from *Paradise Lost*, Morrison began to expatiate on the beauty and grandeur of Milton's style. Then a member told him, outright, that there wasn't much, in his own opinion, which one could say was particularly attractive about the poem. This came on top of an earlier experience, that same day, when, during a lecture on Thomson's *The Seasons*, a vibrant nationalist of a student had called his attention to the fact that nobody in the audience had ever seen his Spring or Autumn; and an even earlier one when his steward, a laggard of the first order, not only ruined the egg and charred the sausages but also broke the spout of his much-treasured teapot. And all that on an unbearably hot and humid day.

16

'There isn't what?' he demanded.

'I mean,' the member replied with confidence, 'I personally don't see anything so striking or worldshaking about Milton.'

There were some who found this amusing. Morrison was definitely not one of them.

'Height of impertinence!' he cried out, red-eyed and red-faced, shaking, his Adam's apple playing. 'Scholars the world over have through the generations hailed Milton as a noble genius and his works as sacrosanct. But you, a fellow from the dense jungles of Africa, brought up in entirely illiterate surroundings, have the impertinence to pronounce on the works in such a way.'

'Will Mr. Morrison please withdraw the reference to Africa,' another interjected.

'Withdraw, my foot! The sooner you and everybody else leaves my house the better,' He stormed into his bedroom.

The general verdict among the student body, including even the most enthusiastic nationalists, was that Morrison had been genuinely provoked and that there was no point in castigating him for the utterance. And the *Scorpion*, the hard-biting students' magazine, kept an impartial silence about the episode.

But for Mr. Keine of Mathematics, the Circle would probably have foundered completely. It was he who revived the idea at the beginning of the current session. He also won over the five lecturers who had deserted Morrison. A rumour was still going round that the lecturers had prodded up Keine, a citizen of a neighbouring African country, to take over the Circle and fashion it the way they themselves wanted it.

'Do we then venture to examine once more the politics of the country in the context of the elections recently concluded?' Keine began. It was the fourth meeting of the year.

'I support that,' came Biere's response. He had volunteered at the previous meeting to introduce the day's discussion.

'How do we begin? Oh yes, the type of persons who have been appointed Ministers. Mr. Ekonte?'

'Thank you, Mr. Chairman,' Biere then took over. 'Well, gentlemen, if my presumptions are correct, you already know who are now in the nation's Executive Council. I fear a good number of them are not quite in a position to discuss affairs of state with good understanding. The most striking of such is the man from my own constituency.'

'Who's that?' asked Lawrence of Botany.

'Eduado Boga, who's been made Minister of Culture.'

'I hear he's not much use,' the chairman came in after a big laugh, after which he called the magic tune of tolerance and open-mindedness: 'But true to the best traditions of the Circle, we must not condemn yet. Let us first ask ourselves whether there is anything that could be said in support of his appointment. ... Yes, Mr. Uko?'

'Perhaps, Mr. Chairman,' said Mr. Uko, a pre-medical student, 'we should approach the question by first admitting the basic weaknesses of the appointment. What I mean is, let's tick off the bad aspects. For example, the man has not the intellectual background to grapple with problems of legislation and government.'

'I, for one, know how he came to power,' I said. 'He exerted undue influence on the electorate. One might of course counter that that is a general pattern! And he went to the extent of planning to destroy, physically, in order to get what he wants.'

'There does seem to be a real danger of our building on a foundation that, to say the least, is very shaky,' Biere said. 'And the worst part of it all is that only very few of those who ought to care do actually care.'

'How?'

'People do such things and get away with them,' he expanded. 'Nobody is going to do anything to Eduado, any more than to a highly-placed official guilty of criminal negligence. No! Eduado will remain the Minister of Culture in spite of everything. And where do we go from there? ...'

'Rather cryptic, Mr. Ekonte,' observed Lawrence behind his pipe. 'May I suggest that we have demolished the man of Culture sufficiently; let's now proceed to the other side.'

'Anybody for the defence? ... Mr. Uko?' the chairman called.

'No,' the other declined. 'I don't feel differently from Biere Ekonte.'

'Nor do I,' said Williams, a young West Indian History lecturer. 'But let's try.'

'Yes, go on.'

'We are all agreed that the man Boga is hardly in a position to discharge with any reasonable measure of competence, the functions of a Minister of State, much less of Culture. But then, let us consider a few basic facts.

'There is a period in the history of any people when those of a soft, gentle and polished upbringing must yield to the tough and rough. It is just like a large family where you have children with all sorts of traits. A time comes when the more rugged and uninhibited stand out as the foremost champions of the family's course. It depends on the issue confronting the family. Now, to get back to the national level, let us when thinking about the politicians of this dependent territory, draw a parallel with the early Americans exploring and expanding in the New World. They could not have succeeded so decisively if they had had learned lawyers and doctors and other intellectuals on the venture. No. Adventure is usually the métier of the rough and tough guy. And now, in the current phase of the history of this country, you have a war on—a war against the forces of imperialism in all its subtle forms and manifestations. May I say here, for the benefit of our white friends, that no offence is intended.

'The question then is this: Who is the best type of soldier for the war? The learned lawyer steeped in western culture who speaks English with faultless accent? The humble, docile schoolmaster wary of change or adventure? Or the careless, dynamic, liberated youth boiling for change? A saint or a knave? A traditionalist or an iconoclast? A civil servant or an independent, self-sufficient businessman?'

'A good point, Mr. Williams,' said the chairman.

'Yes, yes,' concurred Stewart of Religious Studies. 'Without necessarily subscribing to Jimmy Williams's extreme examples, I would agree that a good point has been made. You require for the adventure people who are prepared to throw things overboard. Anglophiles will not do.'

'Does Mr. Stewart mean—' I cut in.

'Wait a moment; I haven't finished. The point is that another issue will have been raised in such a situation: What happens after the battle has been won? What do you do with those who have done the fighting? It may be easy to disband an army, because the ranks have been brought up to obey commands, but you cannot easily disband politicians who mould the public will, except perhaps in a democracy like ours—I mean in Britain and the dominions. With victory, when there are no more battles to be fought against imperialism, the conqueror may turn round to plague his fellow citizens with all sorts of venal acts—bribery, embezzlement, nepotism and high-handedness. What follows after that?'

'They will at least have won Independence for the people!' Keine answered. . . . 'Mr. Ekonte again.'

'Mr. Chairman,' Biere said, 'I'm much impressed by the point made by the last speaker, and I have not the impertinence to attempt to improve upon it. May I reply to the statement which you've just made. Talking of winning Independence, could we rightly consider that a final goal for which every other thing should be shelved? I rather think not.'

'Nor do I,' Stewart agreed. 'Surely the State has to continue to exist after Independence has been won. It will therefore be necessary for the people to have the means of living well; they will need justice and fair play, and they should be exposed to sound principles and ideals. Independence should not be allowed to obscure these other equally important prerequisites—the eternal values. And incidentally, Mr. Chairman, what does Independence mean in practical terms? History has revealed that it is often a mere façade of sovereignty.'

'True!' I said, eagerly. 'We talk of political Independence, forgetting about our economy!' The day before, I had read an article on the doings of a famous foreign commercial firm in a neighbouring country. 'People should not forget that the very power which they claim to have got rid of may turn round at the gate, and come back to befriend those in authority at the expense of the masses.'

'Especially if the rulers are such as are very susceptible,' Stewart said.

'That is the point,' Biere nodded. 'They will receive even from those who were their declared enemies. And it's not just a question of poor education. Even the learned members of the society could be susceptible.'

'Most distressing!' It was Williams again in his candid tone. 'In that event, one loses that which one has fought so much for, before one knows it!'

'The point I want to stress, Mr. Chairman, is that these failings we talk about are not confined to Eduado and his type,' Biere spoke again. 'There is not much in the way of good examples from those who have had the advantage of education.'

'May be, Mr. Ekonte,' the chairman replied. 'But we need not expand today's discussion to cover the latter type of citizen. We had agreed to discuss just the election and the results, and some of the actors in it . . . Shall we recap? . . .'

CHAPTER THREE

Try as I might, I could not detach my mind from the thought of Ruth's misdeed. After the initial flush of anger, the full facts now stood out clear and stark. The letter had been as unexpected as it was brusque in its tone, arriving at a time I was bent on concentrating all energy of mind on the final examination. I loved Ruth—that was the point. And I had come to believe that she loved me equally, perhaps even more. I could not forget that special, sweet twist of the voice with which she spoke my name, or the proud, proprietary tone with which she answered when I called. Biere, the superb cynic, said it was a trick which most female teachers acquired while in training.

She was a certificated, Grade Two teacher on the staff of the girls' school at Oban. I first met her at a Youth Day parade; she was leading a file of elegant and lively girls into the field. Most impressive in their gleaming white blouses, royal blue skirts, and orange berets, they marched on in strict order; and she brought up the rear. She was plump and unsmiling—no expression showed on her black face.

I decided there and then that she was well worth a pursuit.

I brought to it all the art I could muster. She was reputed to be solid and immovable. What did that matter? I was determined to succeed. And I was convinced I would. I would return to the university with the story of my conquest, authenticated with the photograph which I would mount on a stand. My technique would be *simplicity*: no airs, no pretence, no sophistication.

I went on the school's visiting day. Shortly after the small girl had gone for her, she came out looking cold and even antagonistic. 'Who's this person?' she demanded of the girl.

I interposed: 'Ruth Aniedo?'

She agreed; then asked: 'Do you have a message for me?'

'I hope you know me!'

She gave a quick shrug. 'I don't think I do.'

I spoke my name, at which she reacted with one of her rare smiles. I little knew that my name had been ringing a bell among the staff of the school.

We discussed many things that day. On my subsequent visit, she told me in confidence that she too was anxious to get into the university. She would want to read English and History and any other subject I thought she could offer.

'How can we do it?'

'My good friend, Biere, could help you with English. He has no equal in the university.'

'You think he would agree to help me?'

'If I speak to him.'

'You wouldn't mind?'

'What?'

She hesitated. 'His coaching me.'

'Biere is a good friend,' I assured her. 'Or better still—'

'Yes?'

'Why not bring somebody with you, so that there will be one to one instead of one to two?'

She thought for some time. 'I'll come with Edna. She too wants coaching in English.'

Edna was very light skinned—almost palm-oil red; and was quite well-built, especially when viewed from behind. But that was all that could be said in her favour, as far as looks were concerned. Her cheeks weighed tons and were at their worst whenever they bunched for a smile. She was flashily dressed most of the time, thus giving even greater prominence to her fiery skin. And then, she was extraordinarily fond of armless blouses and gowns. I thought that had something to do with the tuft of hair she cultivated under each armpit. Biere charged when the first day's lesson was over and the damsels had departed: 'You and your Ruth conspired.'

22

'Not at all, Biere Ekonte,' I laughed. 'Your friend Roland Medo had no hand in the choice.'

'I trust so.'

'Just the design of a beloved one anxious to protect her interest. Ruth made sure she brought with her a creature of decidedly inferior appearance.'

'Quite clever! But then, Edna seems to have a stronger passion for learning than she, if one may judge from one day's experience. I do not think though that either of them has much chance of seeing the university gates.'

'I reckon too Edna has a passion for the teacher.'

'In that case, she should be prepared to burn her heart to cinders.'

I had myself sensed he did not care much about her; that she had no chance at all. If only she had known this, she would have saved herself all the trouble of coquetry. In the first place, Biere was a lover of simplicity and beauty, which Edna did not represent. He would often declare he was at one with the ancient Greeks who had a common word for *ugly* and *wicked*. 'It's the heart,' he would explain, 'which leaves its impress on the face.' His soul would expand to the glow of the sunset clouds; or the sparkle of water as the stream cascaded through its pebbly bed; or at the sight of the roses which grew close to the university swimming pool.

'Believe me, Biere, you are not of this world,' I once said, trying to tempt him.

Laughing soberly, he assured me he belonged very well. 'I feel however that one ought to keep both body and spirit clean.'

'At your age you're still like that!'

'Why not?'

'You are starving yourself for no just cause. Or do you feel a sense of power in keeping yourself a mystery to the daughters of the land?'

'You speak as if Lucifer were your hero. You were never a true villain when it comes to that anyway.'

A heavy rain came in the early hours of morning. Long and straight, the rods descended on the roof in a steady thrust. Then a fierce wind followed. The water poured into the corridor and into the room.

When at last the rain had died down, I found a broom and swept the water out of the room. Then I sat down. I took my pen; I opened the writing-pad on the table. I began to write.

The first one was to Ruth herself. It had just three sentences—how was she, how were the parents, and why had she not written again. The second, which was much longer, was to Simon Okoromanta, a friend in the railways, Public Relations Division, who knew practically every grown-up girl in Oban, and her love-affairs. The following morning, I dropped the two letters inside the post-box with my own hand.

Nothing came from her; it was Simon who replied in the third week. 'About your girl,' he wrote, 'don't mind the idiot; I can organise somebody else for you any time you are around. They say she is getting ready to go to England to study Nursing—some say Secretaryship. And do you know what? She is to be sponsored by Chief Lobe, that fat, wealthy contractor and prominent P.I.P. man who resides at Gorigori, which is in Doda State, but stays here in Oban most of the time. You must have known him. Some say he is to marry her, as a second wife that is, on completion of her course; others say she is already Mrs. Chief Lobe. I should not be surprised if the latter was nearer to the truth, brother, for the school authorities have already terminated her appointment and the Chief is fuming; he is threatening he will get all white missionaries, especially the nuns, out of the country, starting from Oban, in a few years' time.

'That is the world in which we live! Anyway, I want to tell you now that the girl was not really a butterfly, even though Lobe got her rather cheap. You see, he used his wealth and influence, and he dangled before her the prospect of further studies overseas which, believe me, is more attractive than whatever your university can offer. Don't forget too that the girl is from a very poor family. She needs Lobe's money for training her younger brothers and sisters. You see? Women are children after all; it is easy to confuse them.

'As for the one called Edna, I hear she's left Oban and gone off to live in Portcity. I can't blame her really; she didn't have much of a chance with that your tough friend called Biere, not with those things she calls her cheeks.'

I chuckled.
I folded the letter and put it aside. 'Virgil next!' I announced to myself; *Georgics!*

It was my turn to introduce the topic for discussion at the next meeting of the Social Enlightenment Circle. So far, all the meetings, without a single exception, had been very interesting indeed. The discussions had covered a wide range of topics, including imported religions and international trade. The last one had dealt with an article in a radical daily in which a contributor had put forward a most grotesque suggestion for ridding the land of its numerous ills, which was to organise a single, expensive banquet for the law-makers, both State and National, and keep a couple of undertakers in the precincts of the banquet hall.

The topic which I proposed myself and was now to introduce was: 'The need for men of ideas in an emerging country'. Having read, though with inadequate understanding, some of the works of Plato and Aristotle, mostly in their English translations, I had for some time begun to wonder whether those who preached and educated had actually taken sufficient note of the lessons offered by those teachers of old. And then, there was this recent letter from Ruth. If she had been a girl of principles, mere money would not have lured her away....

I approached the subject boldly and with a feeling of righteousness. It had been acknowledged by all, including even the very perpetrators of those ills against which the masses were shrieking, that something must be done to curb the various malpractices. There were numerous examples of such public denunciations in the newspapers, in public lectures and in students' debates. But the important question remained unanswered. That question was, how to set about it all: how could we achieve a break-through? Nobody appeared to be doing much that could be termed definite.

'It does seem to me that what we need above all is to have in key places a good core of men and women of sound ideals, dedicated to the cause of justice and fair play, who value *principles* more than material wealth. I would recommend to members that we discuss the subject of the need for men of ideals....'

'And women,' Keine added in jest. 'Thank you, Mr. Medo. It has been a stimulating overture. Now gentlemen, may we proceed to the concert.'

Everyone agreed in the discussion that followed that the salvation of the country, in fact of any country, depended on men of ideals. Mr. Williams cited examples from History while another delved into Ethics.

Then Mr. Hilary of Classics spoke:

'Mr. Chairman, having agreed that the need for men of ideals cannot be overstressed, we should, I think, proceed to enquire into what we mean by ideals—or rather, to examine, critically, the nature of those acts which to us appear to be outward manifestations of idealism.'

Eyes turned on him.

'What I mean is this,' he went on, in his sharp, tiny voice which matched his wiry form. 'What on the outside appears to us as an act of the greatest idealism may have sprung from base origins, the opposite of the very virtue which we extol. I don't know if I have made my meaning clear?'

This made me uneasy. The man was certainly ruining the day for me; he was assailing the central pillar on which the whole edifice stood.

'But perhaps we need not press the issue,' he suggested to my relief. 'Not now at least. The essential point which I want to stress is that an act by itself should not be an absolute measure of virtue.'

'Cut that out now, Bill,' Watson intervened. 'I fear we may be getting scandalously deep and sceptical.'

The other returned: 'I didn't mean to spread scandals; or to foul Roland Medo's impressive keynote. Could we agree that I list for discussion in the near future the question of the origins of virtue?'

'I will have left by then,' I cut in. And in the interval of laughter which followed, Hilary reminded me that winged truth follows its votaries wherever they go.

CHAPTER FOUR

'At long last!' I sighed. The final examination was just over.

The sense of release was overwhelming. Never again the tedium and agony of long, sleepless hours of studies, the social privations, and the rest! Roland Medo, you now have the wide world to yourself. In this great expanse you will have to find your bearings, and fend for yourself too. 'You are all endowed with freewill,' a preacher had once intoned, at a meeting of the Students' Christian Movement. 'And you have before you the wide world, with all its pleasures and attractions, and the opposites. It is up to you to choose which direction you'll move. All we've been trying to do for you in your formative years is to expose you to the right influences. The ultimate result will depend on you. . . .'

That was true indeed; I had the world to myself. Who could restrain me? Papa had died while I was still in secondary school. He was a very strict but loving father. He used the cane, and often we would get our own back on Mamma. Yet we all had very good memories of him. After his death, the responsibility for my education passed quietly to Edoha, Mamma's younger brother. It was Edoha who paid my university fees.

Mamma was still very much alive, of course. But then, what could she do about my morals? Except to weep and remind me that had Papa been alive he would have been terribly upset! They had been a very devoted couple, she and Papa. Every night after supper, they would summon us to kneel down together in prayers. They invariably prayed more fervently than any of the children—Roland in particular. Incidentally, the same happened in Biere's family. There, the father and mother insisted on the child saying grace before he could have his meal. We never went so far.

In his last hours, Papa called for a prayer, and we all prayed and prayed. Then he shifted in his bed and groaned with pain; and, speaking with some difficulty, he enjoined us all to live worthy lives, thereby doing honour to his memory. We promised we would. Next, he bade us to ignore all those who might offend us, even in very serious issues. Again, we promised. But now, a discordant, rebellious voice arose in Roland. To ignore them, to forgive them? Just as you did to that pink hound of a man who in front of the son kicked at the father and poured out from his mouth the most execrable names? I was still reflecting on the incident when he began speaking to us by name, one after the other, starting with Alex who was the eldest. '... Roland ... Dom ... Louis ... Dora ...' He was sinking fast. We stood and watched in tears. The priest arrived just in time.

I had intended to spend the three-month interval before the result was released resting and recuperating from the strain of the examination. I would visit friends and places, read some Latin texts in their original and Greek ones in both original and translation, and proceed seriously to look for a replacement for Ruth—Ruth who was nowhere nearer the Niger, much less the Atlantic, now. Ruth was still there, in the very heart of Oban, the more favoured of Chief Lobe's two wives.

I had not gone far with any of my plans before I began to find things really difficult. I needed money for many things, including postage stamps. Enquiries at some of the Government offices at Oban revealed that I had no chance whatsoever of being appointed into the senior grade of the civil service—not until the results were out and I was known to have passed. And in reply to the question whether there were not in fact many non-graduates, native and expatriate, who held top posts in the service, I was warned that such an attitude would disqualify me completely even if I had a doctorate degree in Arts; and an officer in the Security Division of the Civil Secretary's office, a bespectacled old man, went so far as to demand my name and address, for record purposes only, as he put it. But, the young clerk behind him, catching my eyes, shook his head. The latter also ran after me when I had left, to tell me that neither Mr. Okoloma, the old man, nor Mr. Parker, the white man Okoloma served like a slave, had ever seen the walls of a university. Parker, he swore, had in fact been only a sergeant in the army.

What I did was to become a teacher. It was really a case of drifting into the profession. For I merely walked over into Christ High School in Oban, met the principal, and introduced myself. The following week, I was appointed senior Latin master.

Many things were likeable about this school into which I had drifted with such careless ease. There was, for example, the school compound. It looked very trim and attractive with its shade trees, flower hedges, neat lawns and gravel paths. Another was the small, three-room, bachelor bungalow that was my house. Most of all, those children who sat before me each day! How could one fail to love their ways? There were some very small, restless ones. Toothless short-legs was the nickname I had for them. They smiled or grinned or giggled most of the time and called each other names, and knew their declensions very well. At the opposite end, there were the big ones who would approach you like personal friends, and ask for your advice and guidance in matters which had not much to do with the lessons you taught. I had begun to understand them so well in so short a time.

But nobody knew them half as well as did the principal, Father Long. He could tell you the family background of almost every student, and other things. And he handled them with both sympathy and firmness. Always staid and a bit detached, he was nevertheless accessible to all, except that he would not say much, but rather made you speak most of the time. His was a compelling personality; I had never known a clergyman look so tall and dignified unless he was a bishop. He hardly ever carried a cane but instead would remind the staff that just as the pen was mightier than the sword, so also examples were a more positive and more effective instrument than the cane.

Father Long invited me into his office one morning. When I came in he was busy writing, so he merely indicated a seat. Then, shortly after, he took out a telegram from the drawer. He handed it over to me with a mechanical 'Congrats, Roland.'

'What, Father?'

It was true, I told myself seconds later.

'Thank you, Father. But you looked most unexcited about it.'

'Excited?' said he. 'You don't seem to realise that I'm not supposed to be that at my age.' He smiled, warmly. 'Congrats again. It is an excellent result for which we should all be proud.' His countenance turned serious again. 'I hope you'll continue to stay with us.'

'Why not? . . .'

I noticed he was observing me, studiously, as I walked out from the office.

'Just a moment, Roland.'

'Yes, Father?'

'If you don't mind, I intend to announce your success during the assembly.'

I agreed.

'And I'll announce too that you're staying, and not running off into the civil service?'

'All right, Father.'

'Excellent.'

Twenty paces later, I leapt into the air.

Joy had indeed made me mad. Not that I had had any good reason for being afraid, but one could never be perfectly sure—not after Mr. Watson had intimated, candidly, that some thirty to forty per cent of the candidates would fail.

Father Long later informed me that I was entitled to salary arrears totalling nearly twenty pounds for the period I had taught so far. And I informed myself that most of this amount would be invested in Virgil's complete volumes, a possession I had been dreaming of for years. Biere had already started assembling Milton's works, even though he was still unemployed.

From the start, Biere had made up his mind that he would have nothing to do with the civil service, except, in his own words, to be its critic. It could not be said, he went on to admit, that he had much of a choice left after that other than to be a teacher. But he would wait until the results had been released and he knew he had passed; he could not bear the disgrace of failure. My reply had been to request that he stop being funny. Who else could succeed if Biere Ekonte should fail? When the results came out, Biere had a Second Class (Upper), which was to remain a record for years.

Biere's school was situated only two miles from Christ High School, at the opposite end of Oban.

Biere and I set out together one afternoon to watch the opening of the Provincial Festival of the Arts. The ceremony was to be performed this year by none other than the Honourable Eduado Boga, National Minister of Culture. For that reason, what had in the past been a quiet affair was to be preceded by very elaborate arrangements and even a fanfare. There were such ministerial perquisites as posters and handbills, invitations to very important personalities and heads of Government Ministries and Departments, press and radio announcements, and of course security arrangements.

'Fancy all the trouble they are taking!' Biere complained. 'Just because of one uncultured M. of C.!'

I laughed. 'Don't forget that the Honourable M. is a representative of the people and must therefore be seen as well as heard by the people. In short, he must be advertised.'

'Not at the expense of Culture! What is the festival meant for?'

'Let's hurry up, or we'll be late.'

'Late? They are never in time.'

'True,' I agreed.

'They must wait until a large crowd has assembled: they must be seen by the multitude when they appear in their putrid glory.'

We were approaching the stadium.

'Listen!'

Skin drums were throbbing.

'Seems they've already begun.'

'I shouldn't be surprised if they were just warming up; or setting the scene for the Honourable M.s arrival.'

I asked him: 'I sometimes begin to wonder about these things; do you think the educated ones wouldn't do the same if given the chance?'

'They probably would,' he agreed. 'Many of them.'

Tomtom beats rolled to a vigorous, throbbing, rhythm, and a flute wove in sustained modulations. . . .

The music came to an abrupt end. It was like the snapping of a taut rope. The crowd burst into heavy applause.

'They are performing already?'

'I don't think so; the M. of C. still has to arrive.'

The stadium was packed full. There were on one side, women clad in white and pink, wearing party symbols and singing in praise of the great People's Independence Party. Directly opposite them was the V.I.P. section. Some of the seats in that section were already occupied, mostly by State Ministers of State, prominent party men, prominent businessmen, ministers of religion, and top civil servants. Oban was the seat of the State Government as well as the headquarters of Oban Province; and so, although the festival was a provincial affair, it was being attended by a strong core of V.I.P.s. There was a row of vacant seats in the front, directly before the dais, with the pink-coloured canopy over it.

We were hardly seated when a bustle began at the entrance. It developed into a scramble. This was mostly the children, anxious to secure good viewing positions. Then the disorder was overtaken by a general welcome.

'P.I.P. on top! Everybody say, P.I.P. on top!' the voice demanded through a speaker; but in keeping with their democratic spirit, very many held their tongues as the new ministerial Pontiac went sailing towards the dais.

It is enough to record that Eduado Boga did his best with the opening address; and that there was frequent applause. The Permanent Secretary who was responsible for the composition had not been kind, but, resolute as anybody in his position ought to be, Boga went on. Then he came to the final paragraph. 'Our cultural heritage must be identified, enriched, and propagated. We must strive to preserve the things of the heart as well as those of the mind. Only by so doing can we cushion the shock of that interaction of forces which is a concomitant to—'

Thousands of eyes focused on him.

'What is this all about?' He was as calm and unruffled as ever. 'They have not written what I told them to write. ... Let us not go into further formality, ladies and gentlemen; I hereby declare this year's festival open.' While the applause rang, he sat down, took out a handkerchief and began to mop up the sweat from his face.

Biere pinched my thigh.

'Watch his face.'

'What for?'

'He has finished acting, and now he has come back to his real self,' he said. 'Don't you see he looks extinguished, and terribly hostile?'

'Maybe! And so what?'

Eduado Boga's anger was pretty justified in a way. That most arrogant man who was his Permanent Secretary had composed the heavy speech purposely to embarrass him before the public, and before the constituency, and he had very nearly succeeded. For a long time now, Eduado Boga had been complaining to the Prime Minister about Mr. Lukado, Permanent Secretary, National Ministry of Culture, only to be assured on each occasion that Lukado was, in the opinion of the head of the civil service, one of the nation's best Permanent Secretaries. So far, he had found very little comfort in the assurances. And today, he had had to bear the man's conceit nearly to a point of public humiliation. What made the thing all the more upsetting was the fact that the Permanent Secretary hailed from the same State as his Minister. The man had no element of brotherly love in him! Boga swore there and then, openly, that he would get rid of Lukado in a matter of weeks.

Mayor Koko offered his consolation. 'That man has always been as proud as a peacock,' he said.

'He used to be a nice fellow,' another important personality said from behind.

'I know what happened,' shouted Okay Baby, a short, boisterous man of doubtful party loyalty who was popular throughout Oban. Eyes turned on him. 'Lukado has not been happy since he left the Ministry of Lands for the Ministry of Culture.'

'Don't mind Okay Baby,' Boga said. 'We all serve the country, and no Minister is more important than the other.'

The dancers were getting ready to start in earnest. The weather suddenly turned irritable and heavy rain clouds raced over the sky. A violent wind followed.

The rain that came poured down in torrents. It sent both competitors and spectators home drenched and extremely disappointed. For it was mainly the dances—the prospect of seeing the colourful dresses, the ever-changing formations, and the brisk, sinuous body movements—that had brought most of them to the stadium that afternoon.

Later that night, the radio announced that the first prize for dancing had been awarded to the Young Women's Club.

'You heard the announcement—the one about the dancing prize?' Biere asked. It was a week later.

'Disappointing!' I replied.

'Why? You didn't want the women to win?'

'Not without a competition.'

'They appeared before Eduado and he was sort of impressed.'

33

'To think that the officials in the Ministry of Information should have collaborated!'

'Are the civil servants any better than the politicians?' he said, with some bitterness. 'It was a civil servant after all who left Azuka unattended to in hospital. Merely collaborating to give out false news is nothing compared with the other things they are capable of.'

No word came from me.

'And even if they had the best of intentions, they are not free,' he went on. 'They have to depend on Boga and Co. for their rise or fall.'

'Where then lies the ultimate cure?' I asked after some time. 'The Church? But—'

'The Church? How can it help, when they have invaded it too?'

'Truly!' I grunted out.

'Watch them when they come into the church on Sunday. First, they make sure they arrive late, so that they can be noticed by a full congregation; then they make a bee-line for the front seats. And when it comes to collection time, they pay more than others. Try to criticize them and they rally the church members to their side. And yet, some of them have more than one wife. Your co-husband, for example!'

'You're talking nonsense,' I charged. 'And you've not tried to answer my question. Where lies the ultimate cure?'

'The banquet idea would have done the nation a hell of a lot of good but it isn't at all hygienic,' Biere said. 'What I'm sure of is that the solution will come one day, and in its own way. The educated ones who should be influencing others for good do not do so.'

He switched on his radio.

The first news item was that Doda State Legislature had had its life extended.

CHAPTER FIVE

The story being circulated was that Doctor the Honourable Premier, Doda State, wanted more time to clean up some mess in Gorigori District Council. That council, situated in the extreme east of the

State, with the River Niger on its furthermost frontier, had invited tenders for the construction of a new market and several building firms, including some foreign ones based in the country, were bidding for the award, and had begun to make what was termed the necessary approaches. Then, the Honourable State Minister in charge of Local Government and Chieftaincy Affairs, directed that only well-established contractors should be considered; and that expatriate firms must be given a chance, just like their indigenous counterparts. 'Our experience in the past few months does not encourage us to indulge our sense of patriotism at the expense of everything else.' Those were his very words. In their chagrin, the councillors, led by the chairman himself, sent a long petition to Doctor the Honourable State Premier complaining about the Honourable Minister of Local Government and Chieftaincy Affairs' attitude. 'It is,' they said, among other things, 'tantamount to a negation of the spirit of Dodanization, nay of Africanization.' Subsequently, in a face-to-face discussion with the Premier, they went on to hint that there had been some firm understanding already between the Honourable Minister and the monopolistic expatriate firm of Shaws and Sharp, Limited, Civil Engineers.

All this soon leaked out, and the press began to howl. The Honourable Premier ruled that an enquiry should be conducted, but by a few top party men; and that the State elections should be shelved for some months because of the atmosphere.

Barely four weeks later, however, the national radio carried the dramatic announcement that the Doda State Legislature had been dissolved. Clearly, the whole thing had been calculated to take the opposition unawares. It was true that the ruling party had an absolute and numerically comfortable majority in the Legislature. But it was equally true that the opposition wielded considerable influence in the State: it had forty out of the hundred-and-two seats and a good following among the masses.

All that the ruling party, the Real Democrats got in reply, however, was derisive laughter from their opponents. Ojo, the State Publicity Secretary of the People's Independence Party announced: 'We knew their tricks; we had expected the stroke earlier.'

The Real Democrats announced their candidates two weeks later, among them Mr. K. D. Ubakile for Gorigori constituency. Ubakile

35

was an engineer by profession, and a son of Gorigori, and the chairman of the party in that District. Then, the People's Independence Party chose Chief Ezenta Lobe, the well-known business man. Lobe was to stand in place of the former incumbent, who had withdrawn from politics completely.

I just chuckled. . . .

I crossed over from Ania to Gorigori the next day, and talked with Ubakile for over an hour. I went again two days later.

The following week, I was in a position to disclose my plans to Biere.

'My mind is made up,' I declared, for the second time.

'You don't mean it, do you?' he asked.

'I very much do.'

'You, transformed into a politician?'

'Well, don't you believe in the ideals of that party?'

'Oh yes, I do. Who wouldn't?'

'Seriously,' I protested.

'No privileges, no injustices, or corruption? Very impressive. But they need to add "unless it comes from us".'

'A good crop of decent fellows.'

'Well, perhaps. We often laud acts and utterances which suggest goodness, but fail to go into the sources from which they spring . . . A base motive, like ostentation, or self-glorification, can make one appear generous . . . Also, wounded pride can drive one to an extremity of anger and hate. The target of the hatred is made to personify the vice we want to attribute to him, and from this springs what we call virtue . . . Some sublimated vile instinct or exalted weakness, more or less . . . then we come off as champions and lovers of justice and fair play and the rest.

'Do you remember that man, Hilary of your Classics Department? You were present at the debate in the staff common room where he shocked many people. He should have added that it applies both ways.'

'How?'

'That out of a good motive one could proceed to reprehensible acts.'

We both fell silent.

36

'Where did we stop?' he resumed. 'Oh yes, you and your comrades-in-arms.'

'It is a very disciplined party. Nothing like the P.I.P.'

'You would admit anyway that, in spite of its name, this party of your suffers from regimentation. It is the P.I.P. that has democracy as its principal diet.'

'Democracy my foot! What does it mean in actual practice? The white man shouts it at us, and yet terrible things happen right before him and he doesn't do anything to stop them.'

'What do you mean?'

'He rules his countrymen well, but out here anything can be allowed to pass in the name of political inexperience, provided his invested interests do not suffer. There is even a strong rumour that Shaws and Sharp are going to finance the elections for the P.I.P.'

'What's the relevance? And how come that Shaws and Sharp, who are expecting a quarter-of-a-million pound contract in Doda State, should now side with the P.I.P.?'

'Simply because that contract won't go to them. The Premier has ruled so.'

'You sound as if you've really made up your mind.'

'Irrevocably! In fact, I intend to cross over to the other side of the river in a few days to enrol formally. You know that's where we have our ancestral home . . . We live in Bokenu but belong to Doda.'

'Crossing over means Gorigori, I suppose?'

'It follows. But why?'

'Gorigori being where the husband of a certain Ruth Aniedo is being done up for the P.I.P. platform!'

'So what?'

He grinned at me. 'The beast in man.'

I went away transfixed in thought. I too had read Emile Zola's *Beast*, not long ago.

Ubakile welcomed me into the party. He was speaking, he said, as Chairman rather than as the prospective party candidate for the constituency. Then he went on to describe me as a veritable asset, a young lad full of talent and promise, with good education, good principles and great common sense; another energetic crusader on the side of justice, fair play and human dignity. Let there be no doubt about it; Mr. Medo was a true scion of the District. Although his father was domiciled in Bokenu, the family were of Doda State, and of Gorigori extraction. So there was now a welcome reinforcement against the forces which the villain called Chief Lobe was organising for an assault against the legitimate wishes of the people ... My reply was brief; I was very much moved by his speech; and I would do my best to uphold those great principles for which the party stood, foremost of which was the right to rule ourselves.

It was at the next meeting, a week later, that Ubakile went ahead to implement the agreements he had concluded with me.

'We of the party believe in merit,' he declared, with his usual flair for oratory. 'We will not have a semi-illiterate publicising us, as they do in the P.I.P. We want men of calibre, people who can comprehend issues of state and who, equally, are devoted to the nationalist cause. Wherefore, we would be happy to have Mr. Medo for the task of publicising the party in this constituency.' I was never able to comprehend how the engineer came about his florid style of speech.

'Mr. Chairman,' another spoke, 'I am one with you in the views and sentiments expressed. But really, one would have liked our youngest party official—youngest in terms of admission into the party—to go through the usual procedure of belonging before he could be appointed to such a post.'

Shouts of No No succeeded, but in a gay atmosphere. Some took the opportunity to remind the speaker that he could have been more lightly dressed. The young barrister wore a three-piece, navy-blue suit.

'Order, please!' the Chairman demanded, adding a few words about the need for tolerance. 'Our party ought to set the pace in discipline as well as in other things. Continue, Barrister Ugode.'

'Some people seem to want me to change my dress,' the barrister observed. 'They want me to put on a white flowing gown—what they term native attire. Permit me to observe that that's absolute nonsense. Let such people tell me, was the material for the gown made by the natives? Why should I prefer to be wrapped up in white cloth? We mustn't allow ourselves to be ruled by sentiments alone, or to be mere pretenders, like the fellows of the P.I.P. Take the example of that man, our so-called National Minister of Culture, who changed Edward, the name with which he was initiated into the church, to Eduado.

'But that is by the way, Mr. Chairman,' he now said. 'Let me stress that I am most happy that Mr. Medo has joined us, and that he will be the Publicity Secretary for Gorigori. I pledge my full cooperation. All I was trying to say at the start was that the mode of his choice, which admittedly is out of the ordinary, should not be regarded as a precedent.'

When I stood up to reply, I found myself stammering. The words had to make a difficult journey from the heart to the mouth. I had yet to reconcile my conscience completely to my new undertaking. The party's ideas sounded most impressive, and its membership—so many self-respecting citizens—seemed to suggest that it was sincerely out to pursue those ideals. But something was seriously being mooted for the local manifesto about ending once and for all the type of exploitation to which the indigènes of Gorigori had long been subjected. The reference was clearly to the P.I.P. candidate. Though Lobe had lived in Gorigori for well over twenty years now, was a councillor in the District Council, and had built for himself a very successful business as well as the most attractive houses, he was still an outsider. This was surely downright sectionalism, the base metal which would lend serious imperfection to the alloy. And indeed, ploughing deeper still into my conscience, I found another source of unease; a sense of personal injury.

I have always been strongly of the view that our country's principal contribution to political thought is in the field of party names. The citizens have a genius for inventing such names and an even greater one for finding their bearings through the bewildering permutations and combinations of letters. There were at this time, P.I.P., N.P.P., P.N.D.L., N.I.P., all in Bokenu State; R.D.C., R.C.D., C.D.R., N.D.R.D., in Doda State; and S.S.P., N.N.I.S., P.I.N.S., S.O.P., S.D.I., in Sakure State. Add to these the even more complex combinations of letters for trade-union names and it should be clear that the people are geniuses in their own right.

There was one dependable clue, however. Each of the three States had acquired its own distinctive letter. Thus Bokenu had P; Doda had D; while Sakure had S. As a further guide, each letter was in absolute control in its own State, and in no other State. The People's Independence Party ruled Bokenu, with no threat from any other party. The Real Democrats were very well entrenched in Doda in spite of, as they said, the vapourings and menaces from the P.I.P. As for the S.S.P., it had long ago proclaimed itself as firm as the rock of Gibraltar in Sakure, where no other party need venture.

And so, when the P.I.P. put up its posters announcing that the country was indivisibly one, and that any party could control any State and anybody should feel free to contest anywhere, and that the wise people of Gorigori were sure to set the pace in that regard, a secret hand went and scribbled below the poster that Gorigori would do no such thing, but rather would conform to the general pattern.

We put up our own posters two days after. They had a common theme—The man Lobe and his background. The aim was to demolish him completely before building up our man's image. That was part of the main publicity programme.

I crossed over from Gorigori to Ania early in the morning. From there I proceeded straight to Oban. The taxi was a fast one, covering the distance of fifty miles in well under an hour. I went straight to the classroom, without even reaching my house.

The Principal's office auxiliary brought a note to the classroom. That was unusual, I told myself. Could it be about my bodily appearance which, to say the least, wasn't all it might have been, with the early journey and a bit of hunger? The message in the note, that I should see him immediately in the office, did not make things any better.

Father Long smiled his usual half-smile as he looked into my face. Then he indicated a seat.

'I'm afraid, Mr. Medo, I have got a poor type of greeting for you. I had better let you have it right away.'

He took out a letter from the table drawer.

'From the State Ministry of Education. Read it for yourself.'

The scales were still in my eyes minutes after I had read it through.

'I am to warn you, it says, to stay here all through the school term and stop travelling across the Niger to Doda State,' he recapitulated.

'But what I can't understand,' said I in protest, 'is whether they imply that it interferes with my lessons. I've not been missing classes, I'm sure.'

'No, no.' He shook his head. 'And to be fair to them, they have not said so. They are simply against your political activities.'

'But that isn't in line with what obtains in the country.'

'What?'

'There are many legislators I know of who staged their campaigns while they were being paid as teachers, and nobody did anything to them.'

He allowed an interval. 'Well, Roland,' he said, 'I don't think I disagree with you. It's one of those things! I have been warned that unless I get you to put an end to either your politics or your engagement in the school, the school might be removed from the grant-in-aid list. We wouldn't like to lose our grants any more than we would like to lose your services. You see the point?'

I gazed at him.

'Read this.' It was the day's issue of the *Recorder*. He pointed at the editorial. 'Fancy the Irish priests being accused of being agents of the imperialists! I would like you to make up your mind what you are going to do and let me know before the month is out. But don't decide rashly.'

I could only grunt.

CHAPTER SIX

Biere would, most probably, prove unsympathetic, if I knew him well. He would laugh in triumph. There was no point in consulting him. I would see the Provincial Chairman instead, and that at once: cross over to the other side of the Niger in the morning.

That was what I did.

'Victimization pure and simple!' Ubakile pronounced, very composed. 'We had expected something like that all along.'

He went on after an interval: 'You may have noticed how the P.I.P. goes about hunting down its opponents for persecution. Well, let that be a challenge to you. Decide now what to do, or have you done so already?'

I shook my head wearily.

'The elections are quite close on us, and we wouldn't want to lose your services as Publicity Secretary. You've been doing nice work. The posters are in the right places and they say the right things. The Lobe man must be quaking.'

I kept on staring at the bare wall in front of me.

'One must of course feed the stomach,' he continued. 'What could you do for a living if you left the school?'

'Nothing I can think of readily,' I told him. 'Except perhaps—'

'What?'

'Unless one goes back to the university.'

'What for? All the way?' Then he shrugged his shoulders disdainfully. 'That would mean losing you—the very thing we wish to avoid! And in that case, you might as well stay where you are. You see the point?'

'It's out of the question,' I swore. 'I will not bow to the threat.'

'How much are they paying you?'

I told him the gross, and the net, from sheer contempt.

He asked me to come back in the evening, by which time he would have got the Party National Headquarters by phone.

The telephone operators were most cooperative, he said. They had no choice, of course; they were under strict orders to see that all calls from the party were put through without the least delay. The important point had now been cleared. The party had accepted to pay me my salary as a teacher. They would also provide me with a car for the speedy performance of my duties.

'And a driver.'

'That's all right, since I can't drive.'

'And a private secretary.' He gave an almost insidious smile.

'Yes?'

'You need one,' said he with yet another smile. 'Male or female, just as you like.'

'What would the secretary do for me?' I asked him.

'You'll decide for yourself,' was his reply.

A new red Volkswagen saloon driven by a loud and boisterous lad arrived four days later. It pulled up only a few feet before the front window of my office in the party District Headquarters. The driver revved the engine vigorously, grinning with what looked like sadistic relish. Mounted upright on the front fender of the car was a bundle of broom-sticks intended, symbolically, for the national stables. And a flashy female was sitting at the back, all alone.

'Park the car under the tree,' I pointed. 'I will tell you when I need it.'

'I been de think we go go out now,' the driver complained.

'Park the car,' I ruled.

He started the engine. 'I go park her too?' He gestured.

The lady secretary beamed, her head inclined coquettishly to the left, and demanded that the door should open at once, now that she had discovered her man. 'I didn't know that was my oga, Mr. Medo,' she added in a low, apologetic tone which seemed extremely polite of her.

I had not known she was so charming. Minutes after she had come into my office, I kept observing her—particularly her build, her skin, and her face. She for her part went on smiling, as if she was acknowledging the unspoken compliment, or was asking what I thought about the sophisticated hair-do and the tight-fitting gown, with its futuristically high hem.

'Your name again?'

She said Juliana. But I could call her Julie, as did her very best friends.

'Gentlemen of the party!' the Chairman called, slapping on his table. The day's meeting had been summoned to review our stategy for the campaigns, but we had spent most of the time discussing other subjects. And the discussions had been very stimulating. Starting with 'The machination and menaces of the colonial overlord', an article in the day's newspaper, the meeting had gone on to the educational system of the country, and finally to the Kingsway Stores.

'There is something I want to mention in confidence before we disperse,' he said. 'Some time last week, we received a small gift from Mr.

Lukter of the Premier Oil Company. Just a gesture of goodwill to the Government of the State. The point of interest is not the car itself—which Mr. Medo has already commandeered! It is this: the gift seems to me a sure sign that we're going to win. These firms can always be relied upon for their keen political sense.'

'No doubt,' concurred Barrister Ugode ambiguously, adding: 'Mr. Chairman, sir, you too will soon become an Honourable, probably a Minister. Make sure you remember us when you are swimming in the ocean of your ministerial paradise.'

'Amen!' the others sang.

'As you well know, Premier Oil has interests in the liquid mineral deposits in Gorigori,' Ubakile continued, apparently indulging the joke. But to some, it seemed he just did not want to be committed.

'I wonder really, isn't that a dangerous gift?' I asked.

'What? The car?' Woko, the party treasurer, interposed with simulated levity. 'Doesn't it run well?'

'A foe's gift is no gift, the ancient Greeks used to say.'

'You and Lukter are foes—is that what you are saying?' Woko asked again.

'A minute, please. We as a party are seriously dedicated to the cause of Independence, aren't we? . . . Why then accept such a gift from the very ones we're fighting against?'

'Well, I am not a classics man; I studied political science,' said Doctor Jiribe Ijoma, political adviser to the local party organisation. 'It is equally true to say that if aid comes from the devil we should accept it.'

'And I'm neither classics nor political science,' Ubakile said after the laughter had died down. 'I am engineering. For our present purpose, Lukter of Premier Oil may be likened to a scaffolding which one uses for construction work only to dismantle it completely in the end. I do appreciate though the point of your apprehension, Mr. Medo. My contention is that we mustn't allow the party to be worsted by those nincompoops of the P.I.P. when we can muster the means for avoiding that. There are even better grounds to believe that the seat will be ours, but we had better not go into those now. Shall we move out to see the crowd of supporters who are milling round?'

Now it was the month of April, and the pasture was just springing up

44

with tender freshness. Last night a rain had fallen and purged the air of dust, leaving it clean and cool. The ubiquitous palm-trees dominated the view in all directions, the more so as their long, narrow fronds had been washed to an oily sheen; they provided shelter for men and cars. White storks suddenly came flying across. Some detached themselves from the flight and perched in rebellion on the nearest palm tree. Then a lonely, surly one made to perch on a tangled cluster of bougainvillaea, only to fly off again, high into the sky. A cool, quiet breeze coming from the east sent a thrill into the veins. There was something exalted about the sensation I now felt. But there was something missing too: to me it lacked the wholesomeness of a shared feast. Biere was miles and miles away.

We crossed in the ferryboat over to Ania in the afternoon. The driver drove very fast indeed. The car purred on the tarmac with smooth ease and the windscreen glittered in the glare of the sun. He was good at it, I told myself, studying the driver from behind; never mind that he cursed at the least provocation, as when a pedestrian lurched and retreated, or a mammy-wagon took more than its share of the road. By four o'clock, we were driving into Biere's yard.

The houseboy said he would soon be in; then: 'Oh, there he is.' He pointed at Biere inspecting the car under the tree.

'Ro, Ro, Ro!' Biere called, entering the house. 'Where from?'

'Straight from across the Niger.'

He snorted, incomprehensibly. 'You haven't seen your principal then.' He sat down.

'I told you I've just arrived. Why?'

'Make sure you see him; he sent word asking about you.'

'Must be something about my condition of service,' I reflected. 'I'll see him this evening—and put in formal resignation.'

He sobbed; then he spoke, after some time: 'I am delighted to see you again, anyway. I have seen the auto under the shade. And the chauffeur.'

'I can't drive yet,' I explained.

'So they gave you a chauffeur, which is right. Except that he is not wanting in loquaciousness.'

'Why?'

'They gave you a damsel too.' He was now swinging the bunch of keys in his hand. 'Your private secretary, I hear she's called. Sort of for personal and private use.'

'Vulgar!'

'But what then would you say about the people who conceived the idea? ...'

We seemed to have returned, at long last, to the familiar tone and atmosphere, demolishing the thin wall which had stood between us for some time now.

'One hears about the campaigns only from the radio and newspapers. May we hear it from the horse's mouth? What is it that goes on between the Premier Oil and your brigade?'

'What did you hear?' I asked him in reply.

'They bought you people a car.'

I was almost stunned. 'How did you get to hear?'

'I got to—that's all.'

He ordered drinks for two.

He really shocked me after that. Chief Lobe had approached him in person and offered to refund to the party the cost of the car I was using, if only I would stop campaigning against him. Lobe would also see that I was reinstated as a teacher, with all arrears paid. And I would be appointed director of one of the statutory boards in Bokenu State. In the first case, I would have to declare for the P.I.P.; it would not be enough merely to quit the ranks of the Democrats. All these Biere told me, smiling his characteristic cynical smile.

'Can you beat that?'

'Interesting!' I said.

'And then, either in order to strengthen his promises or from sheer self-assertion, he revealed that it was the Premier Oil which was behind your party—just as Shaws and Sharp is behind the P.I.P.'

'Absolute nonsense!' I swore.

He fixed me with his sharp critical eyes.

'Don't choke yourself yet,' he laughed.

'The colossal fool! How could a man with his lack of intelligence come to all that knowledge of the party?'

'Party intelligence! He even proposed a test.'

I turned with interest. 'What type of test?'

'To prove that the information has come from the core of the party.

You are to listen to the radio late tonight, or very early tomorrow morning.'

I sat up in the hotel till late at night, eager to hear the latest news for the day. I was to cross over to Gorigori with the first ferry the following day; there would not, therefore, be time to listen to the early morning news. At last, the drum-beats sounded the signature tune. Then: 'Here is the last news for the day.' The first item was, predictably, something about a certain very important personality spending a two-week holiday with his loving and sagacious mother. The second was about the Minister for Chieftaincy Affairs in one of the States touring the United States of America in the interest of his duties. And then: 'A prominent member of the Real Democratic Party in Gorigori has resigned his membership and declared for the P.I.P. He is the well-known barrister, Young Ugode. In his letter of resignation, the barrister stated that he had discovered that the policies of the R.D.P. are not in consonance with the genuine aspirations of the nation.'

'What?' I gasped.

It might not be true after all. The announcement had come from Bokenu State radio, where the P.I.P. was very much in power. What had the Doda State radio to say? I turned the knob hastily. Almost too late! I only got the news headlines.

'. . . The barrister who was involved in a car accident died a few hours ago, shortly after he was rushed to Kedata General Hospital.'

'What!' I shrieked.

High-life music succeeded.

I switched off the radio, lay down on my back. My heartbeats had become very audible.

Father Long was as understanding as ever. He would like to take me back if I decided to return. 'Provided of course they don't proscribe you.' To which I had replied, mechanically. 'Thank you, Father.' Thinking about it, I should have responded with greater graciousness. Something like: 'I am most grateful, Father, for the way you've treated me all along with sympathy and understanding.' Nobody knew for sure what would happen in the end. I might decide to return to teaching, and to the school. But perhaps it wouldn't have made any difference. Father Long was not a man for sentiment. So I told myself. We were approaching the beach.

The sun rose early, sending the rays through a clear sky to the surface of the river. The water sparkled. A slow breeze began to blow. With grace and dignity, the water flowed on, gentle and unruffled, except where it curled up into waves, like mobile mounds of foam, as the launch creaked and groaned and the propellers churned. The *Tropical* was pretty old. It belched smoke and soot as black as the crewmen.

Everything looked orderly in the *Tropical* this morning—including nature, the launch itself, the crewmen and the passengers. The last in particular! They were mostly of the jovial, uninhibited type, young men crossing from Ania to Gorigori from where they would board lorries travelling to the heart of Doda, and even beyond to the nation's chief port. When they talked about the affairs of the land it was without any trace of bitterness; rather, they merely wondered whether they as individuals had anything against the men of Doda State with whom they traded, or vice versa. With wads of currency notes hidden all over their bodies, and a long journey ahead, they must not concern themselves at the moment with the politics of the States. It was simple common sense.

The launch docked a little after eight. I went straight to the party offices to check the news. The details I got only deepened the shock. And as the days passed, more and more facts began to come to light.

Nobody could guess how it could have come about that Ugode, who was a very sober and calculating young man, had driven into a big oil-bean tree on the right side of the road, especially as that particular stretch was long and broad. Anyway, that was the position. And the attitude of several members of the Executive suggested a studied indifference. At least, the electioneering activities were going on as if nothing had happened.

Tours in the mornings and discussions in the evenings; every day.

'While we face the issue of winning the coming election, let us not forget that the ultimate goal is to see that the country is freed from the shackles of imperialism. It is necessary to keep the nationalist fire alive.' That was now the party's article of faith. It had been composed by the National Chairman himself. It had to be obeyed. There were very refreshing discussions. You could always trust the party when it came to that. Long ago it had started, well before others, to purge the State public service of all white foreigners, and black foreigners too, including non-Dodans, which I thought was going a bit too far. Dodanisation was the word for it.

But the People's Independence Party was concentrating all they had on the election. They had built up a near-perfect organisation in the constituency. Their party stalwarts were of a rather professional class, when you considered their attire, their equipment and their methods. Their symbol was on display at every corner and was guarded by well-built men. And the Bokenu State radio, with its monstrously powerful transmitter, beamed continuously into Gorigori from across the river the list of the achievements of that party in the past five years in the various fields. Some of the claims were true indeed—which made the thing more dangerous. Especially so was what they said about education. 'Primary school enrolment in Bokenu State has more than doubled in the few years since the P.I.P. took over responsibility for the affairs of that lucky State; so also the number of secondary schools and teachers' colleges. And hospitals too . . .' Then they would revert to type, making every maternity home a hospital.

'Let them go on talking; they cannot win,' the chairman stated and received equally resolute cheers. 'We only need to put more money into the campaigns.'

'More money, why?' I cried out impetuously. 'It is shown in my progress report that we have more of the electorate on our side than do the other side.'

'You don't know that the other side is offering five a vote, I'm sure.'

'There I start getting puzzled, Mr. Chairman,' I told him. 'The party has enough spontaneous goodwill to carry it through; besides, hadn't we agreed that certain practices are to be deprecated? And now, we seem to be saying that since the other side is offering five, we should offer six.'

'Exactly,' someone else replied.

'Aren't we wasting time, Mr. Chairman?' another came in.

'Rule by consensus! We'll ask the Finance Committee to issue the funds,' yet another agreed.

The matter was put to the vote, however.

The final phase of the campaign was most exciting. Loud-speakers mounted on vans blared from morning to night, and to morning again, broadcasting vulgar slander or exaggerated praise, sometimes in song. Volkswagen cars went from house to house, to be followed in most cases by a rival's agent. Then we heard of plans to lure voters favourable to us to a banquet. The idea was to keep them comfortable at a chosen spot until the close of polling. We moved in promptly, using oaths and threats. Then, they sent their stalwarts into real action. They were already winning the day, the stalwarts, terrorising, looting and destroying. Indeed they would have swept their way to victory but for what followed.

'Hee pee peep!'

'Ouraah!'

'Vote for—' the same voice called through the speaker.

'The P.I.P.,' came the response, from private houses as well as open places. The thing was infectious.

And then, from the northern side of Gorigori, where the brow of a small hill faced the river, came a different kind of song:

'Down with—?'

'The P.I.P.'

'Louder! Down with?'

'The P.I.P.'

'We are?'

'Real Democrats.'

'We are?'

'Real Democrats.'

'And also?'

'Owners of Gorigori.'

They had come within sight.

'All others?'

'Are strangers.'

'Men like?'

'Lobe, the rogue.'

'Men like?'

'Lobe, the lecher.'

'Men like?'

'Lobe, the bandit.'

'Men like?'

50

'Lobe, the fool.'

'They must not be allowed—'

'—to dominate us.'

'Long live—?'

'The party that's going to save us.'

They went berserk, running, trotting, dancing. There must have been over a thousand of them, both men and women, young and old, breathing fire and shaking their fists into the air.

'Ubakile!'

'He is our man.'

'Ubakile!'

'He is our man.'

'Gorigori!'

'It is our home.'

I bit my lip.

'Tell Lobe—'

'—to go back to his own State.'

'Tell Lobe—'

'—to leave our land for us.' They continued to advance until they were only a short distance from the office. Their tense muscles glistened with sweat. They alternated the singing with dissonant shrieks and ululations.

They later broke into the P.I.P. office, after which they proceeded to look for the party's leading supporters.

The police made several arrests, and started guarding what was left of that building as well as our own offices. Then, with their wonderful sense for the political weather, they cautioned and sent away all those under arrest just before the start of polling.

CHAPTER SEVEN

'They haven't yet announced the cabinet?'

'No; but we expect to hear something any time now.'

'I guess Roland Medo will not be one of them.'

'What leads you to guess so, Monsieur?'

'The fact that he is here in Oban at the moment. He should have been on the other side of the river and at the headquarters of Doda State.'

'Doing what, exactly?'

'Manoeuvring for a ministerial post, or rejoicing at his success.'

'You've failed to note that Roland Medo was not a candidate, much less a successful one; and therefore—'

'What?'

'Could not, even if he wished it, be appointed an Honourable Minister.'

'You say that? But nothing prevents them making you one. All they need do is to transform you into a Chief, without the least bit of the African soil as your domain.'

'Quite right,' I admitted.

'Chief the Honourable Minister R.C. Medo.'

'Sounds macabre.'

'It does.'

'I have begun to detest the whole thing!'

'Repeat that!' Biere exclaimed.

'True!' I affirmed.

'Pretty early,' he went on in his merciless sarcasm. 'You haven't bought yourself a Pontiac; nor have you been allocated any State land, much less built houses on it.'

I frowned in protest.

'I hope to heaven you mean what you're saying, anyway.'

'It's so soul-destroying!'

He glanced right and left. I could not tell why. 'After you have given the Chief what he deserved!'

'What did I give? He just lost,' I objected.

'He holds that you are the architect of his failure.'

'He told you?'

'He told people.'

'That's entirely his look-out,' said I boastfully, then went on with emotion: 'They will always remember Roland Medo—he and his woman.'

'Twenty State Ministers of State and twenty-five State Parliamentary Secretaries!' I complained, shrugging.

'Quite a number,' he merely said. 'And your man, Mr. Ubakile, is the State Minister of Works and Transport.'

'Nothing's wrong about that; my anger is over the quantity. Out of a House of one hundred and two, and a party strength of seventy-four, there are forty-five Ministers and Assistant Ministers.'

'Could have been much less—I agree with you. But we may yet have an increase in the party's floor members, thus reducing the ratio of Minister-to-non-Minister on the Government side.'

'How?'

'Simple process of carpet-crossing.'

The first report came that same evening. Mr. Michael Ojie who had won on the People's Independence Party platform, had now declared for the Real Democrats.

Two more crossed over the next day.

I had had enough. I must quit—escape.

I must salvage what was left of me from this adventure, from the intense and putrid heat. And for effective purification, I must move away, far from the scene. I would find myself a sanctuary, not in the noisy atmosphere of Oban but in the wooded fastness of the country-side.

Umuntianu was the place. We had been reared in that small village. The family still lived there. Umuntianu! It had a longish, queer-sounding name. That was why I had hitherto hesitated to identify myself with it. I merely told enquirers that I came from Oban. It was a common thing among the people of the land. He comes from Ania. Or from Portcity. Or from Oban. Or Labare. Or Sokeba. Hardly anybody would want to declare himself a product of the small, unknown places. I would now. Henceforth, I would call Umuntianu my home town. Right home, then. There, I would breathe an air free from the harsh obscenities and merciless slanders that the speaker spouted every day.

The trouble was Biere Ekonte. He would tease and tease, and probably quote Mr. Hilary to me again. Biere could be ruthless when he had a point against you. But let him do it—let him taunt. What did that matter now? I was leaving and that was all.

And for the benefit of my conscience, there was this big consolation, a point of credit: the residue was clean enough. Those long discussions at party meetings had more than kept the fire alive: they had had me properly baked. What had we not discussed? Each member spoke in his own style. Ubakile, presiding and facing the rest, would intone in a voice that sounded sad and was penetrating: 'It's imperialism all through—imperialism in its numerous shapes.' And then, the others would go off denouncing.

One day, it was:

'Their main concern is economic exploitation—all these white fellows who fill up Oban and profess friendship with our people.'

'Everybody knows that! And they dangle before the people all sorts of tantalizing baits.'

'The educational policy of the country is what irritates me most—if, in fact, it is a policy! It simply stinks. The curriculum has largely Arts subjects with very little of the Sciences.'

'You know why it's so, don't you? They don't want us to have the technical know-how necessary for exploitation of our resources: they want to keep the exploiting for themselves. . . .'

And on another occasion:

'Some of these missionaries are excellent men.'

'Maybe. A few individuals in whom the chord of humanity still vibrates!'

'Force of conscience—no more! They are atoning for the ills perpetrated on our race by their uncles.'

'I think there's a genuine element of philanthropy in it.'

'Philanthropy my dirty foot! It is all imperialism, no more. Religious imperialism if you like. They also want to dominate the spiritual life of our people.'

'Sure! Sure! I agree entirely. We must press for the removal of white missionaries too, except those who are prepared to work under our own bishops and other clergy, and sincerely too.'

'It will come to that,' Ubakile concluded. 'And pretty soon.' He was looking grave, like one suppressing an internal pain, while another kept biting his finger nail and another his lip. One man began a story about how the country's senior civil servants were being enticed, or compelled, indirectly, to spend all their earnings on imported goods, mostly cars and clothes and carrots and apples. At the end, I told the story of Allen, the bully and hound, omitting some details. Moments later, Ugode raised the big issue of higher education in the country:

'The first institution of higher learning they ever started for our people turned out to be a sadist's workhouse. They took in about twenty persons each year for medicine, for example—twenty top brains; and after seven years of intensive studies, only one or two were pronounced successful. The rest were thrown away as unfit. And yet, it's such casualties who later on, on their own resources, found their way into overseas universities and are currently performing wonders, winning medals and things. And the one or two who were deemed capable enough to qualify were merely appointed into the civil service as medical assistants—to serve under white war veterans.'

'Terribly frustrating!'

'That was the Higher College,' I came in. 'Thank God, it no longer exists; instead we now have the university which pursues a more humane policy.'

'Not from the start though—they began by mass-weeding and were forced later on to relent. The same fear of their brothers being displaced!'

'And fear of Red influences, too.'

The atmosphere seemed charged. In the silence that reigned, someone sobbed while another ground his teeth. I cracked my fingers over my bowed forehead. It was a drama I would never forget.

Oh yes, sir, Imperator, I detest your ways now more than before. Please note: from now on your name is Imperator. So then, Imperator, *tu es mihi odio*. You've been doing this and that deed in my native land. Count them, starting with the one in which your prototype, the pink beast of a man, assaulted my father and called him a number of animal names, in my hearing.

We met again a few days later. I gave him the news without a preamble. He listened with interest. He looked sympathetic.

'Thank God!' he said. 'What do you intend to do thereafter?'

I disclosed the rest of my plan.

He gave a grunt, as of resignation.

'Can you come and help me pack?'

'Where?'

'At Uncle Edoha's, where I'm staying. Please come.'

'When?'

We fixed the day and time.

He promised to visit me at Umuntianu before the end of the month.

The taxi, a fairly new black Peugeot station-wagon, pulled up at the point where the approach to our house forked into the broad but rugged road. It sneezed several times. The dust began to diminish. The driver's door swung open. I too came out.

Dora came running, shouting, calling my name. Moments later, she threw herself on me, for a start; then, she caught my hand and held it firmly. Louis and Dom arrived simultaneously.

'Rola!' Mamma cried, arriving at last. She had not been quite decided whether to run or to walk, and was still holding her head-tie in her hand. Her spectacles did not disguise the tearful look to which she was prone in her moments of emotion. 'It's he I'm looking at!' she assured herself.

'Mamma, it is!' Dora laughed.

'And he has brought home all his things, did you say?'

'Mamma, he has,' the other confirmed.

'Lost child!' She came on me in earnest. Winding her hands round my neck, she threw the full weight of her body on me. I made to detach myself, but she held on even more firmly. 'Come home to your own father's house,' she sang.

'Enough of that now,' the driver sighed, scratching his head impatiently. 'Come and remove his things from the car so that I can move,' and he went on to remind everybody that he had not come to witness a family reunion.

We did his will.

'Rola, my son,' Mamma resumed as soon as the stranger had gone. 'You look all bones, but of course nobody has ever known you for your bulk. You got it from your father, all of you.'

'Except me, Mamma,' Dora corrected.

'Rola, it is nearly a year now since you last visited home.'

She was exaggerating. It was only seven months. I had not written a single letter. But they had got to hear about my adventure. I had been

56

so involved in the thing that I could scarcely lift my mind to think about home.

'Mamma, Mamma!'

'Yes, yes; Dorothy, yes!'

'Dominic refuses to carry the big box.'

'Refuses? Why? And where is he?'

'He has gone back to the house. He says people who are in secondary schools don't carry loads on their heads.'

Dom came out again with a towel, which he rolled into a pad. We lifted the box up to his head.

We all began to move towards the house.

'Rola, you won't go away again, will you?'

'Dorothy!' Mamma bawled. 'He hasn't reached the house yet and you're telling him about leaving.'

'Why? He will reach it soon. And I won't let him go away again.'

I was greatly amused. Laughing, I gazed at her, the eleven-year-old girl who was Mamma's exact image: long-faced, heavy, erect, a crisp voice.

The house had been built some twenty years before. I still remembered the occasion. The hammer had pattered on the iron sheets for days and days, and a large crowd had assembled at the scene. Most of them were there merely to watch the experts manipulating the trowels or nailing the sheets of metal together. It was the second such building in the village of Umuntianu, but the very first to have white-washed walls, and a cement floor, and, most important of all, a large sitting-room that could accommodate a score or more persons at a time. Some had felt at the time that Papa was a bit queer. Why should he build such a house, his actual home, in a locality where he was by and large a stranger? I don't think they took seriously his frequent claim to being a model citizen, for whom any part of the country was home.

He had left Gorigori for Oban before he was twenty-five. He was already a carpenter then, and the Public Works Department needed scores of carpenters. They employed him on probation at first. But they soon discovered his worth. That was how Papa used to put it. And not only that, people began to talk about him all over Oban and even beyond. From Oban, he would visit the nearby villages, where he occasionally undertook private work in his spare time. It was during one of these visits that he met the girl who later became his wife. Or perhaps it was the latter who first observed him, for at that time he was, according to his own account, a handsome lad, in addition to being a talented carpenter. He got to know Umuntianu shortly after, through a friend. Thanks to the latter, he soon acquired at Umuntianu a piece of land which was large enough to take four hundred mounds of yam in five places. That was how he began to evolve into a man of Umuntianu, with no strong feelings for Gorigori. He told us the story times without number during his life time, often insisting that we recite it in his hearing, as if he had some apprehension that one day, when he was no more, someone would challenge our title over the land. Nobody had. The house was very much there still, as firm and undisturbed as during his lifetime.

'This picture still hangs here,' I observed, gazing at the enlarged photograph of the newly-wedded pair.

'Why not?' Mamma objected. 'What do you think could have happened to it?'

'Mamma, Mamma!'

'Yes, yes; Dorothy, yes?'

'What about the one of you and Alex and Rola taken when Rola was small? It is still in your room. Rola, you would like to see it.'

'Later. Go and prepare something for him to eat,' she commanded; but they went together, Dora singing *London is Burning*, for the benefit of my ears.

There were two bedrooms on each side of the sitting-room. Those on the right were promptly cleared and swept, and furnished with table and chairs. In addition, I was automatically to take control of the sitting-room. That was partly because at that moment I was the eldest child, since Alex lived with his family some distance away; and partly because Mamma had elected to move over to the outhouse at the back. More or less, then, the house was mine. And on my part, I would care for it. But was there much caring to do yet? The compound walls were still sturdy. The yard was neatly kept. The building walls had very few stains. The floor was as solid as ever. I tried to commend Mamma for these. But she only waved me aside.

'So you thought I would allow your father's yard to be overgrown while I still have my limbs?'

Thick bush grew behind the rear compound wall. A wind was blowing and the leaves gave a gentle rustle. The sun was fast sinking, and the sky had turned into a blazing red, with patches of clouds aglow here and there. And a variety of birds was circling and diving, while others nearby whistled and chirruped. The effect was quiet and soothing, wholesome, forgiving. This was real beauty; a cool and natural setting, with a promise of permanence. *Happy is he who knows the beauty of the countryside.* Happier still if the experience is shared with a kindred spirit.

CHAPTER EIGHT

Biere did not come until five weeks after my return. Before I could tell him what I thought of him, he began to relate how he had left the house very early in the morning, and how the car had very nearly plunged them to death at Ikoto, midway between Oban and Umuntianu. One of the front wheels had come off and the car had bumped into a bridge-head. Fortunately, nobody was seriously injured. But the bridge was closed to all vehicular traffic for several hours. Then he said something very scathing about Public Works men.

'I shouldn't be surprised if that bridge remains like that for the next year.'

'They take their time, those P.W.D. fellows,' I agreed.

'And others' too. They seem to have some permanent grudge against humanity. Last time I saw them doing what they called road-repair work, they were all sitting on the ground, chatting, some of them taking snuff. One young man among them was shouting about people who grab all the money which God had intended for all.'

'The imperialists, no doubt.'

'Yes and no.'

'How no?'

He remarked instead: 'Some people, you know, want us to rule ourselves, while some don't seem to want to commend their future to their own brothers. You know the latest quip at Oban?'

'Tell me.'

'That's how you're going to rule yourselves.'

'They don't appear to have much confidence in their brothers!'

'No. And yet the thing is almost on us—only a year or so ahead.'

'Go and change, man; we'll go out together,' I shouted at him, with a hint of dissent. 'They don't have enough confidence in their brothers because the great lord has destroyed their psyche, among other things. You'll be staying a week or so with us?'

'Why not a year?'

'Isn't this a holiday?'

'What about Mamma?' he enquired now.

'Out.'

'And Dom?'

'Out.'

'And—'

'Out too,' I cut in before he could say the name. 'They are all annoyed that you failed to come as early as I had led them to expect. Go and have a wash while I organise something to eat. We'll go out after that to see Mamma's brother who lives at Siaku.'

'I know of Edoha only.'

'There's another, an elder one, whose name is Ogidi,' I informed him. 'It's him we'll be visiting.'

We decided in the end to postpone the visit till the following day.

The road was barely more than a foot-path winding through the thick bush. A rain had fallen during the night. The vegetation was all fresh and green. A gentle sunlight invaded the air as well as the sodden earth.

'Rural beauty!' Biere mused. 'Very different from the bustle and traffic of men and vehicles.'

'Happy is he who knows the beauty of the countryside,' I quoted.

'Who could that be?'

'A Roman poet—I can't remember exactly who, but it seems Virgil.'

'Very true.'

'And very sweet in the original.' I quoted the Latin. 'The rural environment is an antidote to the tensions one experiences in the towns. It's only there that you can recapture the original native spirit, so relaxed and pleasant. And the human cohesion of village life.'

'An enthusiast's tribute.'

He called out, pointing ahead: 'Look, see that stretch of hills!' There in front of us lay the Abome Hills, monstrous ridges over which lush pasture was daintily spread: imposing undulations clothed in inviolate green. 'The sight is irresistible, man. A matter of aesthetics.'

'Aesthetics, which is poetry.'

'You are right. And sister to goodness. . . .'

The road now cut through the edge of one of the folds. The ascent was short and easy. We would pay for this, as well as for the long descent before us, on the return journey.

Now we were already descending. The ground was stony, and muddy too today, after the night's rain. Then we stood fanning ourselves, looking at the bridge at the fall.

It was an old, rickety wooden bridge, I explained. Nobody had cared much about it, any more than the road itself, since Mr. Stephens, the young, restless Administrative Officer, put up the structure some ten years back. Nobody, unless one should take any notice of what those men called Native Authority Roadmen did to sections of the road with the twelve shovels of sand they dug up each day! Who did not know why? The inhabitants of the locality had, as the saying went, consistently indulged in seriously anti-Government activities, which in precise terms meant voting against the P.I.P. candidate. Not that they had anything against the party itself, they would explain; it was just that they would not accept the braggart and upstart who was being imposed on the people. The plea had however merely angered the authorities all the more. A few heaps of laterite could still be seen here and there along the road.

'So shameful,' came his remark.

'And so, while many hitherto obscure roads in the State are getting tarred, this one, which leads through the heart of the State, is neglected.'

'Some, though, are being tarred by the oil companies—notably Premier Oil.'

'Which to me doesn't seem a particular happy thing.'

'Why?'

'Everything about them is suspect, Biere.'

'Except their roads, which are very strong and therefore make locomotion easier and quicker.'

'In respect of locomotion, if one may digress, the State has done well,' I said.

'How's that?'

'So many new roads have been built and old ones reconstructed within the past five years, while we've been having internal self-rule.'

'That I would concede, but with some qualification.'

'Let's hear that.'

'You should have said something about more percentagings too.'

'It doesn't matter,' I objected.

'Doesn't what?'

'At least we have achieved more within the short time than did the Imperator.'

He did not at first appear to have heard.

'Don't forget he has no intrinsic interest in making you great,' said he after an interval. 'I mean the man you call Imperator and other names. It is our people who ought to have genuine interest in the country's progress.'

We were facing the bridge directly.

The water was shallow, though for little children adequate for a swim. And there were indeed many of them there, naked, splashing, chattering, crying, and the bush around returning a sharp echo; boys as well as girls. Some of the boys, the bigger ones, held their palms joined over their groins while the girls turned their backs to us.

We caught one of the girls unawares.

'Good morning,' she greeted us, with delicacy and respect.

I fixed my eyes on her. She must have been around fifteen; perhaps more, not less. I advanced a few steps. She was very charming; dark-skinned; the hair done in curly waves; beads of water dotting her skin. Then she blew into the air, in an effort to stop the water dripping from her forehead from touching her body. She was simply fresh, like the water itself which, flowing straight from the source close by, gurgled through the bed of pebbles and white loose sand. This girl looked elusive, like a nymph, I thought; and then, as if she had read my mind, she turned round and made to move away, farther in—to vanish. The lower part of her body now became conspicuous, at last. White and pink beads piled on her waist, and below the beads a string of cloth that seemed to have been plastered on her body reached as far down as her lap.

'You, come here!' I called.

Startled, she turned round again, with scores of eyes glinting at her.

'Myself?'

'Yes.'

She threw handfuls of water into her eyes in a shy escape, and began to blow at the drips, just as before.

'How are you?'

'Well, sir.' Her voice was mechanical, yet as fragile as seemed her body.

'Is this our way to Siaku?'

She mustered all the energy in her for a curt yes, after which she disappeared, leaving the eyes gazing at me.

Biere eyed me upbraidingly.

'A nymph!' I exclaimed.

Not one word came from him, and we began to cross the bridge.

'You noticed something round her waist—some concession to custom?'

'I saw the beads.'

'And you know the fate of those mortals who have been enchanted by nymphs, don't you?'

'Tell me.'

'I was impressed by her English,' he digressed.

'Anyway, it's a mark of progress that we should have such an enlightened creature in this remote village. There isn't a household in this area where you don't have one or two children who can read and write.'

'We certainly have done well in the field of education.'

I wasn't sure whether he was being sarcastic again. 'Look at the number of graduates produced in the past few years,' I said.

'Yes.' He sounded mysterious. There was a pause. 'Which could be a potential source of serious trouble.'

'How?'

'Remember what Mr. Rogers said in the university. "Till we exhaust our brothers." '

'The man is an outdated fool.'

'There's something else to it, apart from Rogers.'

'Yes?'

'You turn out so many graduates to meet the manpower requirements of the whole country, only to find in the end that there's isn't one country in fact. Look at that!'

It was a bunch of bananas, yellow and luscious from ripeness, drooping down the stalk.

'I feel like stealing one!'

'Steal? Don't steal, stranger.' The voice came from the bush. An elderly man emerged carrying a bundle of fodder. 'I can give you one to eat.' He plucked four instead, two for each of us.

We came to a cluster of trees, with a glade.

'A shrine.'

'What else could it be?'

'Even in this year of our Lord?'

'Your christianity has not succeeded in banishing the native gods completely my friend. And it never will.' My conscience ruled that it was a case of patriotic blasphemy.

Tomtom beats were pounding at a distance, some poles away to the right.

'A wrestling match is going on.'

'So early in the day?'

'Why not?'

A big roar of applause followed.

'A hero must have been thrown.'

'Yes?'

Harsh voices sounded; then a terrible din.

'Are we safe?'

'Let's hurry,' I urged. 'Usually when a hero is thrown his side resents it even to the point of violence. It is humiliating, especially when one thinks of the scorn and insolence which follows. The Greeks had a word for it.'

'What was the word?'

'Hubris. And, they as a people—the Athenians actually—refrained from hubris; it was the Romans who practised it with barbaric pageantry. . . .'

64

'I wonder what's happening now to our Social Enlightenment Circle?' he asked after an interval. 'If it still exists.'

'Who knows?' I said. 'We should presume it's still there—although it must have been seriously infested with party politics.'

'Tribal alignments, to be more exact. Each side defending the doings of its own tribesmen.'

'And the expatriate members of staff prodding them on from the rear.'

'Agreed, for the purpose of argument. Then, tell me why they should be so foolish as to allow themselves to be prodded.'

'We are getting quite near; see the building,' I dodged the question.

The broad approach was lined on both sides with shade trees. Voices of children rang into the air from the tree tops:

We may differ in the language we speak
Yet we all remain children of the land.

'Seems they've been rehearsing.'

'That National Anthem is just splendid.'

'It is—provided of course the whole thing doesn't prove a self-mocking sarcasm.'

'Why?'

'Look at the situation in the country today,' Biere said. 'Bokenu State for one ethnic group; Doda State for another; Sakure for another. Pure and simple. Anybody who pretends otherwise is unrealistic.'

'It seems Mr. Rogers is being proved right then about the country never being one,' I agreed with him.

'You're coming round.'

We heard 'He-i hi-i!' and a figure dropped from one of the trees and began dashing towards us, full speed, with some younger ones following behind. In another moment, Isaac held me round the stomach and was leaning against my body.

'Welcome!' he panted out.

'You've not greeted my friend!' I gestured, stroking his head with the right hand.

'Good afternoon, sir.'

'How are you?' Biere responded.

65

'I am very well, sir.' He pronounced each word distinctly.

'Looks a very intelligent boy,' Biere remarked as we were moving into the compound. 'Isaac, how old are you?'

'I am thirteen and a half years old.'

'And in what class?'

'I am in standard six.'

'He has been selected to go to college next year.' That was Orienna, his younger sister.

'True?' Biere and I exclaimed together, and the boy confirmed it.

'And father says you will pay for him there.'

'Ta-a-ah!' Isaac railed at her, then ran after her. The small loquacious thing had compromised the big agenda so soon in the day.

Giving up the chase, he returned to join us again.

'Is your father in?' I wondered.

'Yes—except that he is on the afternoon round of the palms,' he replied. 'I'll go and tell him you've arrived.'

'And your mother?'

'She's in the farm, behind the house.'

'Who are those people, Isaac?' she called.

'Come and see for yourself,' he answered her with pious irreverence. We went to see her instead, while Isaac went to look for his father.

She was making mounds for cocoyam seedlings. Bending low, she dug the ground with the hoe between her feet, while the sun beat fiercely on her. Over the mounds, small, winged ants, dislodged from their abode, circled and floated. Some flocked to her body in an unavailing protest.

'How is it with you and the work?' I greeted.

She looked up abruptly, angered at the distraction. 'Oh, is it you?' she asked penitently, and smiled. She brushed her forehead with a crooked forefinger. 'It is so hot today. How is your mother, Roland?'

'She sends greetings.'

The sun began to contract its heat and a breeze came, sending a congealing sensation into the heated muscles.

'You had better go into the house and wait; I must get to that pear-tree before breaking up for the day,' she said, pointing to the tree.

'Who are those, Uruaku?' The voice came from a palm-tree far behind us; and it was harsh.

'Your own sister's son, and his friend.' She sounded quite hurt, as Ogidi's tone suggested he was anxious on his own behalf. Uruaku was famous in the land for her beauty, and she was still young.

'We had better go and meet Ogidi,' I proposed.

Ogidi had descended from the tree when we got to the spot. He had also folded the climbing rope and slung it over his left shoulder, holding the knife in his right hand, the way all tappers do. He called me 'Father', as soon as his eyes caught sight of me. Ogidi always insisted that it was his father, Obiazo, who had re-appeared in the world in my shape. He offered us his knuckles, apologising that his palm was not clean enough.

'One more tree only. Go and wait in the house.'

We offered to wait for him close to the tree.

He unwound the rope once more, and cast it round the trunk. He tied up the ends into a loop. He began to step, up, up.

'There's art in it, truly,' Biere observed.

'Of course, yes,' he agreed. 'Just as in the books you younger ones read.' 'There is more in climbing.'

Perched nearly midway up the tall tree now, and leaning with his back against the rope, he burst into laughter. 'Teach me to read and I'll teach you to climb, my son,' he shouted. 'You people who can read and write books do not know how much others envy you. People have been urging me to go to church. What for? Just to listen to the catechist while others read from books.'

'Very true, Ogidi!' another voice echoed from a palm-tree at a distance.

CHAPTER NINE

Ogidi was slow in disclosing the purpose of the invitation. And I came to find out later that it was part of the tactics he and his sister had agreed upon. He should merely introduce the matter, leaving it to her to prod me on my return.

And so she did. Now and again, she would remind me that nobody could be called a man who had had no direct responsibility for the upbringing of the young. I gave in in the end, though vaguely. I would pay for Isaac in the secondary school; provided I was in a position to do so when the time came.

'And now, my son, you had better begin to think about what to do with yourself,' she then followed up, frowning.

'Mamma, how?' I wondered.

'Find something to do, and also—' She withdrew her eyes. 'You are old enough to start thinking of your own household.'

'Household? At my age?' I exclaimed, abstractedly; my mind was on her first point.

The initial excitement about a quiet and restful life in the village had long begun to wear off. Schools had re-opened at the end of the vacation, and now Louis and Dorothy were away each day from morning to lunch time, while Dom had returned to the boarding house, and Biere called only once in a long while. Quiet and restful indeed; but it was also dull and monotonous. It wasn't the fault of the village in any way. Having exhausted practically all I had by way of savings, there was nothing left for cigarettes, or an occasional drink, or for the requirements of cleanliness and a peaceful mind. Flowers and scenery and birds and sunset clouds and other things—they were still very much there, only the thorns and sand were becoming more and more noticeable. In my helplessness, I had even considered Alex.

Alex might have been able to assist the unemployed younger brother, his own blood. But he was responsible for Dom's fees, and was at the same time remitting fantastic amounts overseas as tutorial fees; and, further still, paying for his wife's younger brother, also in a secondary school. It had been a condition for her accepting to be his wife that he should undertake to train one of her numerous brothers in a secondary school. That was in addition to the two hundred pounds which he had had to pay, cash down, as the bride-price. The reasoning behind it all had been that the salaries which she would earn thenceforth would go to the husband, whereas she had been to the teachers' college at her father's expense. Why Alex had submitted himself to this piece of blackmail I, Roland, could not understand, any more than why he had not considered it time to repudiate the obligation.

'Mamma, did you say something about marriage?' I asked, rounding up the reflection.

'Of course I did,' she affirmed.

'In spite of what your other son has been experiencing?'

'Well, when you set out to marry, we'll make sure you don't put yourself in his position,' she countered. 'But when will you start?'

'When I am old enough.'

'You were born only yesterday!'

'Let me find a job first. . . .'

She concluded by reminding me, once more, that Isaac was now my responsibility.

As if he had been party to the conspiracy between brother and sister, Isaac moved over to our house at Umuntianu immediately the schools closed again on vacation and declared himself my personal servant. He was very efficient at his self-imposed duty. Isaac laid my meals on, fetched water for my bath, and followed me to places. I liked his company. He was ever-cheerful, ever-smiling. 'Yes, sir,' he would say, in response to a question, and his cheeks would bunch into a spontaneous smile, more from good-naturedness than from shyness, his sky-white teeth shining.

He was acknowledged to be the image of his mother. It was delightful to listen to him as he spoke—talking and laughing simultaneously, and yet full of common sense. Still more delightful was the sensation I felt whenever, on a sudden impulse, I tapped his cheeks. Flushed and fresh, the muscles of his body were like the leaves on a tender yam sapling curling slowly and purposefully round the stake.

He was already talking a lot, for the benefit of my ears, about secondary school. Sometimes, he would even flaunt the prospectus at me; or read out the list of recommended books; or recite the motto of the school, 'Pro Deo Pro Homine'. And then, one morning, he informed me he would like to go to the university after he had left the secondary school. He would study Latin, like me, and English, like Biere. Did I approve?

Without replying, I went in to compose an application for a teaching appointment.

The Principal of Amane Community High School replied less than two weeks after. It would be a delight to have me on the staff, he said, among some other things, then went on in a strikingly personal note:

'We do not want to seem indiscreet in our appreciation, but feel you should have a frank statement from us in the hope that the services you will render will be equally unstinted ... If you would call at the office at your earliest convenience, we will discuss the necessary details.'

The school was barely ten miles to the east of Umuntianu.

I arrived a little after eight in the morning. It was the third day of term, yet, from all appearance, they had already got down to the full rhythm of activities. Both students and staff were out in the open field, on morning assembly. I watched from the verandah of the Principal's office. They began to sing, all stiff and absorbed, eyes closed. In their uniform of white and green, and standing on the level, grassy field, they looked like statues. 'Oh God, our hope in ages past,' they sang, in not very musical voices but with the utmost devotion, their faces lifted upward; after which they prayed again. Finally, they marched to the classrooms.

At last, the Principal came onto the verandah.

'Good morning! ...'

'Good morning!' and he turned round.

I introduced myself.

We shook hands.

From the same direction, some one else arrived. He was bald-headed and middle-aged, and white. What could this one be doing here? I protested within me.

'Mr. Lewis ... Mr. Medo.' It seemed as if the Principal had read my mind. 'Mr. Lewis is on our staff—the only expatriate.' It wasn't clear to me whether he was being boastful or remorseful.

I gave the Lewis man a steady gaze which he promptly returned. We shook hands. It was like a truce.

'A minute, Mr. Medo. Let me see Lewis first about some vital matter,' the Principal said. 'By the way, I should have informed you that Lewis is our History Master. Medo is our prospective Latin Master.'

'We won't be a minute,' Lewis said.

'It's perfectly all right.' I had been somehow impressed already by the Lewis man, especially by his calm, almost venerable manner of speech.

70

I was packing. I would leave for my new school the following day.

'They are up again,' Ogidi shouted from the entrance door. 'They may want to set the whole world ablaze this time.'

'Is that Ogidi's voice that I hear?' Mamma enquired.

'Yes, my sister.' He came into the yard.

'And who was it talking with you outside the compound?'

'Do I remember his name? He told me that the box thing which the young ones call radio said there will be another vote soon.' He sat down and took out his snuff box; then, from habit, he began to search for the spoon, starting from the ears.

'Which vote?' I teased him.

He used his thumb instead. 'Ah!' he cried, lustily, and big teardrops came down his eyes. He cleared his nose. 'I value this my snuff much more than the thing they are doing, my son,' he replied at last. 'I hear it will be the last vote before we begin to rule ourselves.'

'It must be that they have dissolved the National Parliament,' I reflected.

'Whatever it is, nobody is going to have Ogidi's vote paper for nothing this time,' Ogidi swore with some vehemence. 'And they must deliver it into my hand'—he displayed his palm—'before I set out to vote for them.'

'You are not supposed to be paid for that, you know?'

'Why? What wrong have I done?'

'Ogidi, remember to thank your father,' Mamma cut in, shouting from the backyard.

'Yes?' he enquired.

'Thank him that our son Isaac has gone to the school.'

'What! My good sister, tell me.'

'Yes; he left yesterday.'

Ogidi burst into a song, rocking in his seat and beaming with satisfaction.

'I haven't paid the fee yet though,' I pointed out, from modesty.

'What does that matter?' he asked in song.

'I merely gave him a note for the Principal of the school promising to pay later on.'

'Just as you decide.' He was now shaking both head and shoulders and stamping his feet on the ground to the rhythm of his song.

'It is the same school in which Roland was employed before he went into madness,' Mamma explained. 'They will agree to wait till he has the money.'

'Of course they will agree,' he echoed, stamping harder still. 'Ogidi's own son will one day be like the great ones. . . .'

'Mind my floor, please!' She began to laugh. So did everybody else in the house.

The election did not seem to attract half as much public attention as had its immediate predecessor. And the reasons were quite obvious. In the first place, being a national affair, its meaning was rather remote from the interests of the villagers. The parliamentarians had to travel hundreds of miles, far far beyond the river, to make their own kind of laws. Nobody knew exactly what type of laws they were supposed to be making when they controlled neither the roads, nor the schools, nor the hospitals, nor the Councils—unlike those who went to the State legislature. So, you might as well stay quietly in your house all the time, and then on the polling day go out and cast the vote for *them*, provided of course they did for you whatever it was they were doing for others. That apart, the overall result of the elections, on both State and national scale, could hardly ever show any change. The party which dominated a particular State legislature would always contrive to win most of the seats for that State in the National Parliament. It was as simple as that. But that was not all. One particular State alone had more seats in the National Parliament than the remaining two put together. What change then could elections effect, really speaking, in such a situation?

It was this last point principally which had recently driven a group of persons calling themselves 'patriotically angry youths', domiciled in Doda State, to found a newspaper of their own. *Harbinger* was the newspaper's name. Right from the start, the *Harbinger* had been dishing out some crisp and scathing editorials which did little service to any of the numerous parties, including those in power. In its very first editorial it had proclaimed that its mission, as the name implied, was to foretell the coming of Independence, with the attendant problems, for the attention of all those who had ears to hear and who called themselves genuine nationalists. That was about two months ago.

And in the next day's issue, the editor got down to real business:

'We draw attention,' he wrote, 'and that with a sense of mission, to a situation in which one of three parts is in a position to control the whole. A part equal to a whole, in short. We wish to emphasise that this is a fundamental issue which must be tackled with true statesmanship—with sincerity of purpose and a sense of give-and-take.

'It would be unfair to hold that the particular State in question is responsible for the situation; in fact, it is probable that, placed in the same position, neither of the other two States would be less unyielding. Everybody in this great land who has had to do with the task of forging the constitutional instrument should search his heart first before laying blame. In the process of framing the constitution, all the States in the country were represented. And the representatives travelled out with a host of advisers, including some females, to a venue that was not fouled by political bickerings. They ought to have reasoned like a people who had genuine interest in building one nation. They did not. What did we see in the end? They allowed the ventriloquist to have his way.

'It pleased the master, the supreme strategist, to hand over the source of political power, which is absolute numerical majority, to one of the three States, his aim being to manipulate the nation from behind his favourite.

'And then, he sets about creating all manner of barriers between the particular State and the rest. Only recently, for instance, a resident in that State said, in an address to a Labour Union, "Let others say whatever they like; the fact remains that you are a different people." What a service to that State! And in the field of education we are always reminded that the people of the State are deeply and philosophically opposed to Western Education. Why are the people not opposed to other things western? one may ask. Like wrist watches, drugs, cars, and so on? Were not the peoples of the other States opposed to Western education at the start? We hold that there is only one answer to all these questions, which is *divide and rule*: it is the policy to keep our brothers, repeat our brothers, of that State different so that we'll never become one. But Mr. Resident and others will soon discover to their chagrin that they are merely postponing the evil day.'

'Touching! Brilliant!' I had exclaimed in my exhilaration. And from that day, I made sure I bought every issue of the *Harbinger*.

One day, Lewis sent his houseboy across with a note asking for my copy of the day's issue of the *Harbinger*, adding that he had foolishly omitted to buy one when the vendor was around. I sent it to him. He returned it not long after, with yet another note, this time thanking me and drawing my attention to a columnist's article on the third page. I sat down on the sofa and unfolded the newspaper.

'Electioneering histrionics are mounting and the actors are getting as weird as ever,' I read. 'Promises are being doled out right and left—we are fortunate they have not gone to the extent of promising free wives. It is necessary that we remind these actors once again about their responsibilities to the nation. And on this occasion, let us examine what steps have been taken to fuse the good peoples of our country into one nation. It is most distressing to have to observe right away that any attempts made so far have merely fallen short of a disaster. . . .

'Again, people have carried from their States of origin to their host States, certain traits which are extremely repugnant; and, consequently, there has been no blending as such. We should be frank enough to admit that one particular group has tended to being outmoded traditionalists, and disconcertingly unfathomable; another group to being mercurial and indeterminate; while the third is irritatingly open-mouthed, often claiming virtues which are yet to be proved. Incidentally, I am compelled by a desire to remain alive (I definitely have no ambition for martyrdom), to refer to the groups in such anonymous terms. So, in the main, we still remain strangers to ourselves. Will those who call themselves statesmen gird their loins and get into the problem of integrating the peoples of this country into one family . . .' The rest of the article dealt with the place of minority groups in the various States.

I found a pen and ringed the whole column in red.

Voices shouting in the next building where some painters were working, reached my ears.

'Let them pay me, and I'll vote for them.'

'It's only Independence which interests me now—let the white man leave our country.'

'Not all of them. Mr. Lewis for example.'

'Lewis can stay. And any others like him.'

'I hear the thing will be in six months' time.'

They whistled, sang, hummed, and whistled again.

'So people like Eduado of Oban will be ruling?'

'Eduado? He is very good compared with the one from my area. Eduado is a kind man, at least.'

'It were better everybody ruled in his own father's family.'

'Let them rule me; I prefer them to the white man,' a new voice dissented.

'You do?'

'Why not? We would then control all our wealth. And we'll feel proud wherever we go.'

'Proud? Not in such rags as your brother now wears!'

An interval of laughter followed.

'And not those of us who can neither read nor write. They will always be cheating us.'

'Your son who goes to school will see to it that you are not cheated.'

'His son? You don't seem to know the youth of today. They are prepared to cheat even their own father.'

They whistled; and they sang again. . . .

'It is Mr. Medo who lives there.' Silence followed.

I was disappointed that nobody would go on with the tune; nobody seemed to care much about me.

CHAPTER TEN

Biere's next letter in reply to mine was full of news. He had made up his mind about owning a car; his recent experiences had led him to believe there could be no alternative. Oban was all quiet after the moderate excitement of the national elections; the populace was focusing all its attention on the coming Independence celebrations. Then there was the latest sensation: Chief Ezenta Lobe had resigned from the People's Independence Party and joined the Democrats, or, geographically speaking, resigned from Bokenu and moved over to Doda State.

'Yes!' I exclaimed, and read on: 'His business in Doda was suffering after he contested against the party, and he wasn't getting much at Oban from the People's Independence; so he changed over. I hear he has been appointed into one statutory board or the other in Doda State.'

I heaved, several times. The news had grazed on the scab of the wound to my self-esteem. It was this very man that the girl Ruth had rated above me! . . .

Preparations for the Independence celebrations occupied a great deal of the school time. As Amane Community High School was in its third year and therefore still comparatively new, it was necessary to start building up its image, and there could be no better opportunity than that offered by the great event.

One morning, the Principal sent for Lewis and me. We should meet him in the office together as soon as possible. We went almost immediately.

'I have a special assignment for each of you,' he disclosed. 'You already know yours, Mr. Lewis: you are to take charge of the school choir. We have offered to sing a religious hymn at the ceremony.'

'I'm attending to that,' Lewis confirmed.

'Mr. Medo, we've just received some bundles of flags and cartons of cups from the District Officer. We want these distributed to the students at the appropriate time. Would you please see to that? They are over there.'

There were over two hundred plastic flags, with alternating white and blue parallel stripes, and about the same number of plastic cups.

'Very nice,' Lewis remarked. 'I wonder what the stripes symbolise, Roland?'

'I'm not sure I know,' I replied. 'I hear, though, they've something to do with fertility and virtue.'

He looked at his watch. 'I have a lesson in a few minutes' time.'

'I too.'

We went out together.

I reached the classroom ahead of the pupils. It was the 'A' stream of the second-year form, and I hated to lose even a second of the forty minutes: they were my best audience in the entire school. The rhythm of the declensions sounded exceptionally sweet when it came from their lips, just as did the Latin doggerel they recited together at the commencement of each lesson. They were on the whole a most pleasant lot—small and brisk and restless; bumpy and noisy, yet full of friendly charm; passing whispers and scribbled notes across in the midst of the lessons, yet grasping what you taught them. They would talk and talk and riddle you with questions on all sorts of subjects.

Today, their fondest subject was Independence.

So was it for all the others too in the weeks that followed.

'They are all very enthusiastic about it,' Lewis remarked. We were in his house.

'Oh, yes,' I concurred. 'And they like the flags—I don't know about the cups.'

'I see that most of them have hoisted the banner over their beds. They are learning the National Anthem pretty well, too.'

'They sing it everywhere, even while washing.'

'You blame them? Independence comes but once. One could add, like many other things!'

'And that would be right.'

'We mustn't allow it to distract our attention from that which we seek to accomplish in these children—to make them balanced, resourceful, honest and God-fearing. That is a point which I'm afraid has not been stressed in the countless bulletins we've been receiving from the authorities.'

I was intrigued. 'Anything just happened?'

'Look at this.' In the day's issue of the *Harbinger* he drew my attention to an article on the back page. It was a report about the Honourable Minister of Education in one of the States overruling a principal's decision to dismiss a pupil on the grounds of gross insubordination, the Honourable Minister's point being that the matter should have been referred to him for ratification. 'An essential fact in the whole matter,' the article concluded, 'is that the parent of the said student is a prominent party man. As usual, we keep the actors anonymous.'

'Upsetting, isn't it?' Lewis asked.

'Rather.'

'Independence cannot cure everything for you. You still will have the type of problem which this correspondent has raised. Plus the incessant bickerings. The noisy, cantankerous bride may be transformed into a smooth, gentle lady just close to the wedding day, only to unfold again, in true colours, immediately the honeymoon is over.'

'My good friend, Biere, often feels the way you do,' I told him. 'With even greater intensity.'

'I'm not intense—no, I'm not,' he countered, somewhat relaxed now. 'It's only that as an educator one feels a sense of outrage about the Minister's action. Have I met that friend of yours, by the way?'

'I don't think so. Perhaps I should arrange to introduce him.'

He was silent, as if he did not want to be committed.

'Speaking with all frankness, Lewis, do you think we have a worse problem in this country than any of those which you have just pin-pointed?' I asked.

'I wonder if you have.'

'Isn't there a more potent force acting against the country's interests?'

'I'm afraid I don't follow,' he said; then, I came out plainly:

'There is a definite flaw in the constitutional set-up which must be removed before we can address our minds effectively to other things.'

He considered for a brief moment. 'You're referring to Sakure State, no doubt?'

'Yes.'

'Well, I'm not a citizen of your country and furthermore, I have no politics in me; but I must agree with you there's a point in that.'

'I hadn't that State in mind actually. My target was the authority that created the situation.'

'You may be right in that too,' he said, most dispassionately. 'I think, though, your people could start helping themselves by solving those problems which fall within their competence. As things stand, they are merely expending their very considerable energy in political bickerings. True statesmanship—that's what is needed of them.'

'He who erected the structure has a case to answer,' I pronounced. 'And his name is Imperator.'

'That at least helps to keep that dead language alive!'

His appraisal of the state of affairs in the country impressed me more and more as the weeks passed. He was objective and sincere, and sympathetic too in a way, invariably concluding with emphasising the need for true statesmen. 'My brothers may have erred in many respects; they may have given you a bad constitution or whatever you call it. But having identified the problem, what do you do about it? Where are your statesmen?' At times, fearing that his remarks might have offended, he would add: 'I trust you relish, as I do, the unleavened bread of sincerity and truth.'

I would assure him that I did.

'The sooner your people begin to build a nation instead of monuments to the god of greed the better,' he remarked one morning. We had just come upon a report in a popular daily about a new ultra-modern multi-storey building just completed in a village in one of the States, by a school proprietor and at a cost of nearly thirty thousand pounds.

'I suppose the owner wants it so,' I rejoined, light-heartedly.

'He surely does! And perhaps even bigger,' he said.

'There's a problem there, I must admit,' I told him. 'Wrong sense of values.'

'Is that all, Roland?' He gave a teasing smile.

'No. And at the expense of students' meals.'

'That's it! It's something slightly worse than a wrong sense of values. And talking about values, Roland, I frankly don't see why most people should not do with my type of car—the Minor, which gives forty miles a gallon.'

'But look, is it not your people and their trans-Atlantic cousins who send the big cars out to our people to buy?' I protested.

'Sure. They want to sell. Free trade. And your people want to buy.'

'That's rather unkind. After all, it's they who condition the people's taste. Part of the imperial authority.'

He was more amused than anything else. 'You haven't been to England, Roland?' he asked.

'No.'

'You ought to go there some time.'

'I would like to. But is there any special point?'

'You would be able to meet many good people there, and bad ones also of course.'

'Oh, I had never implied that there's a lack of men of goodwill over there.'

'You must go one day.'

The pupils went ahead of us, marching in twos, along the new road to the District Office. By the time we arrived they had already taken up their positions on the field. The police band was playing a tuneful march. And, from all directions, more and more school contingents continued to arrive, their respective bands playing too.

Presently, all eyes turned to the left. Breaking loose now, the youngest ones among the school children rushed to the direction, calling: 'Saint Paul's College!' And very soon, the band came within sight, with a host of children on the flanks and in the rear. They were dressed in a most fantastic combination of colours, with frills draping the whole length of their bodies; and yet they were highly disciplined in their formation as well as in the rhythm and tempo of their music. They wheeled this way and that, wound and unwound; and their leader, the master Pied Piper, led them on and on, spinning his baton and gliding right and left.

Then the drummers struck a number of hasty, exciting beats. With that, the movement changed and the music changed. They were playing the now-famous Freedom Song. 'March on, march on, with confidence and strength', the flutes urged. The cornets were the first to pick up the message; and then the other instruments joined in. The tempo soared and the trotting rhythm struck the heart, rocketing it into a fierce longing for freedom.

It took the policemen and the over-enthusiastic boy-scouts, and other volunteers, some time to restore order. In another thirty minutes, the large field was filled up again with disciplined ranks of school children. There must have been at least five thousand, although the papers said ten. They were all neatly dressed—the boys in white shirts and shorts, while the girls covered the seven colours of the rainbow and more. A most attractive sight! I said in my mind. See! You children of our land. A happy future awaits you, dear boys and girls. Your country is growing richer and richer; therefore, you will not suffer the way Roland and the rest had to. There are opportunities for you: there are scholarships and bursaries, in one form or another. You will have better roads, better meals, better books. 'Your luck is great, my children,' I muttered to myself. And I kept observing them in their sly conversations and name-calling and nudging and pinching and sidelong exchanges and all . . . Mamma would have charged that I was misapplying a feeling which would have been more appropriate to my own children. 'At your age, you ought to have had two to three children of your own.' She was never impressed by the plea that I was only twenty-nine; rather she would rejoin: 'Your Papa had Alexander and you at that age.' At which, I would remind her that at that age, neither she nor Papa had ever heard the word university, and that in fact, neither of them had gone beyond Standard Three; then, she would dismiss me with a sigh of irritation and despair. However, she was infinitely less unbearable than the school's abrasive Chemistry master who held that it was a perversion.

At last, the District Officer, an elderly but imposing man who had risen from the rank of District Interpreter, arrived. Confident and unruffled, he walked straight on to the platform, glancing right and left, apparently to make sure everything was in order. Then the speaker boomed. It was time to start, said the announcer who then proceeded to read out the programme. Then the school choir drew up before the dais, facing the crowd, with Lewis between. Lewis had a baton in his hand, and his balding head and his immaculately white shirt glittered in the morning sun. He gestured. The choir of thirty burst into Handel's 'Glory to God in the Highest', the special song they had learnt for the occasion. Swaying and gesticulating and waving his stick, he carried the choir with him. The song soared and soared nobly, into the heavens.

The District Officer stood up again. The police band struck up. Everybody stood up now. The band played the National Anthem, quite well in spite of the leaks in the notes.

'We shall now perform the ceremonial lowering of the imperial flag and the hoisting of the national flag in its place,' the speaker announced in a voice that was devoid of passion. The quiet that followed was funereal. The spectators stared with anxious faces at the red-and-white cloth sinking lower and lower, down the pole, and the new flag, different in both colour and design, rising up and up. They continued to stare until the latter had unfurled at the top, looking virile and fresh. The whole crowd broke out, clapping and applauding and yelling; and many called upon the foe, unnamed, to acknowledge his defeat.

Snatches of conversation occupied the succeeding interval.

'It's better for us to misrule ourselves than continue to be ruled.'

'True.'

'But nobody is going to misrule.'

'Thank God for keeping me alive to witness this day.'

'Really.' He sounded banal. I looked behind. No wonder! He was one of the senior service people—Ministry of Finance, Internal Revenue Division. Somebody accused him:

'When we were fighting, you didn't believe we would win.'

'You've done very well,' he answered.

'Yes, we have. And now, you civil servants are going to enjoy the results of it.'

'How?'

'You will be made Senior Secretary and Deputy Senior Secretary and Senior Assistant what-ever-you-call-it. You will take the jobs which the white man has been forced to abandon. Not so?'

Another said: 'Whoever fought for it and who will enjoy it doesn't matter to me. We are all brothers.'

'No, no, no!' another cut in. 'All I say is that they should remember us when they are enjoying it. After all, brotherhood thrives in letting your brother have a bite.'

There was a big applause for the speaker. I turned round to study him more closely. Our eyes met.

'Hallo, hallo, hallo!' he cried. 'Mr. Medo, hallo!' He dashed towards my seat with his palm outstretched.

'Hallo, man!' And I stretched out my hand, but without similar warmth.

'Look at you! You don't know me again?'

I admitted I didn't quite.

'Think!' he urged, and before I could open my mouth, he announced: 'Councillor Ogamala. We were at school together.'

'Simon?'

'You remember now.' He stabbed my cheek with a finger. 'What ministry do you work in?'

'I am a teacher.'

'What!' he exclaimed in genuine surprise. 'You must go into the senior service and begin to enjoy life, like others.'

I persuaded him to shelve the discussion until another time. Then he gave me his address, assuring me that he would be the first to call in any case, and within the week.

CHAPTER ELEVEN

I was expecting to hear a deep vibrating purr. What came instead was a shallow, throbbing sound followed by a nasal whistle. Isaac rushed out.

'Who's that, Isaac?' I called.

'It's he,' he replied.

'Biere?'

Biere himself answered while Isaac plied him with questions relating to the motor-cycle.

'How come that I see a motor-cyclist instead of a car owner?' I asked, stepping out of the bedroom.

'It's simple enough,' he answered, expressionlessly. 'The car no longer is.'

'What happened?'

'It occurred to me I should rid myself of the nuisance,' he said. 'It was taking up half of my salary.'

'You sold it then?'

'Yes. And at some small profit, surprisingly.'

We heard the sharp, metallic whistle.

'Who's that?' he demanded, rising anxiously. 'Isaac, you're running down the battery.'

The boy made a quick apology. 'I know somebody who has one like this.'

'Who?' Biere asked.

'He teaches in our school.' He added: 'We call him Taurus Gravis.'

'Why?' I wondered.

'He is very fat and can't move fast; so he makes the motor-cycle take him everywhere.'

'Go away!' Biere protested.

'I didn't mean you,' Isaac laughed.

We went on laughing even after the boy had left.

'You're still paying his fees?'

'Certainly, brother,' I replied, in a self-pitying tone.

'I should feel proud of that.'

'Why?'

'He looks so intelligent.'

'He is, certainly. I don't feel proud of my pocket though. The strain is so much. You are lucky you don't have the experience yourself.'

'You may be right but only up to a point,' he said. 'They have already started lining up two of the younger ones, Jike and Chinka, for me.'

'You'll probably have the advantage of State scholarships by then,' I said.

'Scholarships for Biere's relations?' he asked with a sneer. 'You're not being serious, of course.'

'Why not?'

'Talk about something else. How is everybody?'

'Everybody is as he is. Ogidi was here two days ago to see us.'

'I wish I had met him, I rather like the man. You were saying something about Mr. Lewis last time. Shall we meet him this time?'

'Certainly. Lewis is such a wonderful man,' I went on. 'Group him with Father Long of Christ High School and Doctor Benson of the university, and my present Principal—the candid fatherly type with whom one can't help feeling a sense of comradeship.'

'You had better leave it to me to decide for myself. And don't forget, you have included two Imperators in your models of humanity.'

'No; those two are no imperators,' I pointed out. 'They are rather of the missionary type.'

'And what is your missionary type like?'

'Your food is ready.'

Some thirty minutes later, he asked me:

'Did you read yesterday's *Harbinger*?'

'It hasn't yet arrived.'

84

He cracked a bone between his teeth. 'I should have brought it along. Something on the University Students' Union.'

'Isn't it almost dead?'

'Well, no, except in relation to its principles. A columnist was lamenting the fact that an organisation of that nature, with its great potential, was fast foundering on ethnic rocks, as he put it. There is an allegation that some members of staff are seriously aligned behind the factions.'

'He is up to mischief again.'

'Who is?'

'Imperator,' I declared.

'Mark you, the columnist didn't give the colour of the skin of those members of staff.'

'Why? One should be able to deduce. . . .'

'Where has your Imperator been all these weeks, Roland? Tell me.'

I put down the spoon and sat erect, and got my fingers ready, for a moving speech. 'Trust him,' I began. 'He is a wonderful schemer. He has been resting on his imperial height, quiet but watchful. The august wind of change had been blowing mercilessly on him, and so he took shelter where he could watch unseen.'

'A rather nice imagery.'

'Thank you, but let me finish first; I am really inspired. The movement which started many years ago was so insistent that he had to duck and withdraw out of view; but he is still overseeing everything.'

'Very good—except that you've not brought your brothers into the picture. If you don't mind my amending for you, it's they who foul the air you and I breathe directly.'

'Imperator is not unduly upset, mark you,' I ignored the amendment.

'That is because he has already arranged things well enough to meet his end.'

'Do you discuss such matters with Lewis, Roland?' he wondered.

'Even worse matters. And he listens to you all through, after which he states his own views—offers you his bread.'

'Bread?'

'His unleavened bread of sincerity and truth.'

We met Lewis later that evening. He was reclining on a settee in the parlour, resting his foot on a footstool and reading a paperback edition of Steinbeck's *Of Mice and Men* when we entered. We granted his request for a few seconds to enable him to read down the particular page, and I took the interval to draw Biere's attention to the furnishings which mirrored the good man's nature. The general tone was golden-brown. The blinds were of a thick cotton fabric with faint spots; so also were the cushion covers. The most striking of the pictures hanging on the walls was a piece of embroidery depicting a small bird perched on a twig, with the immensity of space for the background. It was so simply conceived, yet the effect was very deep. At last, he closed the book and put it aside with methodical care; then he turned to us.

'You came after all,' he said to Biere after the introductions. 'Roland has been mad about you. What would you like to have? Some Tango or what?'

Our eyes met, and he smiled, while I laughed, much to Biere's embarrassment. I had told him, in plain language and several times, that we as a people had a free choice when alternatives were offered; and that there was no need mentioning several things in the hope that your guest would be polite enough to pick the one which carried the stress.

'Tango then, pure and simple,' he now amended.

'Very good then,' I acknowledged.

'Mr. Ekonte?'

'Suits me very well; thanks a lot,' said Biere.

They remained discreetly formal, throughout, in spite of my efforts to bring them closer. We talked about various things, without much depth. And even when we visited him again a month later, there was no appreciable change. Lewis kept us busy most of the time with a monologue on the great virtues of his elderly cook, Christopher, and the high intelligence of the latter's son, Ike, who was now in a secondary school.

'Oh, yes; he's an admirable lad—Ike is,' he mused, with the inevitable wrong accents on the name. 'I'm sure he'll make a doctorate if given the chance—one of the Government scholarships or something like that. His write-up ought to be first-class.'

'Write-ups are hardly enough in such matters,' I doubted.

'I know. And they hardly are anywhere,' he said. 'It depends to some extent on the priorities of the moment.'

'And who serves on the scholarship board,' Biere added, speaking gently and with superior airs.

'I know.' He smiled a dry, unconvincing smile, crossed one leg over the other. 'These things do happen everywhere, Biere. What I think is particularly distressing in your own case is that the society is pretty young, in terms of development, and there is not nearly enough money to go round; so people feel a keen sense of injustice.'

'In my four years in this country, I have formed the happy impression that the people are simply excellent in many respects,' Lewis said, unfolding at last, on our next visit. 'Frankly.'

'In spite of many things, yes,' Biere answered.

'Oh, yes. And you mustn't forget, Biere, that no country is perfect.'

'I would propose we restrict the award of excellence to the common man. I can't see my way to extending it upward.'

'The common man in your country? He is absolutely admirable,' he agreed. 'Friendly, hospitable, balanced, frank; and above all, with a high sense of humour.'

'Talking about the common man, isn't that the nature of the country folk in most places?' Biere asked. 'Simple and friendly.'

'You don't find them everywhere—not in highly industrialised countries at least,' the other replied. 'That perhaps accounts for my high appreciation of their ways. Last time we visited Christopher's father—who incidentally is still very much alive and strong—he was busy in his farm, even at his age; but then, he stopped what he was doing to take us to the forehouse in his compound, where he offered us Kola and other things. He was relaxed all through.'

'The trouble couldn't be with his type, certainly!'

'Even the big shots too. You can't afford not to admire their expansive airs and sense of humour, and hospitality.'

'Provided you have a forgiving spirit,' I added on Biere's behalf.

'Well, perhaps,' Lewis conceded.

'It depends on how much forgiving one should reasonably do,' Biere took over again.

87

'No limit if you are their collaborator—be you their countryman or an arch-mover from abroad!'

'And none of it at all if you are Roland Medo or his friend Biere Ekonte,' Lewis laughed.

'Seriously, why don't you begin to make yourself part of the country which you so much admire?' asked Biere.

'In what way?'

'Sort of nationalise.'

He shook his head. 'That would be a sham, as far as I am concerned. I am not a racist, as you very well know, but it seems to me the right thing is to keep the races apart for a start, and then work for the closest friendship and mutual understanding between them. The moment you begin to integrate into one political entity, prematurely, without such necessary preliminary, then a struggle for dominance starts—and who wins in the end? No, I remain an Englishman.'

'You are not saying that you support what is happening in South Africa?'

'Oh, no; no!' he objected. 'And nothing in what I've just said should suggest that. The trouble there in South Africa is that there is a deliberate and well-calculated attempt to keep one race in the ascendancy all the time. Let each group, be it a country or just a community in a country, develop and try to tackle its problems; but do not allow one race in the political unit to frustrate the other. Look at your current progress in this country in the various fields, for example—in spite of what you often say! It is true you owe much of it to the pioneering efforts of the early missionaries, but it is no less a fact that the self-help attitude of the people and their extended family system have given that a fillip. An un-understanding government made up of a different race could have destroyed that spirit, either by being overpaternalistic or by frustrating the aspirations of the people. You produce your doctors, your engineers, and your lawyers knowing full well that there is need for them in your scheme of things.'

'You failed to mention teachers,' said I, and we had a good laugh, after which he sent for his steward.

'Beer for one master and tango for two.'

I asked the boy to make the beer a full pint.

'There seems to be a calm in your political atmosphere at the moment, Roland,' said he after some time.

'I think so; I only hope it's real.'

'I hope so too,' Biere came in.

'I too,' he agreed. 'My honest view is that your nation could have been a bit more dynamic, considering all the advantages it has over its neighbours.'

'Things are not moving, really,' Biere said, looking grave. 'Or if they are, they don't at all move well.'

'Some people are very busy working out sums on percentages, for example,' I said.

Lewis burst into laughter. 'Honestly, you two are ruthless. This is a young country, and a lot is bound to go amiss.'

'At the expense of your friend, the common man.'

'Write to the *Harbinger* on these things,' he suggested, smiling. 'I'm afraid there isn't much I could do to change matters.'

'If that newspaper tried to publish half of what it knows it would cease to exist,' Biere pointed out. 'The most it can do is to make sly references which don't seem to penetrate their type of skin.'

'Or write to the *National Standard*. It is quite detached.'

'Detached in the respect that its interests are different from the country's,' I told him. 'Who owns it? Tell me.'

'Imperator—that's what you would want me to say.'

'Well then, it must make sure it defends imperial interests. And the particular contracting firm involved in some of the most current per-centagings is believed to be of imperial origins.'

'You disgust me at times, Roland.'

'It's true.'

'Why don't you try the newspaper of a rival political party?'

'And be charged with contempt of State Minister of State, or of National Minister of State—I am not quite sure the sentence would be the same,' Biere said.

'You are in real trouble then! I have never believed, however, that the press is all that monolithic over here.'

'No. What we are saying is that apart from the *Harbinger*, they are terribly effective when it comes to party politics, and no more. The *Standard* is in its own class of course.'

'They were effective also in the fight for Independence, weren't they?' he asked.

'One must concede them that,' I cut in. 'The trouble now is that the mandate has been discharged, leaving them effete.'

'Just like the brigadiers of the war,' Biere added. 'Effete is a mild word; they have become a positive bane, very many of them.'

'Your views on these matters are rather extreme, Biere and Roland,' Lewis pronounced, amiably.

'But very sincere,' Biere pointed out. 'We are better patriots than the men who live in Government quarters rent-free and all costs paid, who currently parade their own nationalism in public cars, often charging the nation for the service of allowing their noble bodies to be conveyed from one spot to another.'

'How is that?'

'Oh, yes; some even claim mileage allowance for journeys made in public cars,' he explained. 'They also claim what they call sleeping allowance, when in fact nobody asked them to sleep.'

'You two had better shut up now.' The laughter Lewis had been trying to repress overpowered him. 'Roland's fury is directed against my brothers, while Biere wants his countrymen's throats. You do seem to be saying the same thing, though, in the final analysis. And with a measure of truth.'

Night had set in when we left him to return to my house.

CHAPTER TWELVE

I owed Biere a visit in a real sense. He had been reminding me how he had spent days with me, on several occasions. Could I make such a claim? He was right, I would concede, promising I would make it soon. And now, he had written to say that the dialogue no longer impressed; nor did my excuses about the noises of the town.

I had complained to him that I could not bear the sights and sounds. It was not politics: the political atmosphere was cool enough. Oban had lately been transformed into a huge machine which throbbed from morning till late at night. The number of cars appeared to have increased tenfold, with the small economical taxis predominating but facing serious threat from the trucks and mammy-wagons as well as the caterpillars which the Public Works men were dragging up and down. Then, there were the voices of men, noticeably small hawkers and mobile advertisers shouting their wares. Provision stores, wine and beer off-licences, literally littered the town; they served the customers seven days a week, except that they did business through windows on Sundays as a concession to the Commandment. The pubs, too, had increased several fold, with at least one on each street, their loud signs done in white, red, or black. They bore very historic or topical names. One, at a corner street, was called Independence Fountain. Fountain spouted out music all day, more than seemed necessary for the few customers who called there for the bitter-sweet palm wine that came from Lohia. Another, Road to Freedom, had not much in the way of music but made up for it by the quantity of females in the establishment. The hotels had even more alluring names. The Pleasure Inn close to Uncle Edoha's house had just been completely renovated and freshly equipped, and the proprietor, who was Edoha's close friend, had suggested that I could be the chairman for the next guests' night. It seemed indeed as if Independence had given full rein to all men and women with initiative, of whom Oban had a considerable number.

I had felt most uncomfortable at the time. I could not even stay for the night, I told Uncle Edoha; and requested him to send across to Biere the letter I had just written.

Biere had just fired back, in one single and compact page, calling me high-brow and eccentric and other things; after which, he went on to shock me. If I would not come for his sake, I might be interested in seeing the new television set which he was about to acquire. He had decided at long last to buy the thing.

He did underline the last word. It was easy to guess why. Certainly! It was from a sense of guilt. Years ago, when it was being mooted that the country would soon have a television service, and that the Honourable Minister of Culture would soon be touring the United Kingdom and the Continent to make the necessary arrangements, Biere had wondered with a bitter sneer whether the devil had taken possession of the man's head.

'Why?' I had asked.

'There's no money for education and so on, and yet the man has to carry his body overseas at public expense,' was his reply.

'I tell you, the host countries will be only too pleased to have him,' I had rejoined. 'A bit of helping to tidy up the balance of payment. . . .'

And so, Oban and other big towns in the country had long been provided with television, to the eternal glory of Eduado Boga, the Honourable Minister of Culture. All over the town, the antennae peaked the roofs, some rising ostentatiously as much as ten feet on straight pipes. Even Biere had now come to identify himself with the new status symbol. I would go and see for myself.

He was sitting in a cane chair close to his book rack, doing nothing worthy of note, when I reached the house.

'Show me immediately,' I ordered him.

He pointed to his left with indifference. . . .

'A Philips?'

'Yes.'

'And such a toy!'

'The important thing is that it shows the pictures without decapitations.'

'How tall is the aerial?'

'Nil.'

'What do you mean?'

'It's internal.'

'May I charge you with mental aberration?'

'If it pleases you.'

'What paper is that?'

There was on the stool behind him a heap of newspapers over which rested a copy of Turgenev's *Virgin Soil*. He lifted the book, exposing the paper to full view.

'What is it saying about the country?'

He reached out his hand again, for the paper this time.

'The *National Standard*!' I read it. There was something about a citadel of true democracy, with a press that was free.

'So annoying!' I moaned after some time.

'Why? Because it's the *Standard* saying so, is it?' he said. 'Read this one.'

It was the *Crusader*.

The report began with a headline urging the trade unions to gird their loins against injustice.

'This is good,' I remarked.

'Read on,' he urged.

The thing soon petered out. '. . . The meeting ended by passing a vote of implicit and unshakeable confidence in the Government. It also resolved to pursue the cause of the common man until the battle is won, and identified itself with the intentions of the Government in this regard. Finally, it sanctioned the principle of gradualism and pacifism in the attainment of any socialistic objectives.'

'Whoever was talking about socialism?'

'Ask the man—not Biere,' he said.

'What I suppose must have happened in that complex capital city is that some people have started a counter-movement to wreck the trade union front.'

'So divide and rule is not a preserve of your villain, you see?'

'I could concede you the point,' I said. 'However, let's not assume that my villain has nothing to do with it.'

'One never understands in any case what the trade unions are doing in this country of ours.'

'There are far too many of them—far too many names and abbreviations.'

'Most of them sounding utterly unmusical!'

We began listing them on paper, just for the fun of it, and produced:

N.A.F.T.U.	—	National Association of Free Trade Unions
U.F.T.U.	—	Union of Free Trade Unions
A.N.T.U.	—	Amalgamation of National Trade Unions
N.T.U.C.	—	National Trade Union Congress
U.W.A.U.	—	United Workers and Allied Union
J.W.U.	—	Joint Workers Union
W.D.C.	—	Workers Democratic Council
N.O.T.U.	—	National Organisation of Trade Unions
C.W.C.	—	Central Workers Council
U.T.U.A.	—	Union of Trade Union Associations

'This world of ours is full of injustices.' I put the list away. 'Since I came in here nobody has thought about feeding me on anything apart from politics.'

He ordered both beer and biscuits, and the inevitable Tango for himself. I went ahead to prescribe rice with chicken for supper.

'You will be the cook.'

Our programme for the following day, which was Saturday, was quite tight. And we did not help matters by staying awake in bed till the early hours of morning, discussing a variety of subjects including, when we came to females, Mrs. Chief Aniedo the second, née Ruth Aniedo. We left the house at nine o'clock, which was much later than we had planned. We would do the distance of nearly two miles from the school to the heart of Oban on foot. That would give us, me in particular, an opportunity of seeing the town once more. Somehow I felt an urge to see that which I dreaded and detested, in order to reinforce the impression.

There were all along the route posters done in amateurish calligraphy, among other things. The posters carried an invitation to all and sundry to attend the day's big event, which was a football match between Saint Saviour's Grammar School Redoubtables and Christ High School Raiders, the former being the team from Biere's school.

We went straight to Uncle Edoha's house. I had not seen him for some time; I must see him today before he left Oban for the weekend. Edoha was one of those homely characters who believed strongly in regular reunion with the kith and kin. On arrival, we met him chairing a meeting of the Gunpowder Retailers' Association convened at his instance. He had a pipe in his mouth, which looked most incongruous and even dangerous for a man of his trade; and there were empty beer bottles on the stools. He spoke to the comrades as much in English as in the vernacular. Yet Edoha had never been to school, unless one counted the few weeks he had spent in an adult literacy class in one of the less modern wards in Oban. Suspending the meeting on our behalf, he now proceeded to elaborate introductions in which everybody had to declare his name, his trade, and some of his assets. Finally, we withdrew, with the chairman's permission, into an inner room, the one that had been my study, and the children of the house flocked

94

in to welcome us. We stayed there long enough to dispose of a bottle of beer and a bottle of Tango. Then, we returned to the sitting room to assure the uncle that everything was all right.

The time was getting near to noon already. We would visit the library. Closing time was one o'clock. We quickened our steps. But the road was irritatingly crowded. A caterpillar was groaning and grinding on one edge of the tarmac surface, leaving only half the span for other users, men and machines. And ahead of us was the railway crossing. Even in normal circumstances, with the gate wide open, all traffic had to slow down near the crossing. And now, right before our very eyes, the gate man swung the barrier to. The pedestrians complained. The cyclists were furious. From his car, now immobilised like the rest, a driver shouted his recommendation that the Railway Corporation be wound up at once and all the engines turned to scraps and the gateman retired with shame, in the interest of easy locomotion. Then came a shrill, yet soothing, whistle. Faces brightened. The engine head, black with soot as well as by design, was creeping up, with a coil of smoke over its body. It looked like a conjurer at work. And as soon as it had rolled past, the gate swung open, the pedestrians helping the gateman to move it out of the way. There were less than forty minutes now to the closing time. We quickened our steps.

The library was packed full today. They were mainly school children. With sharp, alert eyes they went over the lines of print, or scanned through the newspapers, while the staff attended to the needs of those who wished to borrow or to return books. Biere returned his Turgenev and took a Balzac instead.

'Only one book this time?' the shy girl at the counter wondered.

He returned a most inadequate smile. Then, I came in to make amends:

'It seems he's well known here already.'

'He borrows many books,' she explained.

'My friend wants to register.'

She took out two forms and pushed them forward. When I had completed them, Biere signed the identificaion certificate. Shortly after, I had two books in my left armpit. One was titled *Neo-colonialism and Neo-nationalism*; the other *Trade and Politics in Developing Countries*.

The day was terrifically hot. The atmosphere seemed to vibrate and the sound of engines seemed to ignite the air. We walked into a nearby bar. Freshly decorated and furnished, it was cool and quiet and the proprietor had had the extra good sense to name it The Cool. The beer, as well as Biere's mineral water, was freezing cold. After the drinks, we went out and hailed the first taxi. The driver jammed on the brakes, reached out to the back door handle and flung the door open with extravagant zeal.

The match was to start at a quarter to five. We still had two good hours for lunch and rest. We would rest for an hour—just that and no more—after lunch. So we both agreed; but what we did in actual fact was to lie in bed roaming from one topic to another, until it was twelve minutes past four. When we got to the field a capacity crowd was already assembled. Among them were hundreds of boys from the two schools who were now ranged at the opposite sides, foe facing foe, ready to heckle across if need be. But very soon, they all became united, at least for a brief while, in a common cause: the blue gowns of Saint Anne's Secondary School, second to none, were now arriving. The girls marched on with steady and bold strides, gentle in bearing yet resolute on reaching their position.

The referee ran into the field. He gave a prolonged blast, at which the teams ran in too, one to each end of the field. The game started with a big roar which was later sustained, the fans calling on their favourite team to wake up and do wonders.

In spite of what is usually said about the spirit of sportsmanship, I was quite distressed when the match ended. I lost my bet with Biere, although he was magnanimous enough to commute his win to a playful jeer.

CHAPTER THIRTEEN

Dora was waiting in the house when I returned. Eyiza, my houseboy, was nowhere to be seen.

'I came in the afternoon and you were not in, so I decided to stay,' Dora declared; and she drew nearer and began to remove my shoes.

'What about Eyiza?'

'I don't know,' she replied surlily, then added: 'I don't know why you chose such a person for a servant.'

'You don't like him?' I laughed.

'How can anybody?' She blinked her eyes with disdain.

'How is Mamma?'

'She's well and sends greetings,' she responded. 'And Alex too. Alex gave me a letter for you.'

I read through it; then again.

'They want me at home tomorrow after school! I hope there's nothing wrong.'

'They didn't tell me, but I heard him discussing with Mamma and then they said I should come and give you a letter so that you will visit home.'

'Visit home, what for?' I protested.

Then, Eyiza appeared at the door, grinning at me ingratiatingly. When I wondered where he had been he began a complicated narrative about how my sister had forced him to leave the house, and closed the doors after him. And while he spoke, Dora shouted her rebuttal, calling him a string of names. The truth was that Eyiza had offered, quite seriously, to be her husband, and she had replied by taking possession of the house and excluding him from it. I told her to keep it a secret.

Eyiza ceased to be in my service from that day.

Mamma declared with pride that it was she who had sent for both Alexander and me. She had received some information a few days before from people of the Traco Oil Company that a new road might be built soon which would cut through the family land. Would she give her consent? She had of course refused outright. How could she? Then, they asked her to think again. That was why she decided to send for the two of us. Speaking next, Alex confirmed and gave more details. The oil company wanted a road running from Arare, where they had a big well, to Siaku; and then to Umuntianu; finally to Oban. The representatives who came had indicated they would like the road to cut through our land.

'Even through the compound! Not so?' she interjected.

'Well, yes,' he admitted.

'Nobody will do it while I am alive,' she swore.

'They have an alternative. If we accept,' he pointed out, 'they will pay compensation for everything we lose. And if we refuse, some others will gladly accept the offer.'

'Of course we have refused,' she said excitedly. 'They will not do it while I live, at least.'

'Hold on, Mamma; let's discuss it,' he hushed her.

'Continue discussing if you like.' It seemed as if they had already disagreed before my arrival. Turning round to me, she said: 'Let me know in plain language what you think.'

I began from a very remote consideration. The proposed road would cut through the beautiful scenery between Umuntianu and Siaku, which would be a great pity. And then, to worsen the position, heavy trucks and other machines would start arriving, disrupting the quiet life of the community.

'Disrupting the quiet life!' she echoed plaintively, and her eyes flashed from one son to the other.

'But we as a family would gain,' Alex differed.

'Gain what? Money?' I asked.

'Yes,' he confirmed, seriously. 'Could be as much as four thousand pounds—I made some enquiries.'

'You mean you've been talking with them, isn't it?' she accused him. 'You would then, after surrendering the house and the whole compound, go up and live in the sky?'

He reminded her that Gorigori was still there.

'So that you may have the money, we are to leave Umuntianu and move over to Gorigori! Wicked one!' Her eyes sparkled and she bit her lower lip. 'That's all the debt you owe to your father!'

Dora had been lurking behind all the time, ready to come to Mamma's support whenever the need would arise. She now swore never to go to Gorigori to live; or to leave Umuntianu.

Alex was stubborn. From time to time, as the discussion went on, he threw in a curt phrase that re-stated his stand and ignited her fury all the more.

'You want money; you must go overseas; you will therefore sell everything and everybody in the family!' she came on him at the peak of her fury. 'You, Alexander, have been spending all your earnings on your wife's father's family—you!'

He informed her, calmly, that she sounded incoherent, adding: 'And of course nothing is spent on this family!'

'You have turned into a mean miser.' She was almost singing the words. 'They say my son measures out the day's ration of yam with a ruler. And where is all the money he is supposed to save? Where is it? It ought to have been enough to take ten people overseas, and yet you have nothing either in your pocket or in your house. And now, you want to sell your good father's land. Sell me instead and leave his land and compound alone.' Her voice had cracked—her firm and manly voice which had won her great regard among the womenfolk she led; and tears glistened in her eyes. Dora advanced and stood between her and us, ready to charge.

'That's enough now,' I said, playing the role of mediator. 'Neither of you cared to tell me the full details at first and I did not know that this type of thing had been going on between you. I am hearing this one about going overseas for the first time, Alex.'

He assured me that the whole thing was still a matter of the mind, even though he had thought it wise to inform Mamma. It was quite in keeping with his nature, I told myself, gazing straight into his face in censure, which withered him. He was rather to be pitied. His countenance suggested he had some deep-rooted worry. What else could be the cause than the load he bore: his own brother and a wife's brother both in secondary schools; an intense ambition to go over-seas—all that on his salary; and then, his wife nagging from morning to night, reminding him that boys he had taught in school were now practising as barristers in Oban and Portcity and other towns. I knew Sarah well. . . .

'Enough of it now, Mamma and Alex,' I remonstrated. 'We ought to keep our land and compound anyway, I think.'

Sensing defeat, Alex proposed that the matter be shelved.

He was extremely anxious to go to the United Kingdom to study either Law or Accountancy. That I learnt from a letter he wrote to me weeks after. In that letter Alex became communicative for the first time in his life. He was most unhappy about his status, he said. Well over ten years had passed since he left the teachers' college, and yet he was still just a primary school headmaster with very little, if any, prospect of advancement in life, each one of his brothers having a brighter future than he—just because they had been to or were going through secondary schools. The letter was worded in a touchingly candid tone. The matter had become of such a force that it could no longer be accommodated in his secretive heart.

Some, the letter had gone on, who had been headmasters like himself were already studying one subject or another overseas while others were long back. These were the ones who had been able to save the money or had had somebody to send them over. In his own case he had, frankly, been banking on Edoha, only to discover now that the uncle was an absolute let-down, always bragging about how he had sent a sister's son to a university. It remained for him now, since the offer from the oil company had been rejected, principally by Mamma, to rest his hope on me and whatever his wife had been able to save.

'I am telling you this in the strictest confidence,' he went on. 'That woman has been marvellous. Mamma charges her with sending all her salary to the father's family, but in actual fact she saved most of it. Can you believe she already has two hundred pounds? And she is most anxious that I should go. All I require is an extra two hundred for a start and I'll begin to apply for a place. I am sure I will do very well if I go over. So, please, see what you can do to help.' He ended by informing me that he had just returned from home, and that Mamma had been mollified.

I was not sure whether to feel annoyed or happy, whether to refuse or accede. Either would have been justified. What on earth could have led Alex to expect me to raise two hundred pounds for him? He did not even appear to have considered that I lacked many things I ought to own. Fancy a man with wife and children making such demand on a bachelor! Or was he implying that I should not be a husband and father like him? No; I must not reply in that tone. I would lose him again if I did. This was the first time, since I began to be conscious of such things, that Alex had unfolded his heart to me, and with such pathetic candour; the first time he had come out from the shell of his mind. He would shrink back into the hard shell, perhaps finally, if I should strike his sensitive antennae with an acid refusal. Above all, I must not act precipitately. I would just send him a friendly letter acknowledging his message and informing him that I would come over and discuss things with him, in a week or so but certainly within the month. I might even add that I quite appreciated his feeling about his position. After that, I would set about finding the answer.

'We were talking about a calm only recently, what about all the noise in the press?' I asked.

'Depends on how recent. I remember well, it is some two months ago, isn't it?' Lewis said.

'And two months is enough time for the world to turn completely upside down,' Biere added. 'Especially in developing countries.'

'It isn't as bad as turning upside down yet; it is just that one doesn't feel terribly comfortable about the things they are saying. About the coming census, for example.'

'Oh, that one? Absolute insanity,' Biere agreed. 'People are already planning how they are going to be more in number. Have you ever heard a thing like that?'

'The insanity dates several years back,' I differed. 'The whole structure has its foundations on numbers. And so, you can't improve matters unless you are able to raise your own figure. See what I mean?'

'Rather. But I think you've missed my point slightly,' Biere replied, even though the question was intended for Lewis. 'If one State has seventy thousand adult males it has seventy thousand adult males and that is that. But from what is being said now, it seems people are going to see that more males are born every minute of the day than were ever produced in a single week.'

'And in the event of an admittedly sad game of mutual juggling with numbers, the man on the tree-top will do everything to see that the edifice he has erected is not altered.'

'And having identified that problem, Roland, what have our people done about it?' Biere asked.

'Not much that is impressive,' I admitted. 'But that doesn't extenuate the villainy of the other side.'

CHAPTER FOURTEEN

Alex came over to see me, before I had time to go to him. He was in a fairly agreeable mood.

He was prepared to wait for one more year or so, he said; he had not made up his mind finally. It was necessary to watch the climate first. From all the indications, a lot could happen in the next few months to make one think anew about plans for a better future. . . . I assured him I would do all in my power to assist should he decide then to go ahead with the proposal.

I was as vague as that, and yet he did not seem disappointed in me; rather, he gave the impression that he was merely re-establishing his character before me: he must repair the damage to his self-reliance and pride. Alex went on to hint that he would probably be able, before the year was out, to save a lot more money. 'Within the coming months in particular!' he added, with determination. It was easy to guess what he had in mind this time, from the blue plastic bag that dangled down from his left shoulder: he had been appointed a Verifier for the forth-coming national census. And possibly he might have reckoned too that in the elections into the National Parliament, which would be due within the next twelve months, he would be made an Assistant Registration Officer, Polling Officer or Counting Officer and that would mean another windfall of twenty to thirty pounds. He could even be made two, or three, of them in succession, since, politically, he was discreetly neutral, in the sense that his leaning towards the State's ruling party was not conspicuous.

It was the census, the current sensation, that offered the greatest attraction. 'One pound a day for as long as the exercise lasts.' So the announcement had said.

'Do they know how much it will cost the nation at that rate?'

'They may or may not—what is that to me?' Alex replied with cold indifference. 'Let them pay me my own—that's all.'

'You are not worried about the effect on the nation?'

'Effect of paying me my money?' he retorted, but with a bit of humour; then replied: 'No! As long as I do my work well.'

Surely, he would. He was most conscientious by nature.

'The cost will be terrific!' I pointed out to him.

'What is Roland saying?' He sounded harsh this time. 'They have been eating all these years and the nation hasn't gone bankrupt. Will the few pennies which will drop into our hands empty the coffer of the nation?'

I left it at that. What else could I have done? They had hinted to me that I would be disqualified from all census duties, the reason being that I was once an active, and dangerous, member of the Real Democratic Party. And I had treated the warning with a snobbish indifference. Did they think Roland cared? ... For certain, worse things than mere disqualification had been reported elsewhere. ... But when did I apply to them for a post? ... It was the Principal who had submitted my name, along with those of other members of the staff. And indeed, the final approved list which came from the Administrative Officer omitted two names. One was mine; the other was Brother Badera's.

'Na dem sabi!' Brother Badera made a show of unconcern. 'I go si' don for my house and rest.'

'Me too,' I approved.

'All I want,' he added, 'is that Bokenu and Doda combined should have more population than Sakure.'

'I too, Brother Badera,' I said. 'But how do we do it?'

'Never mind; you will see.' He had turned mysterious.

'I hope you're being sincere, Mr. Badera,' cut in Charlie Agomator, the brash Chemistry master. People often said of him that he carried the acid in his mouth whenever he left his lab.

Badera did not look in any way hurt. 'What I know is that I am a citizen of the country and not of any particular State,' he declared. 'After all, I've spent the best part of my life over here.'

That could not be controverted. He had come over from Doda State some ten years before, with his father who was an employee of the Inland Waterways Department. Then, the latter retired from service and returned to his home State. But the son settled down in Bokenu; and not only that, he would often declare he was bent on marrying from the State of his abode.

Badera lived some distance from the school, in a private house. I went to see him there in the evening, possibly to check on his mood. For I had come to like the man, more so today after he had borne without any show of protest the coarse jibe from the chemist's tongue. He was not in; but I met his houseboy who told me he had gone out soon after lunch. Would I like to see the female relation in the house?

'Sister?'

'So I think.'

'How old?' It was a whisper.

'Hia, oga!' he exclaimed, drawling. 'You people, una deh!' He laughed out. 'You don begin want to know whether if you fit catch 'am?'

'Tell me,' I implored.

'She fine, true,' came his reply. 'You fit come in and see.'

Immediately I was seated, he went to the back of the house. And moments later, he led the creature into the sitting-room. Wonderful! I shivered within me, shrugging in my commotion. She had a delicately fair complexion; and she bore herself with a supple grace as she stepped, holding the fold of her grey wrapper in her hand while her white lace blouse sparkled. And, above all, she was bespectacled.

'Good evening,' I greeted, rising slowly; and when she responded, I stretched out my hand, grabbed hers, most informally, and declared my name and occupation, leaving her with no alternative but to introduce herself too.

'You want Uncle Badera?'

'Oh, yes.'

'He's out. Would you want to wait?' Her voice was inimitably crisp, in spite of the harsh lispings that occurred now and then, and her grammar was faultless.

'You don't mind my asking, are you a teacher?'

She gave a quiet smile. 'Well, yes; but why?'

'Nothing in particular. In what school?'

She hesitated. 'Saint Anne's.'

'Anne's—in—Oban—Second—to—none—in—this—world.'

She looked devastating when she laughed. 'That's what their students claim,' she admitted.

'Saint Anne's? And yet I hadn't seen you before?'

'Must you see everybody in this world?' she asked. 'But I know you. Or, rather, I came to know about you some years ago. You were then in Christ High School.'

I decided to put her on the defence: 'You knew somebody there then.'

She shrugged her resentment. 'I came one afternoon with Ruth but we didn't find you in.'

'Oh, I see!'

A little after, I announced I was going.

'Greet Brother Badera when he returns and tell him I was here for hours.'

'Hours?' She rose.

She saw me out of the door, and gave a goodbye.

'Is that all?'

We stood together for some time and tried to talk about the sunset. Then we heard Osadi, the houseboy, bellowing *In the Mood* close to one of the front windows. Osadi suddenly switched over to a church hymn as she began to walk back to the house.

I met Badera on my way. He asked me to come again another day. I told him I certainly would, very soon, provided he would assure me everybody I had met in the house during the day's visit would be in. He burst into laughter—the old rascal did. And he informed me she would be staying a couple of days, probably for the duration of the census. Her school was one of those which were fortunate enough to lose nearly all their staff to the Census and therefore had to remain closed. Just like Amane Community High School.

'At the rate we are going, we may turn out to be second to China and China alone,' Badera remarked.

'Why?' I asked him.

'Read this.'

I took the paper, the day's issue of the *Harbinger*, from him; and I read:

'Reports reaching us from correspondents in all the States are unanimous in their conclusion that the whole exercise is most unnecessary, to say the least. It is certain that those who hold the reins of Government will do everything on earth to see that they do not lose the very essence of their power, and in such a situation it is difficult to imagine what the others would not do to upset the position. We are objective enough to concede that the virtue of fair-mindedness is not more discernible among leaders of the other States; placed in a position of supremacy, and from what we knew in the past, they would not have allowed themselves to be overthrown. The stark fact is that everybody wants power—and by power we mean also opportunities for self-aggrandisement. There lies the tragedy of this nation.

'To return to the original point, should somebody not have suggested, right from the start, that we save the nation all the expense—of energy, time and money which the present exercises entail? *Just go on sleeping in your cosy quarters and let everybody get on with his normal work: then get up at midnoon and announce whatever you consider meets your aim. Or better still, go ahead and work on any figures which satisfy you; make no public announcements, for fear of unpopularity. But of course, unpopularity is such a passing quality.* Something of that nature!

'The blunder was committed when important people, admittedly from a feeling of political frustration, set about whipping up mass sentiments by linking the census directly with amenities and elections, in their public utterances. The whole thing has now degenerated to political manipulation, for which we of this paper register our patriotic distaste.'

I went straight to see Lewis in his house.

'He's come in the nick of time,' he said, staring into my face.

'What's been happening?' I asked with surprise.

'Oh, nothing. Christopher informs me he has been counted more than once, which I consider to be not in the interest of good accounting. What have you got in your hand?'

'The *Harbinger*.' I gave it to him; and drew his attention to the editorial.

He read in silence.

'What about you, how many times?'

'Once, as far as I know, and in the school.'

'And another as far as you are not aware in the village. It all seems so farcical, but of course it doesn't matter, does it?'

'Go on; let's get your meaning clear first.'

He turned, facing me. 'If, as I believe, it is the pattern all over the country to get enumerated, say three times, nobody cheats really in the end; they just cheat the absolutes, that's all. You could arrive at the right figures by dividing by three in each case.'

'It isn't all that simple,' I dissented. 'You've assumed that the dividing is going to be done in that way. What if the divider should direct his great divisive talents to one or two of the components only.'

'Here comes the nationalist!'

'The pity of it all is that nobody stops to pity the younger generation who are being taught, indirectly, that dishonesty doesn't matter.'

'When it comes to that, your own immediate brothers are more to blame, I'm afraid.'

'How? Why?'

'Well, you see, Roland, they do it with so much fanfare that one begins to wonder what is wrong. Talk, talk, talk! I'm not saying that others do not believe in inflated figures, or that nobody does like inflated figures; what I mean is that the others go about it a bit more quietly.'

'Perhaps. . . . Yes. . . . True!'

'How is Biere? I wonder what he would be feeling about it all?'

'Sad, I know,' I told him. 'I hope to see him this evening.'

'Give him my regards.'

'You've not seen the day's issue of the *National Standard*, have you?' Biere asked.

'No; I don't read the *Standard*—for obvious reasons,' I told him.

'I try to read everything,' he said in a mild reproach.

'Is there anything striking in the paper?' I now asked.

'Yes.' He flung the paper at me. 'It will not kill you. Read at the front page. . . .'

'I foresaw that long ago!' I exclaimed. 'The Democrats grouping into irreconcilable factions! I foresaw that.'

'That's what ought to be happening to the other parties,' he remarked.

'The tragedy of it all is that it's the common man who will suffer if and when the factions begin to marshal for a head-on. They will assemble poor innocent fellows to do the stone-pelting for them. And I bet you, if you check properly, you may discover that Imperator's hand is in it.'

'You are a boor!'
'Call me anything. While confusion rages in other places, his citadel remains intact.'
'I have no energy this evening for idiomatic inanities. ...'
'Send for cold beer. Quick.'
He made it beer and Fanta.

CHAPTER FIFTEEN

'We hold,' the *Harbinger* wrote, 'that this nation is fast sinking into that which we fear even to name. And it could be said that the final count-down began with the recent counting of heads. ...' The Police Officer who led the search team to the newspaper's head office wittily rejoined that the *Harbinger*'s count-down had started much earlier.
After an hour's search, the officer took some of the staff, including the editor-in-chief, to the Central Police Station while his assistant proceeded to seal the offices of the newspaper.

Mamma got to hear about Grace much earlier than I had wished. It was not that I was afraid she would object, for she always did.
Ruth she had positively loathed, partly on the ground that she disturbed my studies and partly because she came from a family where, in Mamma's own words, mother wasn't a female. Ruth's mother had been the fierce type of woman who dominated the husband and waged a sustained battle against those of his kinsmen who dared to intrude. Mamma was convinced that the daughter must have inherited the trait, even though for the moment she appeared quiet on the surface. She was greatly relieved when she heard that Ruth had been picked up by Chief Lobe, whom on that account she described as a human scavenger. She had also managed to hear about Juliana, but that was only weeks after she had gone from my life. It was probably no more than gossip reaching her ears, but she would take nothing for granted.
'Where is the thing I hear you married at Gorigori?'
I retorted that I did not understand her meaning. For I was hurt at her

accusation which was most unfair. I had begun to detest Juliana after the first few days. She was always busy compiling a long list of things to be bought for her the next day, in the interest of continued friendship and secretaryship. And it was not two weeks before I sent her back to Ubakile, the party chairman, who merely remarked that they were all like that. Ubakile would certainly have planted another female on me, probably a full-fledged party spy this time, had I not protested that I was done with female staff. I made Mamma understand my feeling, stressing that I married nobody at Gorigori. Replying, she declared that it was high time in any case I started seriously to look for a wife.

I was so upset that I refused to talk to her again for the rest of that day. And the next day, I went on to swear never to discuss anything about marriage again. Since then, she had not raised the subject. I thought it was because she would not want to create for me an occasion for perjury.

She was certainly very tactful about Grace. She started by serving me my especially favourite meal, which was red beans churned with oil-beans, with a thick dressing on top. Then she said:

'They say Philip Kodi of Eziato who is studying overseas has married a white wife there. I am sorry for the mother who bore him.'

'Anybody could marry anyone from anywhere,' I disagreed.

'But I know you well, you wouldn't do that yourself,' she rejoined. 'And in any case, as things stand at the moment, the safest thing is to marry someone who speaks the same tongue as you.'

'Does it mean, Mamma, you would not tolerate my marrying someone who doesn't?' I tried to tease her.

'I certainly wouldn't, my son,' she replied. 'To marry from a distant land? No, my son! Not with the type of weather we're having.'

'Can we leave it so?' she asked with some anger.

'Leave what so?' I asked her.

'They say they have won.'

'Is it about the census?'

'Yes. They say they have won,' she repeated. 'They have cheated us; we cannot accept it.' She changed her tone. 'So, you see, my son, this is not the time to start thinking about others; let everybody shrink into his house. Finish!'

'Mamma, Mamma, Mamma!'

'Yes, yes; Dorothy, yes?'

'Sarah said she'll make me a new gown.'

'The tight-fist! Did she?'

'Yes. Alex was there when she promised.'

'You visited them?' I asked.

'Four days ago. I came in only a little before you arrived today.'

'You are a lucky child, then, my good daughter,' she remarked. 'To whom did Sarah ever give a crumb? . . .'

'They were both looking very well—he and Sarah. Alex seems to be getting fat.'

'I shouldn't be surprised. Now that it's clear to him that he is not going, he ought to be able to feed himself with his money, if in fact he has it.'

'Going where?' I asked.

'You ought to know; he's your brother.'

'To England,' Dora volunteered.

'Oh, I see,' I said.

'How can he? No; he can't,' Mamma mused.

'He told you, did he?'

'He didn't tell you?'

'Not yet. I was going to ask him on my way back tomorrow.'

'I shouldn't have informed you then; I should have left you to hear it from him direct.'

'Mamma!'

'Yes, yes!'

'Have you heard? Andrew Obaro of Ukuani village returned yesterday. I saw him with my own eyes.'

'The one who is a doctor?'

'Yes. They say he has left Sakure State and will not go back.'

'It must be because of the weather, my daughter.'

'I saw his sister, Vero, and she told me he sold all his buildings up in Sakure together with all the medicine he had in his shop.'

'Is Andrew now a doctor and no longer a chemist?' I asked. An argument ensued. Both of them insisted that every chemist was a doctor. How else could one explain the fact that Andrew not only administered injections but also carried a stethoscope?

'If I were they, I would never have built so many houses in such a distant place,' Mamma said.

'Why? Aren't we one with those over there?'

'You are,' she replied with a sneer. 'But my point remains.'

'Which one?'

'You must never marry anybody who is not of our part. Neither you nor any of my remaining sons.'

She could have spared herself all the trouble. For I came to discover in the next few weeks that Grace, the current idol, was getting more and more distant in her behaviour. At first, I found some consolation in the reasoning that it was all part of the customary modesty and mystique one should expect in a prospective and promising bride. But it soon became clear to me that there was an element of uneasiness, and even of fear, about her behaviour. And the same thing, but perhaps to a greater degree, was noticeable in her uncle, Brother Badera. Badera had now virtually withdrawn from the company of friends; he just taught his lessons—no more. One day, I decided to question him.

'Bro Badera, I have not been seeing much of you of late.'

'See me? Don't I come to school?' He looked both hostile and frightened.

'I mean socially,' I explained.

'Socials? Boh, weather no good,' was his reply.

'What is wrong with the weather?'

He was well on his guard. 'Too much rain and too much cold,' he retreated, brilliantly: it was the peak of the rainy season.

'I'll come over one of these days. Tomorrow?' I offered.

I went three days later, which was Saturday. I knocked several times. A strange face came out.

'Brother Badera in?'

'No, sir,' the stranger replied with extravagant smiles.

'You know where he's gone to?'

'Don't know, sir.' He shook his head in addition.

I thought for some time.

'But I am sure I heard his voice before I began to knock.'

'Ayelo, who is that?' I heard.

'A member of the staff,' I answered, promptly. 'Grace, it's me!'

She came out in a very impressive silk skirt patterned brown and white with a greyish blouse to match. She apologised for her tone and I assured her it was sweet enough. She gave a discreet smile.

'What about Bro Badera?' I asked, still in a thrill.

'He's not in. And I didn't meet him when I arrived,' said she tonelessly, barring the entrance door to me with her buxom body. 'He should be in by evening.'

'Sure?'

'Not sure, but he ought to be. You can try again then.'

'Most brilliant idea. Will you be in then?'

'Until you come.' She withdrew into the house, waving me goodbye with no trace of a smile on her face.

I never saw her again. The house was empty when I arrived the next afternoon. But the landlord was around. Had I come to inspect the building just vacated? he asked in an enticing tone, and in another moment, he was relating the facts, including some I had already known. Badera had vacated the house at very short notice. He had nothing against the man, except that he sometimes paid the rent in arrears, at the end of the month, instead of in advance as the tenancy agreement had stipulated. ...

'But where has he moved?' I asked, ignoring him and his tenancy law.

'Do I know?' He sounded most uninterested.

'And has everybody else that was in the house left with him?'

'What do you mean?' He turned round and looked at me with suspicion.

I went away without answering his question. He started shouting for my identity, and got no answer either. I heard him all right but would not halt or turn.

Mr. Williams, editor-in-Chief of the *Harbinger*, which had now been banned, was sentenced to three years with no option of a fine. The rest of the senior editorial staff had dissociated themselves completely from the editorials which, according to them, represented the views of the chief and his only. That was the story that people told. Then, ten days after, the radio carried the news that Samson Adelu, the deputy chief editor, had been appointed Editor of a government-owned newspaper in the capital city.

I snapped my fingers. I was in Lewis's house.

'Why?' he enquired.

'What do you think about the announcement?'

'You mean about the appointment?'

'Isn't it fishy?'

'Rather, although we haven't all the facts.'

'Divide and rule!'

'Well, yes, it seems the practice is international, and inter-racial, after all. Intra-racial too. You can't blame my brothers this time.'

'No—not directly. The element of personal responsibility is very strong in this case . . . Sheer treachery.'

'It does seem that the Government over there is trying to strengthen its organs of publicity; those boys of the *Harbinger* were a very talented crew. The Samson man I hear is eminently good.'

'In journalism, and also in the art of survival!'

He screwed his face. 'I have been wondering, Roland, whether I shouldn't tell you and Biere right away, before I tell the Principal,' Lewis now said in an undertone of despair.

'What is it now? You know I haven't the temperament for suspense,' I replied.

He was unusually hesitant today, voicing the words with circumspection. 'You were hurt, quite naturally, at the way Badera left without informing friends, and I shouldn't want to hurt you all the more by doing the same thing. I intend to go home within a month or two.'

'On leave, I suppose; isn't it?' I asked after an interval.

'Well, yes. You know I haven't been on leave for almost three years,' he said. 'But it's slightly more than that. I had been wondering really, whether I shouldn't be thinking of returning to England to live. I have enjoyed my stay out here of course, only one must think seriously about one's future. If we must be sincere, the way things are happening out here at the moment does raise problems for people in my position.'

I shook my head. 'I see your last point, very clearly too,' I told him. 'I must say though that this hasn't reduced my shock.'

'Shock? Why? I wasn't going to stay here for ever in any case. No, Roland; it's not a matter that should cause any serious feeling.'

'He who carries a load knows its exact weight, a native proverb says. I'm sure Biere has no idea yet?'

'Biere? Of course not. I'll tell him when I see him again. And I must admit, it's been the triumph of his grim views all through. One should perhaps take it all with an element of humour—not depression.'

'Humour in such a situation would seem escapist, just as distress would be realistic,' I countered. 'I'm for Oban tomorrow or the day after; I'll tell him about it.'

'About what?'

'Your proposed departure.'

'No publicity, please, Roland,' Lewis implored.

'Not at all,' I promised.

We started with the news of Badera's departure, then went over to the fate of the *Harbinger* and its staff.

'I am inclined to dismiss the Badera affair as unimportant,' he then said. 'There is in your resentment against his behaviour the element of disappointed love or frustrated passion. But the *Harbinger* fellows are a most despicable lot, certainly.'

'You were never Roland Medo's ally in many things,' I protested.

'No,' and he shook his head. 'It never occurred to you that Grace and her uncle were only being prudently secretive. To many, including them, life is one long strategy for survival and must therefore have that essential ingredient of all strategies, which is unpredictability. And so, they had to move unnoticed.'

The news of Lewis's impending departure soon shattered his good humour.

CHAPTER SIXTEEN

Edoha ruled that we had acted most immaturely in turning down the offer from the oil company. Three thousand pounds would certainly have enabled us to buy a commercial building in Oban, he pointed out. We could have gone in for a bungalow with twelve rooms or so which were sure to yield some thirty pounds each month at the current high rate, and perhaps more if all the tenants were ready to cooperate. The balance we could then spend in securing another piece of land on which to build a new residence. He was not interested in Alex and his proposal to go overseas to study law—not when the nation already had far more lawyers than was necessary. Edoha wisely refrained from making these remarks before Alex, and before Mamma, both of whom had ceased to see eye to eye with him in most things. He only spoke to me, adding that I could convey his feeling on the matter to the rest. Of course I told him I would do no such thing; and that in any case, Alex had already decided to shelve his plans for going overseas. Edoha then prayed, stubbornly, that the sister and her sons could still see reason, before it was too late, and treat with the oil company. I warned him that the prayer would prove a waste.

And so it did. Work had now begun at last, with trucks and destructive machines grating from early morning to evening, along the alternative route selected by the company, about a mile from our house. It was said that the company had agreed to pay only two thousand pounds in compensation to Karibo Kanu, the well-known produce merchant at Ania whose palm estate in Umuntianu was now being bisected by the road workers. But that was in the first instance only; the unnamed perquisites could be enormous. That particular oil company had no equal when it came to generosity; Karibo could therefore expect great things in the future. It was with such sweet terms that the company's agents got Karibo to accept a mere two thousand pounds.

Like the machines, the workers too were busy all the time, except when they were on official break. Highly impressed, passers-by exclaimed with joy; some invited the fellows of the Public Works, who were nowhere around, to come and see how honest men were supposed to behave: no taking snuff, no name-calling, and no leaning on the shovel! But there were a few who pleaded that the Public Works men could hardly be blamed, in as much as oil company workers were much better paid. Overhearing the remarks, some hot-heads among the newly-discovered honest men retorted, in the vernacular and with faces turned away, that the wages were very low indeed, nearly the same for both establishments; and that the source of their affliction was the small white boy who stood close by all the time, ready to dismiss on the spot anybody who attempted to relax.

I knew the man. I had seen him a number of times. Hanson was his name. He was reputed to have been to nearly every country on the West Coast, even at his age, emerging as something of an expert on the ways of the black working class. He could be a great asset to the company he served, but as far as Roland was concerned he was a nuisance, pure and simple. Fancy the small thing, much smaller indeed than even Roland Medo, putting on superior airs: standing with arms akimbo while he shouted his instructions, often smiling in a manner which suggested a cynical indifference to the toils of the workers. He must be my age, or even younger. What right had he to command and smile with mockery? Why all the pride and confidence with which he bore himself, as if the country was more his than Roland's? But I knew the answer. The *Harbinger* had foretold that long ago—foretold what it called a new form of foreign domination. Later, the correspondent had gone on to lament: 'They have consciously organised these things in the country, our own country, in the way that suits their interests ...' And so, Hanson and his type were still behaving like masters in the land. But it would not be for long. Things were happening already which should make you all to quake and begin to pack finally. What can you do now to stem the rising tide? The wind comes in fierce sporadic thrusts, right and left. Watch out! The murmurs of the masses .... cries from individuals ... the burning editorials ... they converge on you in your hideout.

The great *Harbinger* had been blotted out, it was true. But what had that action achieved? Nothing; rather, more than ever before, there was a serious challenge to the monstrosity of the years. 'The structure must be so rearranged that no part can be equal, or nearly equal, to the whole again.' That battle-cry, which had been composed by the *Harbinger* before its demise, was being sung with relish now. The coming national elections would take account of that. What was needed was a coming together of all the progressives from everywhere; and then, the lever would go up. So it was being reasoned in most places.

Lewis left the country the day before the National Parliament was dissolved. Writing some weeks later, he tried to show that there had been no direct connection between the two events. He did admit however, in a subsequent letter to Biere, that his departure had been influenced by the turn of events, only he must add, with regret, that the heat and insects of the tropics did at last catch up with his appreciation of the common man.

We both missed him. Biere was rather disconsolate. It would have been interesting, Biere would complain, to listen to his views on the illogical party alliances now going on in the rich and promising hot citadel.

The thing was getting more and more confused, with an infinite number of abbreviated names coming into the political vocabulary. The People's Independence Party had recently allied itself with a faction of the Real Democrats into a United Progressive People's Party, or the U.P.P.P.; while the Sakure People's Party allied with the remaining half of the Democrats into the National Democratic Alliance, or the N.D.A.L. Nearly everybody, including even those of the U.P.P.P., acknowledged that the latter alliance was a master-stroke whereby the quiet and calculating men of the S.P.P. had succeeded in thwarting the dangerous designs of the loud bunch called the P.I.P. and the heady remnants of the former R.D.P. But the other side were hardly perturbed.

Thus did the brigades draw up for the great encounter.

The tactics of the two sides were very much alike in a number of ways. Each side began by mopping up the pockets of opposition in the home front. And they did that with a ruthless efficiency. The victims were many; but since it was a domestic matter, nobody bothered much. So, many of the candidates were returned unopposed at the close of nominations, in each of the States. Commenting on the situation, the *National Standard* cryptically reminded its readers that nature does not make a jump.

Petitions and loud protests followed when the U.P.P.P. lost to the N.D.A.L. in the formal electoral encounter. But these soon fizzled out as several of the elected Uniteds, with what looked like the spirit of sportsmanship, declared their intention to co-operate with the winners in the interest of the fatherland; some even crossed over to join the other side. However, there were still many influential ones on the losing side in whom the embers were still very much alive, ready to burst into flame at an opportune moment. And the opportunity soon came.

It came in yet another election, this time for the Doda State legislature. Who does not know the details of that decisive battle? We may just refresh the memory:

The battlefield was Doda State. The contestants were the Uniteds on one side and the Nationals on the other, each calling themselves a grand alliance of parties. The issue at stake was who should rule: who should hold power and all that power implied in the land? There were a few however who exalted the conflict into a noble, patriotic duty. The strangle-hold of one section on the rest must be broken; and with it, the big power behind. Both sides proved themselves gallant and indefatigable warriors the like of whom the nation can hardly ever see again.

Then it began to look as if victory was going to elude the brave Uniteds. Once again? That was unthinkable! And so, they picked up their trump card—they deployed the famous liquidators, their specially trained forces. The liquidators were a terribly efficient guerrilla division, bearing death and destruction. The death-toll was heavy indeed. But the Nationals stood their ground.

Suddenly, all went still, and cold.

Then, rumours began to circulate. . . .

'What's happening?'

'How does Biere know?'

We sat up suspenseful till midnight. Then the radio gave the news.

'Good gracious!'

'It's terrible!'

'I am rather sad, Biere.'

'I too . . . But why?'

'They should have apprehended the whole lot, tied their hands and

118

feet, and dumped them into a common cell, and forced them to remain
there until they are prepared to think about their nation.'

'I do agree.'

I turned to the short wave.

'He is in action already—listen to this!'

'Who?'

'Your friend. Listen to this one pouring out insinuations.'

'Imperator, is it?' he said, indifferently; then he drew nearer. 'Roland,
look, between ourselves—will you please leave that radio alone.'

'He is at it again!' I started gnawing my lip, thoughtfully.

'You are being irrational. The newsreader merely reads what is written for him. What I want to say is that—'

'Speak up, man!'

Biere whispered something about his fears for the future.

Part 2

Part 2

CHAPTER SEVENTEEN

There was a terrific storm during the night. Without doubt it was the worst for years, raging for hours on end and featuring thunder claps and lightning flashes and violent winds.

It began with distant rumblings and responses, like the echo of explosions in a sustained artillery duel. Then a wild wind rose carrying all with it, including sand and dry leaves, and a drizzle. Finally, the rain started pouring in a thick mass; and the earth, sprayed with cold, liquid bullets, began to bleed. The flood, fast and brown, flowed through the paths, into the fields, submerging the crops. Up above, lightning flashes tore open the heavens again and again. Between such flashes, thunder would boom, and the sound would bounce through space, reaching the earth with unnerving reverberations.

All that was before the hour of dawn, and now, the sun had taken control once again.

I rose from the bed, slouched over to the backyard, thoughtfully, chewing-stick in mouth, the leg-ends of my pyjama-trousers sweeping the ground after me. It was an attractively bright morning, with a clear view ahead, even beyond the large cassava plot which adjoined the school compound.

There was a palm-tree at the centre of the plot. Tall grass with richly tasselled apexes encircled the tree, to a height of about eight feet. A squadron of birds, darting across the plot, perched on the grass and began to peck. They were very small and very clever with their beaks as well as with their wings; and they had a most serene combination of colours in their plumage, including a frontal white, like a waistcoat, or a tabard, and a blue rear.

These birds were definitely enjoying themselves, I reflected. And then, as if they had just read my mind, some of them went off to demonstrate: they careened, wheeled, and finally returned to base. Some others went on frisking and preening themselves. And others chirruped. From time to time, they dug their beaks into the stems, and into the tassels, of the grass.

A palm-nut detaching itself from the branch overhead fell on the ground with a thud. The birds flew away, but only to return a few moments later when they had sensed that the danger was by no means real. A gentle wind blew and the grass swayed, dully. Apart from that, the cassava plot lay still.

It was almost three months now since Chimara and her daughters had put the cassava into the soil. I still remembered how she had stood, leaning against her stick and supervising while her four daughters, all married, did the planting. The plants were some two to three feet high now, and the leaves had that lush appearance which was a sure promise of rich harvest. Or rather, that was so up to the day before. This morning, most of the plants had drooping branches, because of the storm.

Old Chimara was there already, I exclaimed in my mind, still gazing into the distance. Yes, it was she, so early in the day. Going from one line to another, Chimara tried to raise some of the plants which had fallen victim to the onslaught. 'Get up; go on!' I heard her urge with strength. 'Get up; the storm is over!' She applied her walking stick this time, with maternal art. 'Get up, please,' Chimara pleaded. 'Your life is not ended.'

There was a child close by at her side. He was her grandson. He moaned: 'Mother, this one is dead.'

'Dead? No,' she protested. 'But don't hurt it.' Then, still bending double and supporting herself with the stick, she went over to the spot, where the child had already plucked off the leaves, leaving only the bare stem. 'Show me,' she enquired.

'Mother, here.' Hiding the leaves behind his back with guilt, he pointed with the remaining hand.

She gave an unearthly chuckle. 'Emenike, this is what you call death, is it? No, my son; it may still live'. She drew closer; and she shook it gently. 'It is only weak. Some have died, it's true, but not this one.'

'Mother, why is it weak?' Emenike asked.

'Because of the storm, my son,' she replied.

'What did the storm do to it?'

'It twisted it. And then,' she added, 'somebody came and plucked off the leaves. The roots are still there and therefore it will not die. It is the roots which are its soul.'

'Ah—ah—ah!' the child exclaimed, greatly impressed. 'So if the roots die it will die?'

'That's so,' she answered mechanically.

I whistled a song, merely to warn them about my presence, then moved closer until I had come to the fence between.

'Mother, I greet you,' I called.

'My good son!' came her response.

'You are well?'

'Well? Yes; your mother may be said to be well.' She paused. 'But what does my being well matter, seeing that I am a setting sun?'

Puzzled, I asked: 'Has anything happened?'

'Whether anything has happened?' she asked after yet another ominous pause. 'These things one is hearing of late about people being killed make one sick—sick on behalf of the young. And you know, my son, last night's storm was only a sign from the gods.' She turned round abruptly, indicating that she had become uncommunicative. And I started wondering whether she too knew that the new Government had just warned the citizens against careless talk and the like.

I strolled up and down, still full of thought. It was nothing to do with the state of the nation; rather, I was worried by the information received the day before, about the new man who would shortly be the head of our school. The thought had survived the night into the morning, propelling me almost unconsciously into the open yard.

A letter from Lewis arrived later that day. He had considered all the facts, he said, and had decided it would not be wise for him to seek to return to the country in the immediate future. Apart from every other thing, he was thinking of re-establishing himself at home, which might imply his finding a wife, for after all forty-two was still quite an eligible age. I was therefore to take immediate steps to dispose of his car. Then, for the remaining half of the letter, Lewis outlined some of his many regrets at leaving the country. He wrote in his concluding paragraph: 'Mr. Uzonaka, the Principal, is an excellent man, certainly one of the best I met in the country. It would not be fair to the rest of mankind, I suppose, to give two such men to your school in succession.'

It was a cautious probe. He must have had the hint already, from where nobody could tell; and now, he would want me to confirm. I did, and on the following day. What was left of Amane with neither him nor the Principal? The students were an admirable lot; Uzonaka had really moulded them into the service of God and Man, in accordance with the motto of the school, sending them to assist the needy and cheer the cheerless in their homes. They were humble, too, generally. I had really enjoyed the years, seasoning the curricular assignments with tales and discussions out of school, with him, and, at times, Biere ... How could I remain? Not with the prospect of the school being headed by a man who could perhaps have been a tolerable citizen had he not undertaken to educate—to give that which he had not. And that would be any time from now.

I locked the letter up in the table drawer. The following day, I took it to the post-office in person. And I watched the envelope slide down the slot, until it was no longer visible.

The new Principal arrived unannounced one evening, which made him look quite promising. But the impression was short-lived, for when he came again the day after, he went from one building to another calling himself Doctor Sohabia, stroking his forehead and grinning like a sage. Everybody had thought that Uzonaka was away on short leave, after which he would return to the school before his final departure. That at least Uzonaka himself had been given to understand by the Amane Community, who owned the school. And now, the Doctor had arrived in Uzonaka's absence.

We had not sensed the full depth of the pots which had been boiling all the time. An influential faction of the community which had founded the school had been seriously worried that the Principal was not a son of Amane soil. Why should they have gone to another town to look for someone to head the school when they had a son of their own alive and well and supremely qualified? Who on earth could claim to be better qualified to head a secondary school than a man who was a B.A., a B.Sc., an M.A., and, to crown it all, a Ph.D.?

He was their luminary—Doctor Sohabia was. I began to dislike him from the time the rumours about his appointment reached my ears. And the dislike deepened as I went on to reflect on his antecedents. About seven years ago, when he returned from overseas, his name had appeared in half the nation's newspapers with a string of letters. 'Another intellectual star returns,' the *Crusader* had announced in bold, front-page headline. Some other newspapers wrote more exciting things, but the *Crusader* excelled them all in its description of the star's titles to fame. 'Dr. Sohabia is a Doctor of Philosophy in Political Science, a Master of Arts in Sociology, and Bachelor of Arts as well as of Science. Before he left the country's territorial waters in quest of the golden fleece, he was already a well-known educationist.' The fact was that after he had left a secondary school of by no means resounding reputation, Titus Sohabia was employed in an equally unimpressive secondary school; and then somebody flung a scholarship, of a very vague nature, at him. The story at that time was that he was going to the United States of America to study both Medicine and Engineering together.

That was the man—Titus Sohabia—who had become the Principal of Amane Community Secondary School. He was always careful to see that the title 'Doctor' did not escape his name, especially on the staff notices; and there were cases where he appended it after his signature. However, he had enough sense of humour to warn the students who called in his office to complain of pains here and there, that his own doctorate had nothing to do with physical ailments.

From all that was known, he had had no clear profession, apart from his attempts at pamphleteering and other such things. Sohabia had written on nearly everything, including Rural Economy, Bride-price, Polygamy, Superstition or Ignorance of Science?, Gestalt Theory as applied to Nation-building, and, latterly, what he termed Idealism-Versus-Existentialism. I never bothered much about him—not since the day I tried to read one of his earlier newspaper theses titled Heuristic Approach to Learning which, in fairness to everybody, was above my comprehension. Biere had described the author of the article as a downright fake.

But there was a quality about his writings which was quite remarkable, all things considered: they were well above the rancour of party politics. He would, for example, point to practices, or malpractices, but never to individual perpetrators. It was probably because of this that he had lasted for so long, and was confident of lasting even much longer. And for his daily bread and social style, he had been advertising himself as a Political Consultant. Many indeed sought his services—ranging from big commercial firms, expatriate mostly, to councillors seeking re-election in their wards. Tall, well-spoken and handsome, he had an almost compelling personality which must account for his having so many clients.

Now that the old order was gone, what future had he? Who would care to consult him again when party politics was anathema in the new order? These and similar questions Doctor Sohabia must have asked himself as soon as he learnt about the change in Government. And it seemed almost certain that he inspired the agitation for his predecessor's removal, in the name of patriotism, the *patria* in this case being Amane.

Father Long welcomed me back to Christ High School after what he described as a pretty long sojourn; and he announced that he was making me the Vice-Principal. There was nothing particularly attractive about the appointment. For one thing, the decision had been forced on the school by a recent ruling from Government requiring every secondary school in the State to have either as its Principal, or Vice-Principal at the least, a citizen of the country. For another, the experience in Christ High School, as elsewhere, was that the Principal did practically everything himself, displaying his Vice to visitors on ceremonial occasions, except of course when, unable to help it, he fell seriously ill. My one great delight, apart from the fact that I was with Father Long once more, was that I lived in the same town as before with Biere who incidentally had not changed school once in spite of the years. And Oban was quite bearable now. Thanks to the new order, as the Government was generally called, the grating sight and sounds of men and their politics were already a thing of the past. 'Nothing that smacks of party politics may henceforth be tolerated; this country has had enough of the tantrums and insanities of people who call themselves politicians,' had been one of the earliest pronouncements of the new Government. The reaction of the citizens had been to invoke God's blessing on even the radio announcer himself.

Biere and I set out on a Saturday evening for an unknown destination. It was not clear to us either what it was we were after. We merely went on talking until we found ourselves in the heart of the town, close to the library building. Then, we turned off to the right, towards

The Cool. The alluring red and blue lights were already playing, and we fell victims right away.

The place was by no means cool; on the contrary, it was positively rowdy this night and besides, the management had introduced a co-educational service, thus altering the character of the pub out of recognition. We retired to a corner where the light was very blue and the table very yellow.

The customers were all in a happy mood. It was said that the management had appointed that night for celebration of the advent of the new order. The highlight would be a grand ballroom dance at which some very important military personalities were expected to be present.

'We drink and go away. Or are you interested in the dance?' I asked Biere.

'Call for your beer and let's go away in good time.'

I drank down a glass. It was still ice-cold, the bottle having arrived sweating. The beer seemed to congeal on the tongue.

Directly in front of us a boisterous group of young men with their girls sat round a table on which there were over fifteen bottles of beer. Some of the girls were chewing something, probably meat, in addition to talking. A fierce-looking, big, pouting one among them started castigating the management for its attitude towards snails, the fact being that the delicatessen had been exhausted long before the group arrived.

'They done hammer them politician proper!' a girl laughed out, then snatched a cigarette from the boy beside her.

'Just listen,' I said to Biere, amused at her choice of words.

'God go bless the soldier boys; they done save we, boh!' She lit the cigarette.

'Amen, sister,' the boy with the cigarettes responded and took out one for his personal use. 'Give me matches first.'

'Roland, you know that girl?' Biere asked.

'No.'

'She was the deputy-madame of one of the Ministers.'

'Well, she's ceased to be—that's all,' I said with levity. 'She too is entitled to express loyalty to the new order.'

'Apparently.' He laughed. 'May we go?'

'Yes.' And yet, I called for another beer.

The waiter, dressed in sea-green, came hurriedly. 'How many bottles?'

'A thousand! Just one, please.'

'And what about the other Master?' he asked.

'Nothing.' Biere waved him away indifferently.

He was of the crafty type, an asset to the management. A female arrived instead, the idea being to raise our consumption. But the scheme proved a fiasco right from the start. Although tolerably well built, she was elaborately painted. Biere turned away his face, definitely, leaving it to me to battle with her.

'You two, I can see una be teacher,' she declared, smiling in an attempt to impress. 'Una no wan' dring dring; una wan' save una money.' She put down the bottle on the table and opened it artfully. She began to pour out.

'Let me serve myself while you go and bring half-size Tango for my friend,' I interrupted.

'Tango!' She sounded outraged. 'When other people de dring beer and hot dring like gin and whisky? A-be, if una no wan' dring make una buy for me.'

Biere asked her with some malice: 'Who are you?'

She again began with a smile. 'Lisabet.' She continued to smile.

'Go and get me the Tango,' he ordered. She must have felt crestfallen at the harshness of his tone, for she did not return.

'I suggest we have had more than enough,' Biere said after some time.

'We can go.' I gulped down the last cup, rose. I nearly lost my balance, but rallied round immediately. The effect was heavily on me—the tingling, sensual pleasure and the floating sensation. 'I haven't had so much beer for some time.'

'Let's go.' He was most unsympathetic. But I ought to have known. He had nothing but reproach for any who took steps, deliberately, to lose his senses.

We left the bar and walked into the main street.

'You are right, Biere.'

'What about?'

'Celebrating. It seems premature.' I hiccupped.

130

'Well, what do you intend to do? Disgorge all the beer you've already swallowed?'

'Question is, where do we go from here?'

'Home immediately, if Roland Medo is not too drunk to make it.'

We hailed a taxi. It stopped and picked me up. He continued to wait for another going in his direction.

I waded through the night with the drink boiling in my head. A feeling of guilt continued to torment me, for hours on end, even while I floated through my shallow sleep. I had never been much of a drinker, and each time I slipped seriously, like this night, pangs of regret quickly succeeded the bubble of jollity, building up to a crescendo when full sobriety returned, in the morning. My head still ached and the overhang in the mouth irritated me; I felt stale inside me. How had I behaved in the drinking house? Had I made a nuisance of myself? Not likely; Biere would have got me home much earlier. Instead, Biere had kept me talking. He himself had said a lot of things too. Yes; we talked about the new order. But we were very cautious in our choice of words; and we talked in the open, away from ears.

Thinking about the new order again, everybody in the country had declared himself happy at the change. Eduado Boga was the very first person in Oban to send his patriotic congratulations to the military who, in his own words, had come in to save the fatherland from anarchy. Then, every other person rose in praises. The civil servants started being really brisk, for once in their lives. Shouting 'Alleluiah!' Yet they were the very people who had served and advised the old order, faithfully, loyally and in all honesty. They had started angling again, true to type. Lukado, for example, had regained his Ministry of State Lands; and Bonye, his former successor to the post, was now in the most unenviable Ministry of National Planning. It was yet to be seen whether Bonye, who hailed from a different State from his rival, would not stir up some trouble.

But the most curious of all the national creatures, as far as Roland was concerned, was Doctor Sohabia, B.A., B.Sc., M.A., Ph.D. Sohabia had started writing again. His first publication, entitled 'The Potential of the Military', was said to have been very well received in higher circles, and he had promised to continue the serial in weekly instalments. How I wished I had the opportunity to tell the man what I felt about him. But probably, he must have known already—from the fact that I virtually walked out on him when he arrived to head Amane Community School.

I was sinking deeper and deeper into reverie. It was the coma of drunkenness: weary limbs and a feeling of nausea, and a mind just half-awake. I must try to retrieve myself from the depression. A warm bath, and then what?

I had coffee instead in the end—thick and black, with no sugar. Then, I folded my hands, staring into the empty cup; full of imaginings ... It terminated in a purer note—a wife, some children, and an after-meal conversation in which everybody joined, the youngest child prattling and pulling at the mother's hair, and the latter making her loving protests, while I observed them with a smile. Blissful thought! Yet it was possible of realisation.

CHAPTER EIGHTEEN

It was Eduado Boga, one-time National Minister of Culture, who, in a wonderful blend of humour and grim earnest, once remarked that although all Ministers were honourable, some were definitely less so than others. He then went on to elaborate. After so many years as a Minister, he said, he himself could hardly boast of anything that could be described as an imposing memorial. His meaning was very clear to most of his large audience. Eduado was the type who spent the greater part of his earnings and takings in caring for the electorate and thereby consolidating his position; and had so far conserved very little against any possible rainy day. Thus it was that when the rain came, it caught him completely unprepared, unlike the ones who had invested in mansions and estates at home and abroad.

However, he had his consolation. Whereas several of his colleagues, including a personal friend in charge of Industrial Development, were now under house arrest or similar harassment, Eduado went about freely, as if he had been publicly acquitted. It was true that at the onset, when the new order was still very fresh and therefore full of zeal, he had, like any other colleague, made himself very scarce, changing from one hut to another, on foot, incognito; but he soon came to realise that nobody seemed to care much about him. So Eduado began to move about like most law-abiding citizens. He even began to use a car once again, except that what he had now was an old, very compact car, in place of the Pontiac, which had long been recovered by the police. And as time went on, he also revived his white voluminous gown, plus the feathered hat, without, of course, the party medallion.

I met him in the bank one morning. He was shouting, laying his complaint before all those who cared to listen. He had come to make a withdrawal. They told him he could take only one fifth of the amount he needed. The order had come from the Government and must therefore be obeyed.

But he drew only imperfect sympathies from the audience.

'Yes, you people have eaten enough!' threw in the lad standing between him and the counter. 'Give others a chance.'

He stared at the speaker expressionlessly. And the latter went on, undaunted:

'Probably your one-fifth is others' fifty times.'

'What about it? Isn't it my money?' he challenged.

'Chief, it's true,' someone else interjected.

'Thank you, my brother.'

'No, I mean you should give others a chance.'

'Ah!' he snorted in his disappointment. 'Haven't we done so already?'

'After you have spoilt everything!' the first speaker said.

'We are sorry for spoiling it. Get on now and do the repairs,' Eduado answered him.

'We will repair it—or the military will,' came in yet another.

The customers around stirred with interest.

'We want them to.' Eduado snapped, as invincible today as ever. Having dealt with crowds, what was this handful for him? 'But the trouble is that some of you people won't leave them alone. You are already putting yourselves forward as experts and advisers and planners and authorities and everything. Very soon, you will begin to deceive them—if you have not started yet.'

The general accusation silenced them all for some time. Then, some-one asked whether he had any particular individuals in mind.

'Keep your trap shut,' he replied, and the customers burst out into unrestrained laughter; and the white bank manager sent an elderly messenger to put an end to the noise. They asked the messenger to go and tell the master that his days in the country would soon be over.

'Whatever happens, we can never be a dumb people,' Eduado said as he was leaving the building.

'Serve them right!' Biere said. I had just told him the Eduado story. 'That's a result of their lethargy over these months. Nothing done!'

'They seem to move on legs of stone,' I agreed with him. 'And it seems to me that they were out at first to do some good things but then somebody came and threw dust in their eyes.'

'The dust-thrower we can very well identify. You see,' he expounded, 'many of the nation's grabbers, the fugitives from justice, are fast returning to the stage, while the slower ones among them are still covering their tracks with the utmost care. It is the parable of the evil spirit.' He looked up into my face; then, he anticipated: 'Don't begin to shout Imperator at me.'

'Of course he is there,' I did shout. 'He has not surfaced yet but he is doing terrible dust-throwing from his fortress. What has happened has been a sad blow to him, and so—'

'You know Nkenne Oli?' he digressed.

'The bearded eccentric of a trade unionist?'

'Yes.'

'He was fuming in the market place this morning.'

'Why?'

'Against the Government.'

'So openly! The halo is gone from the military, really!'

'You know what he said?'

'Yes?'

' "Let me govern, and things will be all right within a few days." Asked how he intended to go about it, he declared that thousands of people ought to be serving life imprisonment on one side of the grave or the other.'

'Still, that wouldn't have brought him to the root source of the nation's troubles. He would still have to battle with the supreme machinator. To a more serious note: the situation is quite complex.'

'Meaning?'

'The Government has serious problems.'

'Go ahead.'

'Three different countries, which go by the name of States, and yet there is a single order for them.'

'I don't follow you.'

'The army is one order: one command: one authority. It follows therefore that there is only one Government for the country, which is the Army Supreme Command. This is an altogether new and delicate feature in the constitutional evolution of this country. You see my point?'

'And how is that a problem?' he wondered, coldly.

'Problem of confidence, number one. And problem of integrating the States into one, number two.'

'You sound obtruse.'

'No; it's you being irritatingly dense today! Try to understand.' I crossed one leg over the other. 'Seriously. The country had long got used to extreme Dodanisation, Bokenunisation, and Sakurenisation. How can anybody, except a genius, reverse the position without grave troubles? Without some outsiders reminding us that we are different peoples?'

He stared into space in thoughtful silence.

'They are proposing that the States be abolished—or rather integrated into one, I hear,' he then spoke.

'Wasn't that what I had been pointing to?'

'One civil service and one—' He halted abruptly.

'In keeping with the army command.'

He shrugged. 'A mere façade!'

'Why?'

'I don't see what that will achieve.'

'What do you mean?'

'First things first, dear Roland,' he said. 'And the first thing they should have done was to get rid of those who have landed us into all this, before the latter could turn round to advise them.'

'Do you want the country united?'

'Yes—very much yes.'

'Now, declare your reservations in clear terms to the proposed integration of the States.'

'In clear terms, merely unifying the civil services of the States, the budgets and so on, won't achieve what we desire. What we need is a unity of the heart, a movement started and sustained in the higher quarters, to make the people feel they are one.'

'You may be right,' I conceded. 'From what is being said, it does not seem the civil servants themselves are happy at the idea. Some are already swearing they will never move out to work outside their own States.'

'Anyway, the main point in that is that each of the States has already organised its manpower to meet its requirements; there has never been any national planning for an integrated service, has there? The moment you remove the barriers you will have one side flooding the other, and the consequences—you see what I mean?'

'Only vaguely.'

'There are genuine fears which must be reckoned with.'

The preamble to the announcement on integration, as carried by the radio, was very touching indeed. Every citizen should feel free to live, work and move about in any part of the country . . . one country, one people, one destiny . . . special arrangements would be made to bring all the sections, no longer States, to the same level of progress within the shortest possible time. . . .

'Heroic!' Eno, the school's History wizard, clapped his hands.

'Why?' I asked.

'The doors are now wide open,' he said with jubilation. 'Fancy preferring foreigners to fellow citizens in their civil service.'

'Quite true,' I tried to reason with him. 'But there is another side to it.'

'Tell me.'

Had I not known him so well, I would have charged him with levity.

'Opening their doors so wide would mean letting in a flood, an act of self-destruction.'

'Say what you like, I shall now proceed to seek appointment in the civil service.'

'As a matter of fact, many civil servants are not very enthusiastic

136

about the integration,' I pointed out.

'That's their business,' he countered. 'But why should they when they are in the service already? Wouldn't you, Roland Medo, want to be made an Inspector of Education instead of an ordinary Latin teacher in this school? Answer me!'

'What for? I am very happy here,' I told him.

'So you say.' The mockery was apparent even from his face.

'In the long run, your career is what you make it,' I added.

'Not without the basic things of life, my good friend. Including basic allowance for your car.'

'Depends on what and what you would call basic. You have enough to eat and enough to wear; and you have good health. Then, you have the opportunity of keeping both the mind and the spirit alive.'

'Senior civil servants have all those things you've listed in addition to others you have not listed.' He added with contempt: 'You and your friend Ekonte hold very queer views at times. Tell me, who has ever invited you to a cocktail party?'

'Why do you ask?'

'Answer me!' he demanded.

'I may have been invited, and you never knew.'

'Answer me!'

'Well, nobody,' I confessed.

'And even if you had the invitation, you would not attempt to go, isn't it so?'

'Why? I'll go.'

'When you have no car?'

'Go in a taxi.'

'Why not on foot?'

CHAPTER NINETEEN

'There has been a revolt against the army . . . the protest is against the recent decree on integration . . . as many as four hundred are feared dead!' Extremely mischievous! In the first place, who in his right senses would attempt to revolt against an authority that possessed guns and bayonets and which had the power to destroy any town, no matter the size, in a matter of hours? And in the second place, only a foreign broadcasting station had carried the news so far. 'Four hundred killed!' Soldiers or civilians? Probably it was just one more calculated attempt to discredit the new order.

I tuned in again in the next hour, but to a different station. The killings, the announcer said, had spread to other towns.

I turned the knob backward. A commentator, who sounded as if he was drunk, was doing an after-news commentary. 'Such then is the present situation of things in that once-promising country. The Central Military Government, which incidentally some of the citizens refer to as the Central Machine Gun, appears to have lost its grip on the situation; and it is feared that what is now happening may well prove an overture to a concert of blood.'

I switched him off, muttering some imprecations.

Confused, I went over to the next quarters where Nayo Eke lived. There was a small group of five, including himself, in the house. The atmosphere was sad and tense.

'You don't look yourself, why?' I asked after the introductions.

Nayo merely shook his head. For the first time since I knew him, he was seriously agitated.

'Trouble, trouble, trouble!' said one of the guests.

'It's terrible,' I echoed. 'It seems it's now over, from what the radio says.'

'Which radio?' another countered, laughing grimly. 'I'm just from the office; the troubles have only begun.'

'Mr. Okara works in the Post and Telegraph,' Nayo informed me in his calm voice. 'Neighbour, there's serious trouble in our land.'

'The telephones have been ringing continuously all the day,' Okara expanded. 'Messages coming through reveal that the fire is spreading to most of the big towns in that State. Don't believe that it is over; or that only a few hundreds have died.' He went into some details about what had happened in the markets and private homes, churches and schools.

'Hunting down our kith and kin,' a woman, the only one in the group, moaned, her legs shaking with impatience, her eyes aglow; and then she chided the five of us for wasting time in discussions when we should be planning for a punitive expedition.

'Why?' I sobbed.

'Why what?' She turned round aggressively.

'Why should those be made to suffer for the sins of others?' I clarified.

'What do you mean?' Eno, the historian, asked resentfully. So far, he had been shocked by the news to a point of speechlessness. And now, opening his mouth for the first time, he went on to warn against what he described as frivolous theories.

'Poor fellows?' I persisted.

Nayo intervened: 'Very many of the survivors are on their way home already, I gather.'

'True.' Okara nodded in confirmation. 'The first batch should be arriving any time now. We'll be going out to meet them at the railway station. I must leave you now: I need to collect a few things for the needy before their arrival.'

'Things like?'

'Bread or biscuits, water, clothing,' the woman said, having thawed at last.

'Has it come to that?'

She attempted to smile but suddenly switched off, self-consciously. 'It has, oga,' she said, even though she had not less than fifteen years over me. 'We should all go out and donate something. That's why I came here,' she added in self-excuse.

'Miss Wilfred is an official of the Women's Christian Association,' Eno informed us.

The night was very dark. But the street lights shone intensely, unblinking. The recent events had awakened everybody, including the electricity staff, to an unprecedented pitch of industry and sense of responsibility. An air of co-ordinated orderliness possessed the entire town. Cars were streaming by continuously, most of them heading for the railway station to render free service to the needy. The drivers were exceptionally courteous today. The pedestrians went hurriedly along the sides of the roads, chatting but not shouting, mostly about the recent doings of those who had all along been their victims' good friends.

'It is most surprising, my brother! Just as you've just said.'

'Truly, they had been our best friends in the country all the time.'

'It is their big men that spoilt them.'

'Politics and nothing else—that's what has turned things upside down.'

'But didn't we say everything had been put right just a few months ago?'

'Why do you ask?'

'I ask because the men you call politicians have come again. It is they who are causing the new wave of trouble. . . .'

We got into a taxi.

The station and its precincts were flood-lit. The crowd numbered thousands. We pushed our way through to the centre where some of the travellers just arrived sat or stood in varying attitudes.

Some were leaning on and clutching at their loads with their hands. These looked dejected, but not despondent. Some others were engaged in conversations relating to their experiences. Many just stared in blank amazement. Close by, some members of the Red Cross, rising to a rare opportunity for service, were collecting food and clothing for the victims; or they were dressing the wounds on the victims' bodies. The leather whips wielded by the attackers had left long gashes and suppurating wounds. Far to the right, some nuns, both white and black, but well apart, were busy feeding the younger ones with rice and milk. A few yards away, members of the Anglican Guild mounted their banner; and behind them, the Methodist Youth Fellowship hoisted a flag. Another sect concentrated on a free gift of pamphlets which warned that the Kingdom of the Lord was at hand.

It was the Red Cross worker who approached me first. Would I like to deposit my packet with her? She must have been over forty-five, and my first instinct was to reject her in favour of a much younger agent; but her tone and manners were delicate and disarming. I was on the point of handing the parcel of biscuits and milk over to her when she suddenly turned her attention to someone else.

'Yes, sir!' She began smiling as she had not done so far. 'Anything for us?'

I looked behind to see the great donor. I hissed, loud enough for her to sense my disapproval. It was Hanson, the oil company road-builder. And he was grinning just as he always did when dealing with his subordinates.

'You prefer him to me, is it?' Before she could open her mouth, I called her some unkind name; then, I moved over to the Catholic nuns.

Some moments later, somebody tugged at my shirt sleeve.

'It's you? When did you come?' I asked, turning round.

'Before you,' Biere said in reply.

'Before me? How do you know?'

'Oh, I've seen Eno and he informed me what time you arrived.'

'Yes, we came together.'

'By the way, Roland—'

'Yes.'

'That man Eno is quite a pragmatist, did you know—'

'What has he done?'

'I was talking with him and he informed me he supports the idea of fitting out an expedition right away.'

Another, pushing valiantly from behind, dislodged us from our position. Before we could even utter our protest, he was already interviewing his guest and scribbling in his note-book.

'. . . Now tell me in a few words what happened to him,' he prompted.

'I was with him in the house,' she faltered. 'They rushed in.'

'With your husband?'

'Yes. They broke in with knives and arrows. He stood up to receive them, and spoke to them in their language. He asked whether anything was wrong and they told him everything. And the next moment—' She wiped her eyes.

'Accept my sympathy, Mrs. Akaji.' The newsman closed his book. The bystanders ordered him to move away from the spot. . . .

We too moved away, to the outer fringe of the crowd.

'What do you think?'

'Many things. Why?' Biere replied.

'Do you think it was pre-meditated or was it spontaneous?'

'Casualties of a brutal mob anger,' he pronounced. 'And the anger must have been inspired.'

'By whom?'

'Enemies of the Government.'

'Be more specific!'

'That's where we begin to part.'

'By them.'

We moved farther away from the crowd, into the road.

'They were never crushed or even silenced,' Biere grumbled. 'Rather, they were let free to insinuate themselves into places. And now they have rallied and struck in an impressive style. So, there we are. You may not agree.'

'When are you coming over?' I asked him.

'One of these days. And very soon—I love those Flame of the Forest flowers behind your school compound.'

'They are already in full bloom.'

'Even a blind man knows that.' He screwed his face. 'It's all fresh and pure—red flowers mingling with the tiny, well-ordered foliage.'

'Nothing world-shaking in that.'

'Blood over a well-trimmed, grassy field,' he mused again, inattentively.

'Rather ghastly.'

'Gentle though grave, I would say,' he differed, his forehead furrowed by some deep thought.

That imagery intruded itself into the night's scattered dreams.

I woke late in the morning. The sun was shooting its rays into the room through cracks in the window shutters. The day was Saturday. I was to supervise the students' morning duties.

Voices were ringing out already at the western end of the compound. I rose hurriedly and wiped my face with a dry towel; then slipped on trousers and shirt. I rushed out in a hurry, in the direction of the flamboyant trees standing in a row just behind the barbed fence.

The fence had been erected several years back. Its main purpose was to keep the students in. But now, by a process of concerted tugging and pulling, with both hands and feet, they had widened the gaps and even broken the wire in places, thus providing themselves with a secret access into the town. Sensing defeat, the Principal had now ceased to bother about the fence; rather, he would merely remark about the manner in which the ornamental trees behind were being misused: those trees were there to beautify the compound and break the force of the wind, not to serve as a truants' corner. Whenever he said such things, the students would burst into ambiguous cheers.

A big rainbow was visible in the sky. The colours blended with the elevated pool of red on the tree-tops into a violent effect. But the silent green of the grass below served to temper the impression. Scattered all over the field, the students went on with their morning duty, which today was grass-cutting. Their knives champed and clashed. Their voices rang.

'See, see, see; a big rainbow!' a voice shrilled.

'Rainbow in the sky!'

'That shows that a big man is about to die, doesn't it?' one boy asked over the noises.

'It's superstitition,' another disagreed.

A prefect hushed them from a distance, threatening he would increase their portions if they continued to argue. They stopped arguing, but only until the prefect had moved away to another section.

'But after all, many big men died some months ago,' the argument resumed.

'And so?'

'Well, may be some more are going to die,' the boy said, laughing carelessly.

'T-fia! Let nobody die again; we have had enough of dying.'

Then, somewhere further down, to the south, a number of boys began to hiss and whistle. This was because a group of girls from Saint Anne's Second-to-none was at that moment passing along the narrow path which ran parallel to the fence. They were all big girls and therefore, in the language of the boys, very capable. But they were all looking grave, which was rather disconcerting. In his disappointment, one boy called out charging that they were no saints but pretenders. And that did it. The tallest of the girls halted and tried to preach about good manners.

They went off, without letting her develop her theme:

'Soror mea!'
'Amantissima!'
'Pulcherrima!'
'Cor meum dulce. . . .'

She led her company on a retreat. Then, some very determined ones among the boys suggested an ambush.

'Hei!' I shouted across in a general reprimand, yet laughing inwardly; and they recoiled momentarily. 'Finish the portion and go over to whatever you are supposed to be doing after compound cleaning.'

Typical Christ High School! They were merciless when it came to heckling the opposite sex. Only recently, a small knot of students had harassed a lone girl, close to the day's scene, to a point of despair. Her saviour that day was an elderly woman who chanced to be passing by. The latter shouted a recommendation that all the inmates of the school should be marched in single file to a butcher's shop where they would undergo some crude surgery. Only then, she said, would the roads in Oban be safe for use by mother's honest daughters.

I watched them from a distance, contemplating at the same time the tree-tops red and green with flower and foliage . . . That was Biere's blood over a well-trimmed, grassy field! Nothing ghastly . . . Gentle though grave . . . It was tame, and fresh—a pure blend, with the red accentuating the effect. This was May, and nature was in bloom once again. The leaves had been washed clean, leaving no trace of dust. The grass on the field, just trimmed and raked, lay like thick, green carpet over the ground.

A group of the smaller boys, sensing that the timekeeper would soon ring for free time, ran off to one end of the field, bouncing a tennis ball between them. Then, the bell came. A general applause followed. The boys kicked the ball high into the air. And they chased after it. Finally, they grouped themselves into two teams. A match was under way.

They were all serious about it, chasing, shouting, laughing, kicking, falling, and nearly every one of them acting as referee. Wasn't that interesting to watch? And pleasant too. They all had the qualities of a sapling—tender vigour, freshness, innocence and charm . . . Call them maidens . . . Mamma would insist it was an expiation.

144

CHAPTER TWENTY

Isaac ran full speed towards the house, a newspaper in hand, grinning, berserk—the way I had once thought I would behave on receipt of news of my success in the degree examination. Presently, he panted out 'Scholarship', and resumed his heavy breathing.

'What type of scholarship?' I asked him.

He pushed the paper into my hand, 'Government scholarship!' he gasped again, then added: 'For me; and for Dorothy too.'

'Thank God!' I prayed, after some time. 'And gratias militibus.'

He looked up into my face, enquiringly.

'For once, they have not only stated but also adhered to a principle in these things,' I elaborated. 'That's why you've got the award.'

'And Dorothy too,' he reminded me.

'Yes,' I snorted vaguely. Isaac was very brilliant in the school. Everybody had acknowledged it. He was exceptionally good in Science and Mathematics, and also in Literature and Latin, which explained why he was given the nick-name Intellectual Amphibian. With Dora, it was slightly different: she was just above average. However, part of the general principles governing the awards was that the education of females should be given a boost, in the interest of enlightened motherhood.

Nothing could equal for the moment the sense of relief which I felt, especially with Dorothy on the list of recipients. Isaac had been manageable, for after the tuition and boarding fees, and a few extra pounds for books, you paid hardly anything more. But for Dorothy, you bought soap and pomade and powder and Ovaltine and biscuits—things which, in her usual lamentation, everybody else brought with her to the school. Dorothy cost nearly a hundred pounds each year while Isaac cost a little over sixty. What was left of my salary in the end, more so after the income tax, at bachelor rate? And yet, I still had to pay my houseboy (in addition to what he paid himself out of the shopping account), and send money to Mamma, and renew the brotherhood with Dom and Louis—the former would be leaving the secondary school at the end of the year while Louis was still in the third year.

The bulk of the burden was off, gratias militibus. I could now begin to save, to assemble the sum of two hundred pounds or more which would be demanded from me as bride-price. And let this be clear to everybody: if I should pay all that amount to the dealer, I would have every right to expect only the best.

She must not be one of three types: first, the money-minded one who would change camp when you dangled the coins; second, the dazzling commodity of a young girl in whose soul there was already a thick coating of filth, at her age; and third, the nymph, the bird of passage, who would keep you at bay with her smiles, your heart panting, while she planned her escape. They all however possessed the basic and indispensable quality of beauty—otherwise why should I have looked into their faces in the first instance? She too would be charming—that, so far, was certain; as for the other specifications, I had better lie down and plan.

But my mind strayed ... I was thinking about the successes of the new order. Count among these the step it had taken in some of the States with regard to the state lands which those in authority, and their friends and relations and associates, had misappropriated. This was one point on which Edoha felt very embittered against the people behind the guns. In the past three years, that beloved wealthy uncle had been allocated five different plots of land, in spite of the official ruling that nobody should have more than two, under any circumstances. Edoha simply adopted the popular device of using different names on the application forms after some private discussions with those who really decided things. And now, he had, in one fell stroke, lost all the plots. For the new Government had decreed, ruthlessly, that all allocations made in the past four years, which was when the racket started, were no longer valid. The most distressing aspect of it all, as far as Edoha was concerned, was that he had already assembled sufficient materials for a really gigantic edifice which he had long proposed for the plot at the junction of former Koko and Ayika, now renamed Ania and Portcity, Streets. That plot had been the envy of even his best friends.

Edoha had a passion for building houses, or what was known as landed property. He already had enough of them to keep him in reasonable comfort up to the end of his life; or to sustain his one wife and five children for years in case he should depart from this life abruptly. But he was not a happy man. Edoha was always grumbling about plots which needed renovation, and defaulting tenants, and development tax, and water-rate. To be fair to him, up to a point, he was only being fashionable. Buildings, buildings, buildings!—that was what almost everybody had been talking about. And so, the Minister in charge of State lands had become the most popular man in the cabinet; and the mere fact that you were from the same village with that most honourable of them all was a passport to social importance. To tell the whole truth, though, Roland Medo did once apply, on the appropriate form and through the official appropriate channel. And I would have been delighted if I had succeeded. It was later explained to me that I had failed to follow the application up. The rascal who told me this said he was a personal friend to a personal friend of the Honourable.

If only the Government had gone further than merely revoking the leases! I thought. Couldn't it have started enquiring into how many buildings each individual had in the State, in the country, and then outside the country, against the background of the owner's income? 'The warriors of liberation had been allowed to make away with their loot.' Biere was right. What, for example, could happen again to Doctor Anibado, Chairman of the National Finance Corporation, who on an annual salary of two thousand pounds bought a brand-new Mercedes car every six months, or less, and had a row of flats in the national capital and another row in Portcity? They said he was being considered for an economic mission to Europe and Asia. Another was Mr. K. K. Orejo, proprietor and principal of a secondary school, who spent more of his time arguing with building contractors than attending to the needs of the school. Orejo had just completed yet one more modern mansion—the sixth, it was said. Only the week before, the students under his charge had gone on hunger-strike, accusing both himself and his well-nourished young wife, and the numerous relatives on both sides, of living solely on the students' rations, in addition to other things.

'How can such people be brought to account when the Government is falling into a bloody disarray?' I asked myself, aloud, and rose. An hour later, I was in Biere's house. . . .

'We may even begin to expect a counter-stroke from them.'

'What leads you to say so?' I asked him.

'It's quite easy to perceive. The military has been compromised by its woeful failure to satisfy the expectations of the masses in most respects; and so, it has rendered itself vulnerable. But the worst thing about it is that it has left the arch-what-do-we-call-them to regroup.'

'You may be right,' I conceded. 'But you seem to forget that the Government lacks the support of the real arch-what-do-we-call-him, without any doubt. Which was a terrible thing: it has to face that in addition to its other weaknesses.'

'It's in its interest that it should lack the blessing of your Imperator—that's what I should have thought, if it was a really nationalist government.' He picked up the day's issue of the *Crusader*. 'The atmosphere is congealed right now. Read this.'

The article, culled from a foreign newspaper, hinted at a general sense of drift and a presentiment of fear in most parts of the country. 'No one, except the most naïve,' it went on in the concluding portion, 'would be surprised in the event of another eruption. The overture having been what it was, one begins to wonder what the full concert would be like. The thought itself unnerves. But of course we know that the country has always had the good luck of stopping just short of a full ...'

'Distasteful journalism,' I protested, flinging the paper back at him.

He shook his head in affirmation, smiling at me indulgently. 'What I dislike about it is that it has failed to tip us off on the nature of the eruption which is feared—whether it will be by the masses or within the ranks.'

I picked up another paper lying on the floor. I opened to the middle page for the day's columnist.

'Oh God!' I shrieked, and flung the paper yards off. It was Doctor Sohabia on *Manpower Planning*.

'Time?' he asked.
I looked at my watch. 'One o'clock. No, not quite; two minutes.'
'Shall we listen to the news?'
I nodded assent.
'B.B.C.?'

He switched on and turned the tuning knob, just in time for the time-signal. Then we heard:

'A major army revolt ... Some shooting was reported in the barracks.'

Then, the news came in detail. ...

Two days passed during which reports continued about deaths in hundreds.

'I only hope,' said Biere dismally, 'that the shootings in the barracks do cut across ethnic groups.'

'We can only hope, no more,' I agreed.

'And that they confine themselves to their barracks.'

'There doesn't seem to have been anything to the contrary. But the trouble is that when they have done with the barracks they may want to repeat it outside. Whoever it is ...' The words were wiped out of my mouth by yet another report that bodies of the dead littered the streets in hundreds.

'We now have yet another New Order for the nation, as a result of the conflagrations,' I said. 'I hope it will satisfy him—satisfy the archplotter, and give us a breathing space.'

Biere held his lower lip between his teeth and depressed his left cheek. 'It was easy to foresee from the start that there was going to be further bloodshed,' he stammered in his pain, 'but that was not the type of thing—' He shrugged again; and again. 'People are still dying. What have they, soldiers and civilians, done? Why should honest men and women be dying for the sins of others?'

'What exactly the killers want I don't know.'

'Nor when they will be satiated, if ever.'

'I'm even beginning to wonder whether, in spite of what he may have wanted, Imperator could have a hand in this thing, which has claimed thousands of lives and is still claiming more.'

He did not appear to have heard. His mind was somewhere else. ...

Later that day, the radio announced that thousands of civilians had been gunned to death in a renewed orgy.

'At the other end,' the announcer said an hour after, 'the natives have started lynching the stranger elements in retaliation.'

CHAPTER TWENTY-ONE

So many people that I knew had of late begun to behave in a strange way. It would be interesting to take a census of the whole of Oban. The latest was Nathan Edeogome, the third-year student who threw his breakfast out of the refectory window, ran off into the open, and started calling down God's anger on anyone who would in future prescribe a train journey for him. Nathan had lost his father and mother in the train on their way down to Oban. Hundreds of people had died in fact, and it was a miracle, wrought through the Red Cross, that brought him home and alive in the end.

We took the boy to the hospital in Biere's car. The psychiatrist said we should expect more of such cases.

The car was a Peugeot saloon, brand-new and shiny grey. It had been purchased the week before. Biere had produced less than a quarter of the cost while his father paid the remainder. This afternoon we would take it to Umuntianu at my request. I was to pay for the fuel while he saw to the other things, unspecified.

Straight from the hospital, we halted at the Mobil petrol station at that end of the town. A girl came up, briskly, and began to enquire about our need while at the same time inspecting the inside of the car. Biere whispered, right into my ear, that she must be one of the security girls. The girl had already switched on the meter and was now asking us to confirm she should fill the tank to the brim. That would have meant more than two pounds, whereas I had budgeted for fifteen shillings at the most.

'How many?' Biere teased.

'One gallon,' I said. Meanwhile, the meter was rolling precipitously down to two.

'Two gallons now,' and she terminated the current with a jerk. 'How many more?' She gave a broad smile.

'Fine girl,' I complimented. 'Should I marry you?'

'Roland, let's hurry!' Biere cut in with a big frown. 'Put in two more gallons,' he ordered.

A young man, probably in his late twenties, appeared from the station building. His hair was unkempt, his dress almost in tatters, and his steps sluggish and wobbly. He yawned, and yawned again. 'Please attend to the masters well,' he said to the girl. 'I no well.' And when I asked what exactly was wrong with him, he replied 'everything'. Then he began to grind his teeth, and his eyes turned bloodshot. Hands over his head, he went away, into the street. The girl told us how he had reached Oban only a few days before, after losing all his belongings. He had escaped with his wife by ingeniously disguising himself as a lunatic, which he was now, in fact, steadily turning into.

The vehicle ran smoothly. The distance was only thirty miles each way. We would certainly be back in less than two hours, including the time we would spend in the house. For once, it was thanks to the oil company: the road had been widened and tarred and the surface was smooth, and the journey was a pleasure ride. We would surely be back before four o'clock, in time for the meeting at the town hall in the evening. It was something to do with the welfare of the refugees who, in less than three months, had nearly doubled the population of Oban. We had agreed we should attend. And not just today's, but all subsequent meetings too.

The car was purring effortlessly at fifty miles an hour on the overdrive.

'Beautiful machine,' I said.

'The Peugeots are nice,' he agreed. 'And cheap too.'

'At nearly a thousand?'

'Less twenty-five. But with very high second-hand value. This one could, for example, turn in as much as four hundred after five years—'

He shouted 'Lord!' and I cried 'Mind!' Simultaneously, the brakes gave a wild screech. I hit my head on the dashboard....

The engine had stopped running and the car was tilted to one side, less than a yard from a ditch on the edge of the road. We stepped out.

He was very much composed, while my heart kept pounding.

'See, see her!' I gasped, pointing at the figure that stood giggling meaninglessly a short distance ahead, by the edge of the bush. Did she know she had just escaped death by a hair's breadth? It was probably her whitish blouse which had caught our eyes, just in time for Biere to swerve.

'She started to cross the road when the car was close,' he complained.

151

'This car has no horn,' she countered. 'And its engine has no sound.'
We both eyed her furiously.

'Come and kill me with your car.' She stretched out both her hands in an entreaty. 'Come and kill me.'

'Woman what is wrong?' I asked.

She gave a loud shriek and disappeared into the bush.

Almost immediately, an old man arrived through the footpath on the opposite side of the road.

'I heard some sound. Is it your car?' he asked with compassion.

'It is,' I said.

'Anybody hurt?'

'No.'

'The sound was terrifying,' the old man remarked.

'Do you see that woman who has just gone away?' I asked while Biere went on inspecting the car.

'Lilian, isn't it? I saw her well enough.'

'The car nearly ran into her.'

'We thank God!'

'But is she well—sane, I mean?' Biere asked.

'Why?'

'She just dashed into the road. If the brakes had not been very good she would have been killed on the spot.'

The old man gnashed his teeth. 'Nobody knows what exactly you young ones think about the things happening.'

'Which things, father?'

'The things happening to our own blood.'

'They are terrible!' I said.

'Terrible? Is that all?' he wondered, twisting his lips to the left. 'My days are few, my sons; and I can no longer do the things that are proper to the youth.' He brushed the cutlass in his hand on the hard surface of the road. 'That woman called Lilian is my own brother's wife.' He was almost singing now. 'A brother from the same mother's womb! And she was one of the best women in the land. She loved him and he loved her, and they had four children. Now, she has only one child left—the youngest at that. And no husband!'

Ogidi and Alex were in the house when we got there, and they both joined the rest in a race to see what they believed was Roland's car.

Ogidi's disappointment was more apparent than anyone else's, even Dorothy's. He had thought that at long last the sister's son had become one of those who owned the four-wheeled thing. He had even gone as far as to conclude that I would take him back to Siaku, right into his own compound, in it. It was true Edoha had a car, but who saw Edoha these days, not to talk of Edoha's car? And then, Ogidi turned his back, away from me.

He was in a queer mood today. He began to pluck at the metal prongs on the calabash bowl in his hands. . . .

'Ogidi, you are making music while the land is aflame?' Mamma remonstrated.

'Why not, my good sister?' he insisted. 'Music may be for dancing.' The prongs burst into another concert. 'It may also serve to console the heart.' He did a staccato.

'I must be going, my sister,' he said, to the rhythm, after some time. 'I have seen you, and you are all alive and well, for now. That's why I have come.'

'You've done well,' she acknowledged.

'A good thing, Rola came in too while I'm here. And with his good friend. The sky is terribly overcast, my sister.' He slapped on the bowl with his right palm, indicating the end of the performance.

The town hall was nearly full by the time we arrived. And, as the newspapers would put it, there were people of all walks of life. These included former Ministers of State and former party leaders. They were all cheery, and, inevitably, loquacious. And although everybody was free to dress in any way he liked, nobody in fact appeared in any form of robes. And everybody was free to sit anywhere.

We found two empty seats close together, directly behind a man and a woman and towards the back. As we drew the seats to position, the metal feet brushed on the floor with a grating sound. The man was the first to turn. Our eyes met, and he gave an instinctive half-hearted smile followed by a mechanical greeting, which I returned.

'Husband-in-law!' Biere then whispered into my ear. 'With her by his side.'

'They too must have fled!' I whispered back.

'From Gorigori? There couldn't have been much fleeing in their case,' he said.

She too turned. She withered when our eyes met. Biere held his hand over his mouth; then he bent down his head, looking into my face from a low angle.

The dais in the fore-front was at the moment a scene of unco-ordinated activities and indecisions, various people moving up and down, consulting, arguing and even quarrelling, aloud. A struggle for leadership on a most bloodless scale had ensued. It was one Aneke Oyioma, alias Okay Baby, who seemed to be winning. As lively today as ever before, the baby argued his points left and right, very audibly, his countenance showing the full gamut of emotions. Above everything else, he was reputed to be fearless and forthright, and quite sincere. He was very popular with the public too. He alone, for example, had been able to tell honourable men their faults without incurring their open wrath.

'No, no, no!' Okay Baby shouted over the noises, his body quivering. 'We are not women; we are not women!'

'Let's get started,' shrieked his rival.

'That was what I was about to do when you began to raise problems,' he retorted.

'Well then, start,' the other urged with sarcasm.

'Give me the bell; where is it?'

Someone else came pushing through, the bell in his hand. Okay Baby took the bell from him, put it on the table, and then stroked the ample hair that crowned his five-foot-five, after which he adjusted his glasses.

The bell rang, for some seconds.

'Ladies and gentlemen!'

The voices began to die down.

'Yes, Okay Baby,' many voices answered.

Hands clasped, as if he was nervous, he said: 'The day is going and we mustn't allow darkness to overtake us.'

'Truly!'

'It is necessary that there should be a chairman for the occasion,' he said; and he added craftily: 'Or has anybody any other suggestion?'

His many supporters proposed him and then shouted him into office.

Oyioma recounted in his opening address the misfortunes which in the past few months had befallen the kinsmen. It was the work of providence that some had been able to escape and were still able to breathe. Gratitude must go to all the good samaritans who had helped these to save their lives. The problem now was how to sustain the brothers and sisters whom the Great Almighty had led out to the land of the fathers. Such people must eat, drink, and be clothed. They required help—indeed generous help. And that was the main purpose of the assembly. He would, subject to general approval, like as many people as possible to speak on the subject. 'But,' he ended, 'let me say this to you right away. No matter how sweet our tongues may be, they will not go far in helping the destitute brothers. We must give them something material and substantial.' His language was admirably neat and precise. Yet he had had no education beyond the secondary school. And by profession he was what they called a local business man, dealing in miscellaneous hardware, from nails to pails. But you could hardly see him without a thriller, often by Edgar Wallace or Peter Cheney, in his hand. Those who spoke immediately after were definitely no match for him.

The first was Eduado Boga. Eduado had succeeded in building up some permanent image among the population. The truth of it was that he was generally a humorous and sociable man. He loaded his speech with proverbs, mostly rendered in the vernacular and therefore fresh and penetrating. The second speaker, a woman, claimed that she was representing the world's motherhood. But she soon proceeded to contradict herself. 'If the men of this State,' she threatened, 'prefer to be wives while we become their husbands, then we are prepared to go up there and ask them why they did that to our children.' In a characteristic style, the men, who were in the majority, asked her to remain what she was, except in her own family. The third recounted how he had lost everything he owned, including land and commercial goods.

Somebody gave an account of an incident one morning when he came out of his house to find he had been surrounded by armed men, some in uniform, and how in the end he managed to escape through the solicitude of friends in the host State. 'There are still good men over there—even now. They are there and they are many. I would not condemn them wholesale. No!' A heavy silence descended. 'I lost everything, it is true,' he continued, 'but I must say what I feel is the truth. It was a wild fire. Even the people who lit it know it.

'However, I do not mean that we should not take precautions. For the fire may yet start in a fresh blaze which may reach our very homes. We can never tell. . . . I must thank you all for the efforts you've been making on behalf of those of us who are refugees. It gives us confidence, making us feel that we are going to survive.'

'We are going to survive!' many voices echoed.

'Three or four more speakers and then we'll ask the ladies to go round with containers,' the chairman announced. 'Yes? Quiet, ladies and gentlemen!'

Biere's hand shot up into the air.

'The next speaker,' he shouted over the voices, 'will be a teacher. Mr. Ekonte! Listen! . . .'

Biere looked taller, and thinner, than he actually was as he stood on the dais facing the assembly, dressed in striped casual shirt and grey trousers. And there was wonderful discipline in his oratory: it was unaccompanied all through with gesticulations. He was not speaking on behalf of the teaching profession, he said, gravely. He was speaking as an individual who, like many others, was gravely upset by recent happenings.

'And now, let us get down to the matter before us. First of all, I must associate myself right away with the chairman's view which was very precisely worded: indulging in self-pity, or merely licking our wounds, will lead us nowhere. We need first of all to take steps to resettle our kinsmen who have been forced out of their places of abode. We need also to think about our safety here in our homes. Then, and this is the main point of my speech, we should also sit down to reflect upon the causes of the situation in which the country has found itself. . . .

'We should be honest enough with ourselves. Maybe some people here may feel offended, but the truth remains in spite of their feeling. It is the misdeeds of our brothers, among others, which have brought about all the trouble. What is necessary now, if we are to avoid even worse incidents, is a firm intention of amendment, without which we'll be seriously hampered and frustrated in our endeavours in other respects. There is no need my flogging the point, Mr. Chairman.

'It is most unfortunate that there has been no logic in all the killings we've been experiencing. It's mostly innocent ones who have been shot or hacked to death—people who had very little or no share of the so-called national cake. One could of course argue that this is only in accordance with the general pattern and irony of human affairs; that it is the innocent civilians who are usually the greatest victims of war, while the bellicose protagonists survive. . . .

'Those who may have known me for some time will testify to the fact that I am not a man of passion. But I feel deeply about what has happened. Why should one part of the nation be singled out for such gruesome sacrifice? The least we should expect is a guarantee that such things will never be repeated. Had it stopped with—' He checked himself. 'But again, let us think within ourselves what gave rise to it all.'

When he took his seat minutes later, and while the applause rang, four men rushed at him. Two of them just offered their hands, another went punching the air before his face in congratulations, and the fourth opened his notebook and introduced himself as the local correspondent of an unnamed American journal.

The speech had certainly opened a new angle. Hands went up. Then, Oyioma declared he would welcome more than three more speakers, in keeping with the wishes of the assembly. The first, second and third speakers lashed out, mercilessly, on 'looters and conspirators, and the men in public cars driven with public fuel and by public drivers'. The next demanded that such people should no longer be allowed to appear in public places. He was all the more disconcerted when the very persons he had in mind burst into laughter; and Eduado Boga even proposed that such people should also be stripped naked, publicly, if that would save the country, or raise the dead.

'Last speaker!' Oyioma now announced.

I raised my hand and also caught his eyes.

'Yes . . . remind me, your name, please? . . . Mr. Medo is the Vice-Principal of Christ High School.'

'Congratulations for the excellent speech!' she said, sidling towards me. The meeting had ended at last and the crowd had poured out into the open. They stood in scattered groups discussing.

'Ruth! I could hardly recognise you,' I said.

'Why?'

'You are attired like a regina, believe me.'

'You haven't changed, Roland—you and your friend,' she charged with fondness. 'Except that—'

'Complete it.'

'You've begun to grow a beard. What for I do not know.'

'Beard and hair together. I am sad,' I told her.

'What about.'

'The events in the land.'

'They are terrible,' she remarked.

'Is that the only changes you've noticed?'

'Another is that you no longer care about anybody,' she said.

'Including you?'

'You know very well.'

'Can I? Should I? Answer me.'

'You live in the college?' she jumped.

'Yes.'

'In the Vice-Principal's house?'

'Correct,' and I nodded. What was she after? I would try.

'When may I expect you?'

She looked right and left. 'Good night; see you again,' she said, hurriedly and in a low voice.

The fool of a man was advancing.

CHAPTER TWENTY-TWO

Okay Baby said we had nearly ruined the alms-receiving ceremony of which he was chairman by attacking the men of influence the way we had done. They it was who had the stuff in their pockets, after all, and it would have been a disaster if because of our loud-mouthedness they had refused to dip their hands. Countering, we reminded him that the men had very thick hides. No amount of rudeness could have deflected them from their purpose, which was to exhibit themselves and their wealth.

Then, Okay Baby confessed he was one with us; he had merely pulled our legs.

According to him, the greater part of the sum of twenty thousand pounds raised in Oban so far had come not from the indigenes but from expatriates, notably of the big trading companies. Premier Oil alone had donated five thousand, while the two commercial banks in the town paid a thousand each.

Were they being sarcastic or what—these companies who were now doling out money for the dead or dispossessed? I objected. But Biere differed:

'We need their money.'

'Doesn't that compromise us?' I asked.

'Nothing is compromised. Let's wrench the money out of their hands. . . .'

Rounding up, Okay Baby described the argument as an unnecessary waste of words. Government, he said, had already accepted the donations and issued letters of thanks, but only to those who paid ten pounds and above.

That was a week after the meeting. Today, we were gathered in the town hall again. But it was nothing about the welfare of refugees this time; we were attending the inaugural meeting of the Area Emergency Council.

I had received the first intimation of the day's meeting that very morning. The letter just said that I had been appointed a member of the Area Emergency Council, and that I should attend the inaugural meeting fixed for three o'clock that day, and without fail. I got to know in the course of the day that Biere too had received an invitation. But in his own case, the thing was couched in a tone of positive command.

I got to the hall ahead of time. Even then, a fairly large crowd had already assembled. They stood or sat in small knots, discussing, speculating, swearing and making some positive suggestions. Ekenkwo Elu, the current hero among trade unionists, was in a far corner of the hall shouting recriminations on the former leaders, or 'the old order', while

159

Eduado Boga, Chief Lebo and Nnanta Agomo listened and laughed. In the middle, Doctor Sohabia, Doctor Anibado, and yet another doctor, Makamadu, sat rocking with laughter. And to their right, there was a cluster of men and women, which included legal and medical practitioners, prominent businessmen and contractors, and a leader of a religious sect of local origin, all eagerly exchanging platitudes and blandishments. Then, behind this last group, sat Biere and Okay Baby, and Amos Isiguzo, the librarian in charge of Oban Public Library. Okay Baby was busy amusing the other two, with both his mouth and his fingers, when I joined the group.

Soon after, a young administrator bumped in. He mounted the platform with unabating speed and called for attention. Then, he declared he had been sent to inaugurate the Council. By whom, he would not tell anybody, but rather proceeded to read out some names.

There were seven of them. The fourth was Roland Medo; and the sixth Biere Ekonte. Those, he announced, had been sent the wrong invitation, for which he was apologising on behalf of the authorities; they should proceed at once to the office of the District Officer for something that was extremely urgent.

The guards at the entrance led us into the office where two army officers with grave countenances were already waiting. Biere was the first to enter; then Oyioma; then myself. Moments later, the rest began to arrive. They were Professor Makamadu, Doctor Sohabia, Ekenkwo Elu, and Philip Udo, a pharmacist. One of the two officers glanced at his watch, impatiently, while the other, a short, heavily-built lad, demanded to know why we had come in late. When we told him what had happened, he struck his baton on the table, several times, after which he roared out. The civil service was grossly inefficient, and must be pruned. How could the so-called District Officer bungle matters to the extent of mixing up the two meetings?

At last, calming down on his own, he proceeded to address the seven of us.

First, he introduced himself. Major Nzellia, he said; and the other was Captain Abo. He had come in person to deliver an important charge to us. We had been chosen on the recommendation of the secret eyes who had been watching all our movements and public utterances.

'Mr. Medo, for example!' he now turned to me, to my great be-wilderment, 'you delivered a particularly agreeable speech last time at the meeting on refugee aid. We liked your analysis of the part which imperialism played in the long history of the troubles. And the others, too, their speeches were well in accord with the thinking in the military. That is by the way. . . .

'What we have done so far is to set up an Area Emergency Council for each administrative province in the State, plus five others for the big towns, including Oban, the capital city. They will advise the State Government on the feelings of the people and on the appropriate action to be taken. You know we have never been politicians,' said he, speaking now like a human being. 'We have no machinery as such for ascertaining the people's wishes except perhaps from official reports. That's why we considered it necessary to have the Emergency Councils.

'Now, let's come to you.' He shifted in his seat and removed his hands from the baton, for the first time. 'I don't suppose you know much about the membership of the Emergency Councils—except perhaps for the fact that you went into that hall in error. We have in them some people with infamous pasts. That is intentional. We need to carry as many people as possible with us; and then, to keep an eye on those who might be suspect. You see what I mean? I know that it raises some security questions, but on such matters you can never really make a fool-proof arrangement.

'Now, in actual fact, it's on the seven of you that the Government will depend for advice. That is as far as Oban is concerned—there is a similar committee for each of the other Provinces and big towns. Please note too'—he took up his baton once more—'that your assignment is to be kept secret. We shouldn't let the parliament called the Area Council know that there's another body that is virtually counter-checking on its advice. I have come out into the open with you, and I trust your actions will bear out the trust. It would be quite easy for us to do it in a different style. You see what I mean?'

We stared at him, enquiringly, while the armed soldier behind him glanced from one face to another. And then, rather than explain, he went on to appoint himself chairman of the eight-man committee, and he announced that the next meeting would be held at six o'clock the following morning.

After some argument, we succeeded in getting him to change the time to evening.

I travelled back to the school in Professor Makamadu's car, Biere taking the opposite direction. The professor proved to be a simple and amiable man, certainly not what I had thought of physicists. Still more impressive was his Mercedes car which had remained in an almost immaculate condition in spite of its six years.

'Prof.', I said, 'these things that have happened emphasise the point that we have one great untapped asset—I mean we of this State.'

'Which is?'

'Manpower.' And I added: 'It is amazing how we've been feeding the other States at our own expense.'

'Well,' he drawled. 'We don't mind all the hardships of the moment, provided something is achieved in the end. You follow the point, don't you?'

'I hear the Central Machine Gun is being assembled for action in case we don't yield,' I said. 'In case we persist in saying that we cannot submit to its authority in the present confused situation.'

'Nonsense!' he said, coolly and yet seriously.

'You don't think they will?'

'Let them try. But how can they, with all the contrasting elements there? Cynicism, morbid fear, and even a genuine feeling of guilt and so on. Look, Mr. Medo, I've lived over there for over twenty years and know these things only too well.'

The car stopped. I got down.

'It is sad to reflect that it was our good friends over the years who did such horrible things to us, isn't it?'

He switched off the engine and postponed his departure. 'We shouldn't be sentimental about these matters,' said he. 'It's been a patch-work all through, bits of artificial alliances and marriages of convenience. It's good that things have come to a head at long last—the only regret, as far as I am concerned, being that the bloodshed is not fairly distributed. Let's fight the issues now to a conclusion.'

'Our main headache all over has been the ventriloquist. I don't know if you agree.'

'Certainly.' He nodded.

I invited him into the house but he announced he was in a hurry.

As soon as I entered, Zaccheus, my latest servant, informed me that a certain lady had called immediately I had left the house. She had refused to give her name; she only left a note.

He took out the letter from his pocket.

My guess was correct.

Ruth came again in the afternoon the next day. They were on a fund-raising campaign, and besides she wanted to see a relation in that section of the town; and so on. I refused to listen.

She sat directly opposite me, seemingly uneasy, in the inner room which was my study. Her face averted, she kept fanning herself, delicately, and the bangles on her wrist gave a faint rattle. Her attire was quite simple today; no doubt she was still conscious of my taste, I thought.

'How are the offspring?' I asked, after I had begged her, for the fifth time, to stop bothering my ears with generalities.

'They are well.' She tried to study me from the corners of her eyes.

'How many now?'

'Five.'

'Thou art then a matriarch,' I said. 'Verily.'

'Roland, you have not changed much,' she remarked. 'Except for the bushy hair and beard. Why don't you go and see a barber?'

'One day perhaps.' Then, I added: 'No, I've not changed—unlike you! You are no more Ruth Aniedo, for example.'

She fell silent, taking me in with her biggish eyes, her sensual lips twisting in a smile of protest.

Something which had been developing within me for some time now propelled me forward, towards her.

I grabbed her hand, and she remained still, almost limp. Next, I held the gold beads round her neck. She warned me: 'You will break it, Roland.' Then standing up, I held both her hands, and drew her towards me. She stiffened a bit, feigning displeasure. I pulled her again, harder. 'Leave me alone, Roland!' she whined; and I told her I would not obey her command.

I pulled and pulled, until she had stood up; until our chests had met; and then, I threw my hands around her. And with that, she exploded and a sudden vigour came into her.

Her body burned and quivered. She squeezed and crushed, and she whined.

'Ruth, why did you leave me for that fool?' I blurted.

She went dead still. Her eyes glistened and then the tears brimmed over.

I held her gently now. I began to fondle her plump beauty. Ruth was a beauty, except that she lacked the subtle extra: the polish and elegance and enlightened simplicity, which one found in the more cultured type. Lebo's money had never been able to buy that for her.

'Did you ask why I did it?' she breathed.

'Yes.'

'Well—'

She wiped her eyes.

'Go on, tell me.'

'But, I cannot tell you,' came her voice again.

After another interval, she said, with bitter resolution: 'I must be going now.'

'Going home?' I asked.

'What else can one do? The children must be expecting me . . . Do you know, Rola, what he says?'

'Who says?'

'He. That you are the father of my children!'

'What? Don't go away yet.'

Biere came over to see me some days later, bringing with him a letter which he had just received from Lewis. He gave me the letter to read for myself.

Lewis began by apologising for the time lag, nearly four months, then went on to explain why he chose to write to Biere alone in the first instance. 'Do please, set about preparing Roland's mind,' he wrote, 'so that when he receives his own letter, maybe a week or so later, he may be disposed to read it and not merely consign it to the flame in his anger against Imperator and his brothers.' Finally, he got down, in a more serious tone, to the events in the country. It was sad indeed to hear about the conflagrations. Little did one imagine that the initial rumblings and tremors would develop into such dimensions. He was sending his sympathy through Biere to all those he had known in the country who had now lost a relation or other. They, of his own country, had had their problems in the past. Nation-building was by no means an easy task. 'And,' he concluded, 'there doesn't seem to be any better line of action open to you than to dedicate the lives lost to the cause of building the nation.' Biere had already made a marginal note which read 'That's exactly what we are out to do!', in red against that particular portion. And then, in a post-script, Lewis hinted that he was applying to the World Council of Churches for an assignment in the country in connection with refugee aid.

'All this nonsense about their having had their own problems in the past!' I sighed. 'They seem to imply that they would want every other country to pass through similar experience.'

'Reduce your venom; the letter is from Lewis,' Biere scolded. 'And moreover, we've passed the stage of angry excitement; we must now face stark realities.'

'That's exactly what we were trying to do until this letter arrived,' I replied. 'The State Government has been facing with courage the issues before it, least of which is certainly not the refugee question.'

'Correct,' and he nodded.

'Look at the thousands that now fill the streets! And yet, normal life continues.'

'It is indeed amazing,' Biere said. 'The Government still has things well under control.'

'It's because it's been doing the right things—so far at least,' I said.

'Yes, but only since the troubles began,' he amended. 'Before that, it was completely detestable, as far as Biere was concerned.'

'The other side are talking of plans for the future, and nothing about the present.'

'They may be sincere, mark you,' he suggested.

'How sincere? Or is it sincerely ignoring the needs of the dispossessed thousands?'

'Oh, no—that isn't my point,' he retorted. 'Nothing could excuse that. What I mean really is in promising things for the future.'

'When we should all be dead?'

'We can't all die so easily.' Then, he resumed his point: 'The trouble of course is that nobody can take chances again. That's where the crisis of confidence comes in.'

'There's a suggestion I'm thinking of putting forward when Major Nzellia's committee meets again,' I hinted to him.

'On what?' he wondered.

'Something to do with security.'

'Give me an idea, or you won't?'

'You see, so many thousands of people roaming the streets raises serious security problems. We don't know who is who. You see the point, don't you?'

'You will propose identity cards?'

'Something more sweeping. All those who don't belong to the State should be made to move out, and leave us to plan with confidence. You see my point?'

He thought for some time. 'They are security risks, is that your point?'

'Yes, and you will agree.'

'Including foreign nationals?'

'Oh, yes; yes!' I confirmed. 'They perhaps more than the others.'

'Priests and nuns and doctors?'

'Don't be silly! You know whom I have in mind. The commercial and diplomatic and foreign aid people, who usually have hidden roles.'

'Try proposing it; I will support you,' he said. 'Though a serious issue would be raised by such a decision.'

'Whatever it is, it should not deter us,' I told him. 'Since the people of the State have all returned—to a man almost—what could be the objection to their own people going home also, and peacefully too, unlike with us?'

'Propose it and I'll support you,' Biere repeated. . . .

The committee amended the proposal in the end to exclude all foreign nationals, mostly on diplomatic grounds.

The lesson was just starting. A student raised his hand.

'Excuse me, sir!'

'Yes, Mbelede?'

'How do you think the present trouble will end?'

166

I laughed. 'How do you want it to end?'

'Sir, should we not have revenge?' another interposed.

'You want to fight?' I teased.

'Yes, sir,' came the chorus.

'But revenge alone doesn't lead you far, does it?'

'All right, let it end in peace,' Mbelede prayed.

They turned and stared at him with contempt. Some began querying him for his seeming levity over such a serious matter, while some called him a coward.

'The trouble is that you boys don't know what war is, apart from the things you read in books, or see in the cinema,' I cut in.

'We want it, whatever it is,' they chanted.

'Nor have I of course,' I went on, ignoring the interruption. 'But from what is learnt, it must be a most dreadful experience.' I had in mind a letter just received from Lewis in which, after praying to God, fervently, that there might be no shooting war between the two sides, he had gone on to describe a scene in the Second World War. He had come across an open field pitted with bomb craters; there were parts of human bodies scattered here and there; and one of the victims was later identified as a neighbour and good friend.

'We do not mind!' Ebenezer Dikuku vowed, biting his lips.

'Don't you?'

'No!' many voices joined.

'Shall we get on with the lesson, please.'

Ebenezer stood up with a frown. 'We don't have much interest in the lessons any more. What are we reading for?'

'What then would you suggest we do instead?'

Cosmos Obana, the class prefect, took over.

Opinions were divided among members of the Oban Emergency Council. That was what Major Nzellia said. Some, led by Doctor Anibado, advocated an outright and permanent break with the Centre. There should be no talk again of patience and reconciliation and all such cowardly nonsense: people should have the courage to face the issues before them. For how could you be reconciled with a man who had done such terrible things to you? At the other extreme, there was a small crop of elderly and respectable citizens who held that people should continue to think in terms of one nation in which the wounds of the past would be forgotten. And true though it was that the doings of the other State exceeded all bounds, Bokenu citizens, at home and abroad, could not, if one would only search deep into one's heart, be described as saints or models. They put the arguments in such a crisp and convincing style that it was difficult to call them traitors. Then, midway between were those who advocated that everybody should still keep an open mind, that the people of the State should press their points without any assumptions, one way or the other. If in the end it was found that there was no possibility of agreement, then—all that information had come to the major by way of Intelligence Report, and he thought it fit to read it out to us at the day's meeting.

As soon as the meeting was over and we were on our way home, Biere said to me: 'That is exactly our trouble.'

'What is?' I asked him.

'That Anibado and his type should have been allowed to surface again.'

'You know I'm not particularly fond of him. But what has he done this time apart from voicing his opinion?'

'He made sure nobody touched him and his assets even in the new order. But then, he hasn't been feeling completely secure all the time, in spite of his being mentioned for an economic mission overseas. And so, he is anxious that the position should get even more confused, so that nobody would have the time to enquire about his ill-gotten gains. The point is he knows very well that to attempt the thing he is advocating, that is, an outright and permanent break, would land us in a terrible mess.'

'That's the pattern all through, if one may quote yet another doctor—Sohabia,' I said.

'Incidentally, that man Sohabia looks like a man of all weather,' he observed.

'A crook of all weather,' I corrected.

CHAPTER TWENTY-THREE

It was being rumoured that the military leaders in charge of the various States would soon meet to talk face to face and without their guns. But people dismissed the story as just one of those things, on a par with a recent one which said that one particular State had acquired some twenty jet bombers and that the pilots were waiting for an order to take off for another State capital; and another which hinted that some daring young men, of this same State, had abducted five top men of the other camp.

Major Nzellia had refused to discuss any of the earlier rumours, and would not confirm the current one. It was not part of his duties, he said, to give out information to the public. Rumours however very often had foundation in fact, he added.

But whereas the other rumours had stirred the populace to wild jubilations, the one about the meeting was received with mixed feelings. Meeting? What for? Were they going to raise the dead or repair the damages or what? But of course, let them meet, if only to learn our feelings. Others thought that once the leaders met face to face without their guns and shook hands and embraced each other in true African style, and drank together and made jokes, then all the torments of the motherland would be over. This latter attitude prevailed among members of Nzellia's Special Committee, which caused the major some serious concern.

'Let me warn you right away,' he spoke out at last one morning. 'Nothing is going to come out of it, even if they meet.'

'Which would be disappointing,' said trade unionist Elu.

'The fact is this,' Major Nzellia went on, ignoring the other, 'they may meet and take decisions. But who will implement them? Not the civil servants.'

'Exactly! That's what is happening over there,' came in Doctor Sohabia with his characteristic opportunism. 'It is civil servants who dictate things over there, which is a tragedy.'

'Actually, it goes beyond that,' I countered. 'It is my sincere belief, and I know one or two people here share it with me, that the military, on both sides, are serious and conscientious in most of the things they do. The trouble, to my mind, is that they are not as free as they ought to have been. The real operators of power are outside the command.'

'Thank you very much for acquitting us so creditably,' the major said. 'The point is, we mustn't allow such rumours about meetings to distract our attention. We have problems and problems to tackle ... Yes, Professor Makamadu, you have some proposals to put forward at today's meeting. May we hear them.'

'Yes, Major; I have,' confirmed the Professor in his soft voice.

The summary of the proposals was that the State Government should withhold its very considerable contributions to the Central Government.

Lewis wrote again. There were four full sheets, quarto-size. He was happy to acknowledge receipt of the two hundred pounds which I remitted to him in respect of his car. Then, we went on to many other things.

I began replying immediately I had read through, but only mentally as yet. The civil service of our country? Yes; it was still functioning despite all the trouble and confusion. It had stability, thanks to its foundations, one would agree; but much of that was due to inaction, lethargy and effeteness. 'I am directed to think,' and similar things. Most uncreative! The top echelons build their personality around cars and other luxury items which promote somebody's industry. . . . How I wish you were around to hear my voice! But of course you have already admitted some of the facts, some time ago. Your economic interests and a stable climate for commerce: once these were guaranteed, then my friend Imperator would be prepared to be human. A fair deal that. But if not, well—I know you will smile and call me an ultra-something, which does not hurt. . . . But please, I miss you, seriously.

An hour later, I picked up the pen, opened the pad. The heart came into full play, tempering the mind. The written words were dispassionate: they just had punch and speed, which was a matter of style. 'He would be a fool,' I wrote, 'who would hold that our contact with your civilisation has not done us a lot of good. What about your literature, for example? Not to talk of the more obviously material aspects. Medicine and science, too. Nor would I be so foolish as to state that everybody from *his country*, to use your exact word, is a villain. Yours is a society where solid Christian principles have been entrenched over the generations: indeed, the individual has in him much that is admirable. . . .

'Let me thank you, once more, for your expressions of sympathy and good wishes, as well as for the concern you show about the refugees. We are striving hard to get the refugees assimilated into the community. The problem is rather overwhelming, but something is being achieved—in spite of provocations from several quarters and thanks to the assistance from several others. The Christian church bodies have been particularly helpful. While on this, it is a pity your application to the Church Missionary Society has not yielded any result as yet; however we, Biere and I that is, are happy in the knowledge that you still hope to succeed.

'I do expect to hear from you soon, please—just as we are anxiously waiting for whatever is going to be the next step in the national crisis—I mean now that the leaders have met and agreed and then dispersed to disagree. You see the point? And one last thing, couldn't you have done something to bridle that man with harsh accents who in yesterday's radio news-commentary was complaining about trade ceasing to flow in our country? I am not sure whether he is not implying that the channel should now be dredged with blood.'

I read through, at the end of which, I nodded with satisfaction. Then I put the letter inside the table drawer, for the moment. I would take it to the post-office on my way to Biere's.

Among the privileges associated with Biere's vice-principalship of his school was a self-contained, four-bedroom bungalow with a neat, grassy lawn and a huge garage. His predecessor in the quarters had been an Australian-born Chemistry-cum-Bible-master who cultivated it with the utmost industry, devoting as much time and thought to it as he did on all the other things put together. It was he who had the whole yard enclosed with a high and thick hedge; he also planted some colourful creepers at the back, wih thorny bougainvillaea arching and obstructing the back exit from where some unruly young ones often burst into his privacy.

'It's wonderful here,' I remarked, looking round. 'Really.'

'Why?' Biere asked.

'Cool, green, quiet.'

'The bush behind is.'

'And the lawn is smooth.'

'Is that all?' He pointed to the neighbour's quarter, some hundred feet off. 'You hear the noises?'

'Well, yes. What's happening?'

'They have been having a party there since morning.'

'Who?'

'Virginibus puerisque.'

I laughed.

'I'm not amused,' he objected, folding the magazine he had been reading. 'People make merry in these critical times.'

'Why not? Isn't that good for the nerves?'

'They have ruined my Sunday's rest for me.'

'Biere, my brother, never you forget that we are a nation of great spirits; and that a true Bokenuan, in particular, hardly succumbs to problems.'

'Turn round, Roland!' he called, in a very low tone. 'See?'

A man had just emerged from the neighbour's house wobbling, and was now heading steadily for the bush. Then, the man halted, midway, as if he had just changed his mind. He coughed, and spat; and shouted something about a people being very determined; after which, he urinated. Three more emerged, simultaneously.

An open-air debate followed:

'We have to be careful.'

'Nonsense. There's nothing they can do to us. Nothing!'

'It is mere bluff—nothing else,' another agreed.

'You call that a bluff?' said the first speaker. 'So you have not heard that they are building up?'

'Nonsense! Have we been asleep ourselves?'

'Left to me, all the mess would have been ended long ago.'

'How?'

'Stop sending our money to them.'

'Exactly!' cried the one who was still urinating. 'They will collapse in no time.' He hiccupped.

'You hear them?' Biere asked uneasily. 'Last time the matter was discussed in the Special Committee it was unanimously agreed that the step, though seeming inevitable, was fraught with grave dangers.'

'They cannot last a week without our money,' the man shouted coarsely into the air, at the same time buttoning up his trousers.

'Listen to that man!' Biere moaned. 'Any intelligent person should be able to realise that it isn't as simple as all that.'

'He is not intelligent, that's all,' I said.

'You know him? Mr. Agoka. He's supposed to have a Master's degree.'

'There are more highly-qualified ones, when you come to that. Sohabia for one.'

'Or Anibado.'

'Biere, those two men are no use,' I agreed. 'Do you know what they were trying to propound a few days ago?'

'No.'

'That we should change the lingua franca immediately.'

'To what, if one may ask?'

'Anything other than English, apparently.'

'And what say you?' he asked accusingly.

'You ought to know I don't carry my venom to such sensational irrationalism.'

'What they are after is to make sure they are riding on the crest of mass sentiments,' he said. 'No more. Anibado in particular. I believe they know enough to realise that it would be impracticable to switch over to another language just like that; and, equally, that the utterance hurts nobody. All they want to accomplish is to "belong" to the mass feeling, thereby shielding themselves.'

There was a knock at the entrance door.

'Who?'

'Visitors.' Another said: 'Red Cross.' Both voices sounded clearly feminine.

I was there before him.

'Yes?' I asked with simulated gravity.

'Excuse me, sir, we're from the Red Cross,' the smaller one said, timorously. She was dark-skinned and corpulent, with a rather masculine look on her face. 'We are collecting money for refugees.'

'Won't you come in and introduce yourselves?' I fixed my eyes on the elegant, slim one behind. 'Anybody could start collecting money in the name of refugees.'

Biere ruined the joke by paying as soon as the girls had entered.

I paid ten shillings, which made it a total of five pounds in the past seven days.

CHAPTER TWENTY-FOUR

The argument sounded convincing, on both sides. Henceforth, Bokenu would keep all the money it had been sending to the Centre. That included revenue raised in the operation of railways, electricity, and postal services, and, most important, from customs and excise in the State. The amount was enormous. The Centre would collapse in no time. It was hoped, however, that before long those over there would realise the true position and come to terms with the State; they would begin to say: these people have a genuine grievance; so, let us indulge them a bit, especially now that they have got us on a very delicate spot.

But what if they should decide in reply to adopt a hard line? some asked. And that was exactly how the other side reacted. They said: All right, if you so decide, we will not talk much but just discontinue the services which we render in your State. You see? Remember, always, that you derive your strength from us; you will cease to be all that mighty the moment we decide to bridle you. And you see, we know about your grievances and about your problems, but let us not over-stress these things. So, from henceforth, until you withdraw your decision to keep to yourself alone the money intended for all, no ships will be allowed to call at any of the ports and you will have no communication with the outside world. So think again; in the meantime, we are leaving you a few openings in the hope that you will use those to communicate with us about your change of heart.

It was already two weeks since the last ships docked at our ports, and now we had virtually no communication with the outside world.

'We have not seen you for months now,' Dora accused me, like an adult, gazing at me with annoyance, her eyes twinkling now and again. She had learnt to dramatise her friend, Mamma, perfectly.

'Isn't it only two months or so since I last visited home?' I said in defence.

'Mamma is very anxious and has sent me to find out whether you are alive.'

'That's why you had to leave school?'

'We're on mid-term break,' she explained, coldly, then reverted: 'You would not send word to anybody.'

'All right, tell Mamma that you saw me and that I am not alive.'

'Everything is getting scarce and you don't bother to find out how she has been managing all these weeks,' she complained.

'She told you to say all that?'

She would not answer.

'What and what are getting scarce, tell me.'

'Everything,' she repeated. 'Especially salt and medicine, and meat. It is because of the blockade. People are feeling unwell everywhere. And many are dying.'

'Do you think that people outside our State fare much better?' I asked her. Part of our duty as members of Nzellia's Special Committee was to play down the effects of the blockade.

But Dora would not allow herself to be browbeaten. 'Do I know?' she sneered. 'You will ask Mamma when you see her. Or ask any of the sick.'

'But surely people do get ill from time to time. You can't blame everything on the blockade.'

'Rola, it's true. Her tone had turned mild. 'The sickness is new, and it attacks the young and the aged more than any other group. They turn yellow and their bodies are swollen and watery.'

I sobbed in a painful admission. There were two such cases known already in the school. One of them, the son of the night-guard, had soft, watery skin and bloated cheeks. The other was a first-year student. The doctor who examined the latter in the hospital had said that the thing was still at an early stage; he had also pronounced that the disease would soon be widespread among the population, adding something extremely pedantic about syndrome and the rest.

Dora insisted that I should go with her. I told her I couldn't. She pleaded she was afraid to go alone. I pointed out to her that fear was not part of her nature. Then she disclosed the nature of her fear. There were very many soldiers on the way, and they were all armed with guns; and not only that, they said terribly sinful things and called people terribly sinful names. It would be risky to go home alone so late in the day. I told her I had seen her point.

Mamma was out when we arrived. It was said she had gone to the Mission. The priest had appointed her to a small committee of church women which would advise him in his new assignment of seeing to the parishioners' stomachs in addition to their souls. She should have been back by now, but she had indicated she might have to proceed from there to a funeral.

'Who is dead?' I asked.

'Oh, I forgot to tell you!' Dora exclaimed. 'Ogoma.'

'Which one?'

'The one who is Udebonam's wife.'

'Yes? Ogoma, that grand stately woman whose words were always loaded with meaning! Was she sick or just old?'

'She was old and then sick.'

Mamma returned a few minutes later.

'Mamma, welcome,' I greeted her.

'My good child,' she responded, adding: 'So she managed to drag you here?'

'Who? Dorothy?'

'Oh, yes—she I mean,' she confirmed. 'She has brought you to see us. Isn't she a great daughter?'

'Mamma, we brought you some salt,' the other declared, which won her further praises.

'Mamma, they say Ogoma is dead?' I asked now.

'Yes, indeed; she's dead,' she confirmed, mournfully. 'The great one is gone.'

'Was she sick for long?'

'The thing caught her—the thing they call Kwashiorkor.'

'I thought it was just age.'

'No!' She shook her head. 'What kind of age? Ogoma was not all that old.'

'But Mamma, it's possible she had been sick long before she died. Everybody now attributes the least bodily ache to lack of meat and salt.'

She shook her head again. 'Ogoma had foreseen it well before her death, my son,' she said.

'Mamma, wasn't she the one who once said that churchmen were a queer lot who let good music go to waste?' Dora asked.

'She may have been,' she replied indifferently. 'She had a quiet sense of humour.'

Then, she changed the topic: 'I hear Uruaku too is terribly sick.'

'Uncle Ogidi's wife?'

'There is no other one.'

'Mamma, what is wrong with Isaac's mother?' Dora asked.

'She has a disease of the stomach, I am told. But the more terrible thing is that there is no medicine for her.'

'None in the stores?'

'The price has gone up many times and who has all that money to pay?'

She turned round to me: 'Roland, if you want your mother's brother's wife to live for another week, go straight and see her and find somebody to treat her.'

We were still discussing when an errand man arrived from Siaku.

'Yes?' Mamma gasped.

'She's gone—Uruaku is gone!' the man panted.

Tears swiftly filled her eyes.

The funeral lasted only two days, which in normal circumstances would have been an offence of the magnitude of a crime. For Uruaku was descended from a great paramount chief, and then, from her mother she had her other assets—her beauty and personality. And yet, her funeral had to be rushed. This was partly because the customary perquisites had become as scarce as salt: cows for the guests and cloth for the effigy were difficult to procure. Add to that the atmosphere of tension and fear which now eroded the spirit, robbing most human activities of a sense of purpose. And then, there were soldiers all over the place, strictly enforcing the ban on loud noises, whether of mourning, of merriment, or of dispute.

Soldiers, soldiers, soldiers. All the time and everywhere. Guns in hand or over the shoulders, and their boots thudding, they paraded the roads, went into the offices, into shops, and into the hospitals. The most impressive were those on road-check duties. These brandished their guns proudly, and some their bayonets too, for everybody to behold with fear; nearly all of them wore steel helmets with mesh camouflage. They were well-built and lively, but very severe in look, feigning cruelty and bellicosity, as if those were the most essential qualities of the profession. They searched nearly everything you had on you. Then, they went over your car, including the boot and the pigeon-hole, and even under the carpet. And when in the end they thought it was time to let you off, they slapped at the car in disappointment: they would certainly have been much happier if they had found a machine-gun and some rounds of ammunition, and a hand-grenade into the bargain, for in that case, they would convict you on the spot as a traitor, an agent of the other side.

They were mostly young recruits, aged between sixteen and twenty-four, enlisted within the past few months. The response had been overwhelming, and the recruiting officers had had to apply their whips. The idea was to eliminate right away any who proved soft or temperamental, and could not bear the strains and hardships and privations of combat. Yet they continued to rush in, in thousands, all bare-bodied, only pants, their skin glistening with sweat, yet cheerful and determined, each prepared to leap even up to the sky if that was what would give the qualifying score.

Nzellia, now a Lieutenant-Colonel, announced that another Special Committee, which he would not name, had beaten us completely this time. That committee had made a very sound recommendation about the next step that ought to be taken in the crisis, which was that the State should 'mobilise the spontaneous mass feeling into a tangible, compelling force'. The suggestion had already been accepted by the authorities, and mass rallies and demonstrations would follow soon. It was for members of our own Special Committee to see that the demonstrations in Oban had the expected impact, bearing in mind the position of the capital city in affairs of the State.

'Suggestions, gentlemen!' he called.

We discussed for hours. . . .

Doctor Sohabia described what followed as the charging of all the positive and progressive forces. The streets of Oban were packed full from morning till late in the night with groups of demonstrators—men, women, schoolchildren, trade unions, and others, each group carrying a banner which had, among other things, some deadly inscriptions intended for the distant *other side* and some pious sentiments for the Government and people of the State. They sang and swore, and gestured with both their hands and their heads, and promised to die if it should come to that. Then, at the end of each day's demonstration, they would proceed to burn some effigies. And thus, for the next few weeks, the streets of the town were covered with charred remains of effigies as well as with discarded posters and handbills.

But there was a lot of restraint among the demonstrators. Just as the organisers intended, the people never went into real mob excesses. For example, they spared all foreign-owned business houses, including the commercial banks, confining themselves to such threats and violent gesticulations as were necessary to make the expatriate managers quiver, except that they later followed that up by withdrawing, in a very constitutional manner, all their personal savings from the banks.

'Excellent organisation on the part of the committee,' I observed one afternoon.

'Quite,' Biere agreed.

'The various elements of discontent—political, economic and so on—have coalesced.'

'You prefer that to Sohabia's own expression?'

We had met to review the position, after three weeks. Lieutenant-Colonel Nzellia was as yet lighting his pipe, in defiance of a fierce wind; so, Biere and I took the time to discuss. And now, having heard his name called, Sohabia turned round. But before he could get out of his mouth what he had in mind, we heard a sudden burst of singing in the street below the building.

Everybody looked out through a window.

'Schoolgirls,' the colonel was the first to observe.

179

'Secondary school,' I amended. 'Let somebody go out and speak to them.'

Someone proposed Biere.

'You are not being serious!' Nzellia guffawed; then: 'I would have thought Roland Medo should be the one.'

'Who am I that should disobey an order to parley with our daughters?' said I, and went out, leaving them all laughing.

The girls were from Saint Anne's, Second to None. They had all forms of weapons, including ferrules and wooden clubs, and even high-heeled shoes. Dressed in green long-sleeved shirts and jeans, they marched with tight faces and resolute strides, their banner raised aloft. Just behind the standard-bearers, someone carried a poster with the inscription: 'Give us guns; we too want to be soldiers. Give us the chance.'

I managed to halt the procession.

'You want to be soldiers?' I asked them together.

'Yes!' they declared.

'Why not pilots too?'

'Pilots too.'

'Why not the navy?'

'That too,' they confirmed, seriously.

I shook my head. 'You had better leave those things to the boys for the meantime and carry out guard duties for us.'

They shouted their resentment. Then, the heavy one in the rear called for the school song, which the rest picked up, singing with pride. And after that they sang another song in which they called upon Africa and the world to listen to the cries of the sorrowful and to excuse what was about to happen. . . .

Later the same week, the world's radio stations carried the news that the Centre was mustering a huge force for a quick and decisive action on the State. This was in addition to the step it had just taken to split the country into many more States.

CHAPTER TWENTY-FIVE

I am alone in the house, thinking, tugging at my hair, and my beard; thinking and thinking. I feel depressed. We are in serious trouble. Everywhere is tense. A war is imminent. More deaths, more bloodshed, and worse commotion than ever before!

Again, I scratched my head, and rubbed my palm over the lower jaw.

This growth has become quite a load. The beard is manageable, more so as it makes you look very masculine, and lends you age and weight and gravity, and all that. But the one on the head gives you a sinister, ghostly appearance, and besides, it is a big weight—so big that at times it sets the nerves on edge and causes the head to ache, especially when you are worried, just like now! And yet, I mustn't put a comb in it. No; not until things have broken the pleasant way. Let that be the visible sign of my grief, and my mortification, if you like, for the sins of others: those who have brought about all the confusion and bloodshed.

'You fool of a man, do you think anybody takes notice of your appearance?' an obscure voice, in me, queries.

'What does it matter whether they do or not?' I retort, stubbornly; almost audibly.

I stood up; and began walking up and down. Again, I scratched my head. . . .

The constitution was one of the principal causes. A part equal to a whole! But that inequality has now been removed. It was removed with the creation of many more States. So it looks, at least. The question people are asking is whether the thing is genuine. Probably yes; perhaps no. There's the rub. You must reckon with the least fear or doubt; you cannot afford to take chances. Every move on the other side must be suspect. Sakure is now six States; Doda, two; Bokenu, three. That would have been excellent, in normal circumstances. I would have leapt up to the sky and hailed the New Order as a conqueror and invited Imperator to take note that he has at long last been successfully dislodged from his hide-out. . . . But for this element, the absolute lack of trust! A crisis of confidence. And the arguments are sound.

181

Then Biere came in. He was looking totally downcast and pretty emaciated in addition. And he did not make things any brighter for either himself or me with the copy of Hemingway's *For Whom The Bell Tolls* which he had in his hand. He collapsed into a chair, put the book aside; then invited me to sit too, in my own house.

'You have not heard, have you?' he said.

'What is it?'

'It has begun!'

'What has?' my voice faltered in anticipation.

'The heat has now developed into the incandescence of war,' said he slowly and solemnly, his face screwed up.

I pondered for some time. 'They've attacked in the end, have they?'

'From four different points, though very few know as yet. I got that from Colonel Nzellia himself.'

Again, the picture which Lewis had painted came rushing through my mind: Bloodshed and utter destruction ... planes whistling ... bombs exploding in salvoes on buildings; and then, yet another bang, a very big one ... the whole area was littered with bits and pieces of human bodies twitching with some residual current of life, some of the survivors groaning or sobbing, bleeding, and clutching involuntarily at their shattered parts, the gangrenous flesh. Lewis had of course written about a war between the greatest nations on earth. This one could hardly ever come to that, for neither side, even if it had the heartlessness, had the capacity for such doings. It would certainly be a brief war. That was what everybody had said in Colonel Nzellia's Special Committee.

'Have you any idea how the sides are getting on?' I asked.

He shook his head. 'I was with some of the Intelligence boys before coming over here. They don't feel the present pressure from the other side will last,' he said.

'But seriously, had we any alternative?'

'I have one serious apprehension,' he said after an interval.

'Yes?'

'The fundamental issues which gave rise to the whole chain of troubles will now be relegated because of the present preoccupation.'

'I know!'

'The war will provide a near-perfect cover for my villains. And the longer it lasts, the better for them.'

'What about my man?'

'He is to be treated as secondary—I have always said so; the primary blame goes to the citizen-devil. If you like, you may call the former a calculating adventurer fishing in troubled waters.'

'He's certainly doing much more than fishing; he is troubling the waters too,' I differed. 'But—are you going?' He was now standing.

'I have an appointment with the Intelligence boys,' he explained. 'I could come back later in the evening.'

He came the next morning instead.

'I ought to tell you, Roland. I am being tipped for one or two things,' he confided.

'Who by?' I asked, anxiously.

'Well, Government,' he replied. 'The authorities remain extremely pleased with our views which, as they say, accord with the original views of most of the military.'

'Fare thee well, then, Biere Ekonte,' I said. 'But only after you have named the nature of your calling. Or am I not entitled to know?'

'I am required to prepare inspiring literature for the new nation.'

'And what does that mean in plain terms?'

'I don't know yet,' and he laughed. 'It was only yesterday that I had the first hint. I have started to gather materials for it however.'

He drew out from the pocket of his trousers a typed sheet of paper, which he tried to thrust into my hand.

'What is that?' I resisted.

'You may wish to read it.'

I unfolded the paper before my face, and read:

The battle rages with many a loud alarm and frequent advance and retreat;
The infidel triumphs, or supposes he triumphs,
The prison, scaffold, garotte, handcuffs, iron necklace and lead balls do their work,

The named and unnamed heroes pass to other spheres,
The great speakers and writers are exiled, they lie sick in distant
lands,
The cause is asleep, the strongest throats are choked with their
own blood.
The young men droop their eyelashes towards the ground when
they meet.
But for all this liberty has not gone out of the place, nor the infidel
entered into full possession.
When liberty goes out of a place it is not the first to go, nor the
second or the third to go,
It waits for all the rest to go, it is the last.

'It's convincing.'
'And topical!'
'Who's that?'
'Whitman. Do we have the time and disposition for a critical
analysis?'
'We may manage.' I glanced through once again, for the essential
points. 'First of all,' I now said, imitating the dry and high-pitched
tone of Mr. Nicholas, the English lecturer we had in our first year in
the university, 'what and for whom is the selection intended? Mr.
Ekonte, will you please tell us.'
'Inspiration, sir,' he replied. 'And for the top ranks of the army; each
one of them should have a copy. Then later on, for some civilians
too.'
'I see! Don't you think that it is charged with pessimism, that it fills
one with great forebodings?'
'Explain.'
'The war has just started, as we know, and only at the borders. We do
not hear any gunshots; we do not feel the effects, and yet you propose
to present to those placed under your charge the full dimensions of a
major war.'
'Get on first and I'll answer you in the end.'
'Who has bargained for all those terrible things—garotte, scaffold and
iron necklace, whether literally or figuratively? The picture is in fact
that of a Roman conqueror, represented by the infidel, leading his

victims into savage captivity. I hold it will serve more to unnerve than to embolden.'

'Finished?'

'Yes; now, reply.'

'The point is well taken,' he began, nodding several times. 'I would, however, have liked you to consider it along with the latter half of the poem where the counter point is made that although such terrible things could happen, liberty would still not be gone; the spirit is still not crushed. This latter is the crux of the matter.'

'I only hope your charge will understand it so.'

'With the military, there ought to be no problem.'

'Why?'

'Being professional soldiers, they must have been taught the full dimensions of war.'

'You amuse me! How professional are these boys most of whom have been assembled only in the past few months?'

'Well, let them begin to learn it now,' said he, seriously. 'As for the rest, that is the civilians, anybody who is not prepared to go the whole length to prevent what happened in the past from happening again might as well give up the struggle right away. And in any case, we need to educate people on the issues involved so that they know why exactly they are risking their lives.'

'Seems rather late, since the war is already on!'

'I have an idea that a body is being set up which will handle the whole issue of educating the people.' He paused, seemingly awaiting my reaction to the information.

'Really!' I merely uttered.

'It will be known as the Publicity Bureau, or Plobe for short. Its duty will be to give a correct interpretation of the nature of the war, thereby counteracting all such propaganda, from within or without, as could demoralise the fighting boys.'

'Yet another body! They are getting innumerable,' I observed. 'Area Emergency Committees, Special Committees, and now the Plobe! The military have a flair for committees, haven't they?'

'Let's drop that point for the meantime. Any other objection or question?'

'Yes, there is. Tell me, Biere, who is the infidel?'

He said with a mysterious smile: 'I did think about that.'

'And—?'

'There is the fear that many people may, from either mischief or naïvety, hold that he is the one who took up his weapon to kill, more so as that one has his own view of God and will not be converted to Christianity. No, my infidel is of a much more dangerous and much more sophisticated type. He is possessed by a vile, unscrupulous, conquering spirit.'

'Go ahead, man!' I applauded.

'His chief attributes are avarice and greed; love of lucre and power. Let us personify the spirit; and let us give it a name.'

'Well, in my thinking, that must be a soulless name.'

'We may call it *id*. So, we say that the infidel is a man possessed by *id*.'

'Excellent. But do you think you will be able to put the point before the populace?'

'Why not?'

'Why not?' I repeated. 'I fear the men with id will frustrate you. Like the clever thief who joins the crowd of pursuers in shouting "thief", they will hide their identity and start shouting "infidel" louder than others, no doubt focussing attention on the sensitive issue of the death recently of the kith and kin. I imagine exactly the same thing would be happening on the other side.'

'Tell me, how would you classify your villain? He is an infidel too, isn't he?'

'Oh, yes; certainly. A Christian infidel. No contradiction.'

'Elaborate.'

'He does not practise the Christian virtues of justice and universal love and brotherhood, and equality of all men before the Maker. That is number one. Number two, he is possessed by *id*. Wherefore, he is doubly an infidel: Imperator is an infidel. Worse even than those countrymen of ours whom we have been castigating.'

'Placed in the position of the white plunderers, many of our people, here as well as on the other side, might prove even more ruthless.'

'Quite.'

'Wouldn't it be right then to say that Imperator is, essentially, neither white nor black?'

'Essentially I would agree. He is just an international type of infidel.'

He nodded several times, like a lizard does. 'Haven't we now achieved a perfect fusion of ideas, Roland?' he asked. 'The local or national exploiter, the international exploiter, be he white or black, red or indigo, is our villain. And conversely, there are excellent men here and there, black or white.'

'Lewis for example. That I would always concede.'

'You would do well,' said he, regarding me with a wily look, 'to help in propagating such a view.'

'Which view?'

'Vision rather,' he amended. 'The vision of a new society free from the menaces of *id*.'

'How does one begin, Mr. Visionary?'

'Join us in the Plobe.' He was serious.

'So you are in it already?'

'It is only just being formed,' he explained, calmly. 'I was asked just four days ago to start it, and to set about recruiting some seven more soldiers of kindred spirit.'

'Roland Medo is to be one of them, is that your point?'

'Very much so.'

'Go and tell them I am not at home.'

'But you very much are,' he rejoined with an attempt at humour which I stifled with a grave countenance. 'Shall we speak about it next time?'

He got no reply. I simply waved indifferently as he was leaving.

When we met again he was full of apologies.

'Frankly, I am very sorry,' he repeated.

I poured myself another glass of beer, drank down, then asked him coldly:

'What was it?'

'The way I introduced the matter.'

'How did you?' I offered him a Tango, which he readily accepted.

'I was not sufficiently frank,' said he. 'You see, I had very strict warning. "Every member is to be screened and screened and screened before he can be admitted into the Plobe," were the exact words. As a matter of fact, the others who were proposed with you simultaneously are still undergoing screening, without their knowing it; you are the only one of the seven on whom a definite decision has been taken. You must join, Roland.'

'Me?'

'You must, please.'

'All right, when?'

'Immediately.'

I paused, just to heighten his suspense. 'There will be eight members in all, you said?'

'That's correct.'

'And who are the others, if I may know?'

He hesitated, and I frowned. Then he spoke: 'Your friend Sohabia is not there.'

'He has been dropped as a concession to Roland, no doubt. Go on!'

'You feel he is a humbug. The authorities are a bit more diplomatic than that: they say he is a man of very mobile attitudes.'

'Who are in?' I demanded.

'Professor Makamadu is one, though it is feared he may not be able to devote sufficient time to the Plobe in view of his more directly professional contributions to the war. Okay Baby too.'

'Only two so far.'

He gave the remaining names in quick succession.

'So your task has been to clear me, has it?' I now asked, aggressively. 'Clear me before admitting me.'

'You're being absurd,' he protested. 'How can I propose and then clear the same person?'

'There lies the absurdity—and yours, too. Anyway, count me out; I'm not joining.'

'But I have given your name already.'

'Take it back. That should be simple enough. As a matter of fact, since our views are identical, there's no need for me to join too.'

'It's not just a matter of views, Roland,' he pleaded.

'But of?'

'Service—people to propagate the views.'

I kept on tugging at the beard.

'I must have hurt your ego terribly, for which I now apologise.'

'There is nothing to apologise for, is there?'

'I gave an undertaking that you would join.'

'Go and tell them that Roland Medo has bluntly refused,' I shouted at him.

CHAPTER TWENTY-SIX

He kept on pleading, for days. How could he do without me? he would ask. I gave in at last. Then he gave the remaining details. The new assignment would be full-time, and we would cover not just Oban but all the provinces. As for Colonel Nzellia's Committee, it was to be assumed that that no longer existed.

'Your assignment in the Plobe,' he went on, 'is with the youth.'

'Yes?'

'Both military and civil.'

'You've mapped all that out?' I wondered.

'The Bureau Chairman did.' He looked up, into my face.

'You are the chairman, aren't you?' I pursued.

'Well, yes,' he stammered with modesty. 'Or rather, until another one is appointed. I need your services, Roland.'

Smiling, I promised I would give them to him. Then I asked: 'What is it by the way, I am expected to be doing to or with the youth?'

'Lecture them,' he replied. 'Give them edifying talks.'

'So many words seem to be being flung about these days. Inspiring, edifying, and so on. Too many words and too many ideas! This committee today and that tomorrow, and yet another one the next day.'

'That should only be expected. We are still trying to evolve a system. Nobody was prepared for the situation we now find ourselves in.'

'What exactly do you say that Roland Medo is expected to do with the young ones—and I hope you include both sexes?'

'Boys and girls, soldiers and civilians, yes,' he confirmed. 'And the task before you is to put a definite accent on the moral aspect of the war. You know what I mean.'

I gave a thoughtful snort.

'Schools have long been closed as a result of the war.'

'What is the point?'

'Schools are where one could get the young ones assembled. The assignment seems impossible right now.'

'I know,' he agreed, then added: 'Yet it must be done.'

'Unless one goes to the barracks and the war-fronts and battlefields.'

'You would be very much on the right track.'

'A very dismal track too,' I mused, running my hand over my head, and my face. 'Thousands and thousands of boys are now getting depraved and brutalised in the camps, not to count those who die unburied in the battlefield each day. I often feel sick when I think about it.'

'But then, it is the youth mostly who fight in wars.'

'But not such yam saplings as we are now recruiting and sending into the battlefield with very little training. I suppose too that applies to the other side.'

'What alternative would you suggest?'

I had none ready. He proposed one himself:

'Except perhaps to conscript all those in our midst who led the country into the present troubles, and send them into the thick of it.' His tone was vehement, and he bit his lip. 'They should be the ones dying on the battlefield. However—when do you take off?'

'For the battlefield, is it?'

'I suggest the day after tomorrow. There will be a meeting of the Bureau tomorrow.'

'Is that the invitation?'

'Beginning of it. Please make sure you are there.'

'What else can one do but to resign oneself to the methods of the chairman?'

He looked offended at the remark.

'How are they getting on at the front?' I digressed.

'The situation is not quite so bright, I am afraid,' said he sadly.

'One could almost sense that! But tell me more.'

'We're not on the point of being vanquished, but it is a fact that we have not made the progress we had expected,' he replied. 'The forces against our side are quite enormous.'

I visited all the main Command headquarters, six in number, plus a few of the camps around them. Then I began to visit areas near the war zones, starting with the more northern ones where the position had become very tense with the invasion of an important town there by troops of the other side. The Commanding Officers were both polite and diplomatic; they would not let me advance beyond a short distance from the Command headquarters. That was, as they put it, in my own interest.

But at one sector, the officer in charge indulged my zeal and curiosity.

The guards at check-point had actually ruled that I must turn back, and on foot, leaving my car for military operations. Then I told them about my mission and presented my identification card. They lowered their guns and announced that I could take the car back. Or better still, would I like to take one of them to the base camp to see the officer in charge? I said I would. Three of them came into the car, all with guns.

The officer in charge was a young lieutenant. He declared outright that he knew about me and my mission. Then he issued a pass which would take me to the very last location farther on, just before the scene of the actual conflict.

All seemed quite normal along the road, and even as far as the location. There were soldiers everywhere in their green uniforms, bustling and whistling, full of good cheer, as if they were not taking the war seriously. There were vehicles moving up and down, some conveying wounded soldiers, including ones with freshly-bandaged hands and feet and foreheads, from the emergency first-aid centre to the nearest hospital a safe ten miles behind. One mini-bus was heavily decked in front with fresh, yellow palm-fronds, indicating that it bore some corpses within. Yet, in spite of all that, the general atmosphere seemed almost normal. Face to face with actual realities, with idle imaginings giving way to stark facts, what else could they do? I asked myself, staring at a trio who were smoking one cigarette between them. Two of them counted the puffs as the third smoked his turn. They cared for nothing else at the moment but the cigarette that was aglow in the colleague's mouth.

Predictably, the orderly at the entrance to the commandant's office was hostile. He simply dismissed me as yet another idle civilian, then went away. Then a corporal came out of the room. He was tall and slim and light-complexioned. He turned his eyes abruptly into my face. 'Morning, sir!' He made to salute in addition but as his senses overpowered the instinct, he merely held a hand suspended midway.

'Good morning. How are you?' I responded.

'Very well, sir.' He smiled a modest smile. 'I'm sure you don't recognise me again.'

'My student somewhere?' I asked, face screwed up.

'At Christ High School. You taught us Latin.' He spoke with obvious reverence, choosing his words carefully. Then he disclosed his name, just before I did so; and I gave the remaining details. He had been a keen boxer and a good athlete, graceful in manners and well-bred. He still looked a good lad, even here—neither depraved nor brutalised, perhaps. There were certainly happy exceptions, like this one.

'What can we do for you?' he asked me.

'I've come to address you, so what you can do is to get the soldiers to listen,' I told him.

'Sir, you must see the camp commandant,' he pointed out.

'Where is he? You people are full of names.'

Smiling at the remark, he conducted me towards the room. And soon, we stood before the Commandant, he giving a very elaborate salute. The commandant was a sturdy young man, very restless, issuing orders right and left.

'Yes, next! What can I do for you, man? Are you the one for the lecture?'

I tendered my card.

He read aloud, after which he shouted: 'Yes, we have been expecting you. Now, Corporal Kurama'—he pointed at my escort and former student—'go and call me Second-Lieutenant Pipia. At once! You hear?' He was most unorthodox in his methods. The corporal, anticipating him, was already well outside the door.

Pipia came in shortly after to find him still talking.

'Here is Mr. Medo and here is Second-Lieutenant Pipia,' he now said, pointing at the two of us simultaneously and with both hands. 'Medo has come for the lecture; Pipia, you will take him along. But make it short. We do not know how the weather is going today. Where is the file? Orderly!' He had ceased to think about us.

In no time, the soldiers were assembled in the field, which was a school playground heavily camouflaged with palm-fronds so that it looked like an integral part of the forest. They were seated on the ground, in a careless attitude, muttering and chattering, and whistling even in the presence of the lieutenant. I told myself: They have definitely carried their innate egalitarian spirit into the army. 'Order, order!' Pipia called, shrilly; and they reacted with what sounded like a contemptuous 'Yes, sir!' Then, hands akimbo, the small-sized lieutenant introduced me and announced my mission.

The talk began in a conversational style.

This war, in which many lives were being lost each day, and because of which they, the soldiers, had had to shelve their education ought to be given a name. Could someone suggest one?

They said several things. One particularly boisterous young lad shouted that it was a struggle to put an end to nepotism, and they cheered, and the lieutenant called for order. I told them they were all correct, in a way; it remained to harmonise the various statements into one central theme. We were out to prevent the events of the past from being repeated; nobody would want to see the killings and flight and other things again. Therefore, we must stamp out the root cause of the troubles—which was greed and injustice and ambition and love of power. 'Not so?'

'It is so!'

'If we are to have a happier future, such evils must not be allowed in the new society.'

They okayed again.

The future belonged to them, really. They were fighting their own war, not anybody's. It was for them to make the nation what they desired to be—free, happy and dynamic, led by honest men. 'Honest and fair-minded men, civil or military.'

A stealthy hiss, as of protest, rose over the many voices.

'Let it therefore be our motto that we fight not just to destroy the lives of the other side, but to achieve a happier future where nobody is oppressed.'

Laughter, definite laughter, followed. And somebody called: 'In brotherhood our army falls!' And then a hand shot up.

'Yes, Private Uwa?' the officer called.

'Sir!' the private gave a powerful salute, then turned his eyes at me.
'Suppose they too say the same thing about themselves.'
'Who?' I asked.
'The other side.'
'Well, if they could say so and believe in it sincerely, the war would then end.'
'In our favour?' the private asked.
'Yes. And in their own too,' I replied.
But it was too subtle for him, and for the officer. The latter gazed at me for a brief moment as if scandalised. And many more hands went up.
'Yes, Okorokoba!' Pipia called with enthusiasm.
'Both sides would win? I don't understand,' Okorokoba said.
There was almost a boo. Pipia threatened several things, including court martial. But the voices lingered on.
'What is wrong with both sides winning?' I resumed. 'Nothing really, provided it means both sides getting to a common goal. You see what I mean?'
Private Okorokoba shook his head in doubt. They booed and called on him to sit down. Pipia intervened and tried to counter the impression by announcing to me that the private was a very intelligent lad who asked very intelligent questions. . . .
An orderly came running, a note in hand. The murmurs died down and anxiety took over as Pipia read the note. Many folded their hands across their chest in sad anticipation.
'Battle order!' Pipia called out, pocketing the note.
They dispersed, completely, in a matter of seconds. They filled up several vehicles, some hanging on the sides. On the whole, they were cheerful and composed, forgetting for the moment their domestic grievances. They sang as if they were going to a football match, or an athletics competition, and not to kill or be killed. One particular song they sang more than any other. It was that requesting the daughters of the land to be more cooperative over the matter of body contact. And there was an intense sense of order about it all, the drivers ready at the wheels as the troops poured in. Then the vehicles drove away, one after the other.
The attackers had made a surprise move which brought them within

shelling range of the camp. It was even reported that their advance platoon was only four miles away. The reports came from fleeing inhabitants of the area who now jammed the road. There were hundreds of them, mostly the old as well as women and children. They had only a few of their belongings, on their heads or hands, in addition to the very young ones they dragged along; some took livestock too, mostly the disciplined goats and companionable dogs. They trudged with weary, reluctant steps, the more elderly ones biting their lips and grinding their teeth, and sobbing from time to time as they ate their sorrow in their hearts.

'Destination unknown!' I sobbed.

'Sir?' the driver answered.

'Shouldn't we pick one or two of them up?' I suggested. 'The trouble is that one doesn't know where to take them.'

'No, sir,' was his answer.

He manoeuvred the car skilfully through the crowded road.

'Stop; let's pick up this small group.'

The rattling of small arms was clearly audible already. We had not heard it before now because of the engine. Silence intervened between the two of us.

'But I believe that's our people,' he spoke first, referring to the sound of the guns.

There was a deep boom, and the earth vibrated. Then another, much nearer. The driver looked at me and shrugged his shoulders, jumped into the car, and shrieked a frantic appeal for me to jump in too. Close by, a small child toddling at the mother's side fell down with shock and began to scream.

The third explosion must have occurred only a hundred feet from where we stood. And with it, a tumult of confusion and near-despair arose among the escaping crowd. What would happen if the attackers should send the mortar-bombs right into the crowd? Surely, it could not be that they didn't know the crowd was there. There must be much good still in their hearts, whatever one might say ... Some whistling and hissing this time; then the shell exploded right before us. This took four lives on the spot and wounded several others, including a young woman who lay now on the ground in a pool of blood. The woman seemed unaware of the injury which the hot metal fragment had left on her hand; her attention was completely taken up by the child who lay unconscious by her side. The metal appeared to have struck the latter full impact.

We took both in the car.

The child died some thirty minutes later, just as we were reaching the hospital gate. And in her grief, the mother began singing her story. She sang it even while the doctor was treating her own wound. Her name was Maria. She had lost her husband while the child was still in the womb. And when the child was born, it was male, and she called it Ikenna. And now, Ikenna was gone too. She had no husband and no child. Maria broke into a loud, unrestrained wailing, and the tears streamed her eyes; and she summoned the Maker to come at once and take her own life too. In all this her voice rang smooth and the cadence was tuneful indeed. Her eyes showed a subdued radiance, and her bosom heaved with the rising of her voice. Wasn't she a beautiful woman, this sorrowful widow now rendered childless too? I said to myself. Light-complexioned, long-faced, symmetrical in build, and with a strong but pleasant voice, even in sorrow. But the soldiers who were around had other views.

'Who is that mad woman disturbing the patients, eh?' demanded the formidable-looking sergeant on duty.

'She lost her child,' someone apologised on Maria's behalf.

'And so what?' Looking all the more irate at the reply, the sergeant moved forward and the speaker vanished completely from the spot. 'What about those who die fighting everyday, eh?' he continued. 'Does she think they have no mothers?'

There was no reply.

'Doctor, send her away.'

The doctor looked up and smiled, for a fraction of a second.

'But where is her husband. You?' He pointed at me with contempt, but turned dramatically into a kind being when he learnt I was not.

Part of the functions of the Plobe was to sustain the morale of wounded soldiers. That particular duty had been assigned to Joe Anoke, who was a psychologist by training, and his team of co-opted experts and field staff. However, every member could assist whenever there was an opportunity to do so. I therefore took advantage of my visit to the hospital to go round the wards.

The guards on duty would not let me go beyond the civilian wards at first. It was the order, and that was all. I then tendered my card. That transformed them into polite humans. They even sent one of their members to show me round, starting from what they termed the worst-cases ward.

The patients in this ward lay in various attitudes depending on the nature of their injuries as well as their individual temperaments. There were cases of serious amputations; these lay immovable, gazing intently at visitors as if the latter had just arrived from the other world and they were anxious to have the latest information. There were several shell-shock victims who droned and screamed with impatience, even while conversing. Five still lay unconscious in the stretchers long after the bullets and fragments had been extracted. One patient who had lost a leg was busy reading the *Life and Teachings of Christ*, while another with a bandaged chest read the *Sorrows of Satan*. We came to a patient with a shell-injury.

'I go show them one day!' he crooned, nodding his heavily bandaged head. 'I go kill them; kill them; kill them!'

'You go kill them,' the experienced nurse echoed. 'When you recover, you go kill them.'

'Ha, big master done come! Give me—' He touched his lip with the thumb and middle finger together; then blew with his mouth. 'Armada boy! Na me!' he boasted. And now, he rose from the bed and advanced with considerable speed towards me. 'Oga, big master, give me.' His face was tense and turgid with desire.

'I do not smoke, unfortunately,' I tried to apologise. Perhaps he had not heard, for he was still making the gesture; so I shook my head and gesticulated with the hands too. Then he turned hostile, and even looked violent. The urge had transformed this boy, a teenager, into a beast ready to pounce.

'Armada, see!' another called, to my great relief, holding less than half a stick before him. And the boy pounced. The effect was instantaneous, like water on a live coal. I ordered a few packets for the ward. That put them in a good mood, and they began telling stories of their experiences on the battlefields.

The stories pointed to what looked like a good sporting spirit between the two sides. Like this one:

'Go on pushing this time; when you are done we'll turn round and show you hell,' one side cried across during a lull.

'You will show us hell with matchets and catapults, is it?' the other returned.

'You wait and see.'

'Fools that you are! They send you to war without guns and you agree to go. Look at your uniforms; they're all rags.'

'Lazy ones! What have you achieved with all those arms on you?'

'What have we achieved? I have part of your land—that at least is something.'

'But you can't carry it home, can you?'

'That's true, my brother,' the other conceded. 'You've spoken the truth. Come over here and have a cigarette for a reward.'

'Send it over.'

'No, come in person.'

'Then let the cigarette smoke choke you to death.'

From that point, the forest rang with raillery and imprecations, followed by explosions and whistling of bullets; a real orgasm of fire.

'In the end, however,' concluded the narrator, 'our side successfully routed the other, inflicting heavy casualties. But in a counter-attack a few days later, they chased us out again, and started mortaring the next village where we were regrouping. And the inhabitants fled unprepared.'

Okay Baby's special assignment in the Plobe was to keep up the spirit of those who were forced to flee their homes because of the war. This took him to the various refugee camps situated in market squares, village halls and school compounds. It was in the course of such visits that he came across one fine lady, according to him, who enquired whether he knew of a certain man, a good Samaritan, with unkempt hair and beard, whose name was Mr. Medo. I gave some description which he confirmed. Okay Baby also gave details about the location of the camp.

I went to the camp three days later, in the company of the Refugee Officer for the district.

There were well over three hundred persons in the open school hall. A few of them had bamboo beds which also served as seats; but most lay on the bare cement floor, their mats spread all over without any order. They stared at you as you approached, with varying expressions on their faces, ranging from stubborn hope to total despair. Two small huts, one at each end of the building, served as the kitchen, but a good many, not caring for form, set up their potstand in the front of the main building where also a number of children were playing and shouting and crying. Of the children, some looked happy and healthy, thanks to the resilience of infancy; but many looked lean and sick, with pale skins. These latter were the ones that cried, and their mothers, unable to provide a more effective cure, merely tried to hush them into silence. All alone near the right end of the building, an old man with a long grey beard sat on the bare ground under a tree, grinding his teeth, silent, except when he muttered his complaints against those who brought about the situation in which a man of his years must abandon his homestead, the symbol of his existence, and sleep in the bush on a strange soil. By his side a woman, one of his wives probably, sat consoling and upbraiding him.

It was the woman who told us more about the old man. He had been behaving very strangely in the past few days, she disclosed. In the hours of deep darkness, he would spring up from his seat and reach out his hand for his household idol, which was nowhere near, and then he would begin to sing his sorrow. Last night, the song was about how the cock would crow and the owl would hoot, and he would take up his climbing rope and tapping knife and set out on an early round of the palms. He had continued to tap the palms even at his age, for not only had it enabled him to retain his erect form and his health, it linked his soul to that of his beloved father who himself had been a tapper of great renown. All that was no longer possible! he had moaned, sobbing, biting his teeth. And when dawn came, the old man had sat up cursing and spitting, lamenting the fact that the thoughts which had passed through his mind during the night had been nothing but an echo mocking his longing for home.

The figure I had been searching for stealthily with my eyes was now advancing towards us with quick strides and a bold smile.

'Maria?'

'Sir?' she answered in a low, yet penetrating, voice; and then she began to contract with shyness.

I regarded her steadily. The ringed neck! Lord, I had not noticed that!
A current ran through my body.

'It is nice seeing you again.'

She had withered at my gaze. 'Let me go and tell Mamma,' she said.

As she moved away, I held the Refugee Officer's eyes. And she came
back in less than five minutes with two others.

'Mamma, this is the man I have been telling you about,' she said
moments later.

'This? My daughter told me everything. I can only ask God to thank
you for me, my son.'

'It's a pity about what happened,' I remarked in reply. 'It is nice to
note now that she has accepted things the way they turn out to be.'

'What else could one have done, my brother?' She had addressed me
more appropriately this time: for she certainly was no more than
twelve years older than Roland Medo.

'And how have you been getting on?' asked the Refugee Officer
now. He appeared to be well known to the inmates of the camp,
from his familiar tone. He took out his notebook and pen, ready to
record.

Maria took over: 'The natives continue to be very kind to us. They
give us food.'

The Officer recorded diligently. 'That's very good. Yes?'

'But only as much as they can afford. We need much more, and some
clothing too.'

He did not write this time; he merely said that the Government was
trying its best.

'Nobody says it isn't trying,' Maria retorted, in faultless English. For
the first time, perhaps from the force of her emotion, she was speaking
unguardedly and betraying her capabilities. 'What I am saying is that
not much passes down to us.'

'Why?' I interposed.

'We don't know—perhaps the Officer should know,' said she. 'What is
certain is that we get very little from the Government. For instance,
when they say they are sending you a stick of fish, you find that
threequarters of the stick has no fish on it. I don't know if it is the
Government, or its agents, or what, that eats the three-quarters.'

'The same complaint everywhere,' the Officer tried to dismiss the accusation. 'Camp Supervisors make away with food intended for refugees, and so on! Nobody can prove anything.'

'How I wish Biere was here!' I mused.

'Who?' the Officer asked.

'Nothing.' I turned, facing him direct. 'Part of the problem really is that we cannot find sufficient food for the refugees in competition with the requirements of the armed forces.'

He nodded his approval.

'The other part, perhaps more serious, is that the distribution is faulty.'

'How?'

'The organisation is not all it might be,' I charged without restraint. 'People know this but nothing appears to be happening about it. The Central Committee doesn't have a hand directly in the doings, I am sure; it's the local organisations.'

A lively debate followed, the Officer taking on the whole lot of us, and proving himself a keen debater indeed. It all ended on a more or less friendly note.

'Sir, how about your people?' Maria now asked.

'They are all quite well, I think,' I replied. 'I have not seen them for some time though.'

'Greet your wife and children for us when next you see them,' the mother said.

'How can I?'

'How?' Maria sounded bewildered.

'I'm still a bachelor—that's what I mean.' Our eyes met, and she smiled—a shy but interested smile. Even in the midst of war, in trouble and suffering, these things do exist! I thought within me. And then, her mother began to laugh, seemingly registering her approval. Only the girl, Maria's sister, kept frowning in a maidenly austerity that was insensitive to all that was happening.

'Fine people!' the Officer remarked as soon as they were gone.

'Rather,' I said mechanically. 'They would have been much finer, though, had your organisation cared for them better.'

'I think I should arrange for them to leave the camp,' he offered. 'You would like that?'

'And go where instead?'

'I can help to get them fixed up in one of the war establishments—like Fuel or Food Procurement.'

'What a solution!' I remonstrated 'And leave the rest to suffer, isn't it?'

'The trouble about refugees is that they are never satisfied.'

'Stop that jargon, my friend. Give them a fair deal and they will be satisfied.'

He appeared not to have heard me well. 'There's every hope, however, that the Church Relief bodies will soon come to our aid,' he added.

'Your aid, I know—not that of the refugees!'

We entered the car, slammed the door. The driver began to fumble in his pockets for the ignition key.

'Who will distribute the food and clothing when the Church bodies send some?' I asked.

'That can be easily arranged; let them send it first,' he said.

'Arranged by whom?'

'By us, of course,' he replied in an equally harsh tone.

'Indeed!' I stroked my beard. 'That is what you people must never be allowed to do.'

The driver broke in announcing triumphantly that he had found the key, right there on his lap.

'Drive fast; I have a meeting in an hour's time,' I said to him.

'One whole hour!' He switched on the engine.

Then, he switched off, paused, listened.

"I thought I heard some sound, like a war plane,' he said; and we listened. . . .

The faint buzz began to develop into a swelling roar accompanied by a sharp, whistling sound. A heavy, unearthly silence took possession of the immediate vicinity as the supersonic jet circled, causing the heart to pound and the head to throb. I found myself ducking behind an oil-bean tree.

The camp was one wild confusion. People ran up and down, right and left, and someone shouted: 'Don't run or it will see you,' and got the reply: 'Stop shouting, you; it will hear you.' Then I saw Maria dart across, and I watched her dive behind a cluster of shrubs. The plane had now appeared directly over the camp: fish-shaped, shining, flashing, roaring and whistling. From all directions, animals, mostly stray

202

livestock from near-by homes, began to bleat and bark and cackle. But they all went silent when the boom occurred.

'It's got me!' a voice cried, and corrected: 'No; it hasn't!'

The explosion sounded again; and again, and again. Smoke, dust and confused cries rose into the air; and as if in reply, the plane fired its cannon down to the ground. A tumult followed, mostly from the more hysterical ones who lay flat on their stomachs in the bush, clinging to any solid object around, including twigs.

A nearby hut was set ablaze and three of the inmates were killed. But the camp remained surprisingly untouched by rocket or bullet.

CHAPTER TWENTY-SEVEN

The discontent among the soldiers in Captain Okenna's camp had survived the bitter battle fought for several days, unlike many of the soldiers themselves. And nobody still alive could bear his ways any longer. Okenna had systematically eliminated the more outspoken of the malcontents by sending them on assignments on which they were sure to meet their death. And he had continued to surround himself with his own blood relations, like Pipia and Okorokoba—people who would collaborate with him in the practice of diverting supplies intended for the fighting boys. And then, just recently, at a time of the utmost danger, Okenna had ordered the company into the field of battle while he himself escaped with his relations to the far rear. He was nowhere to be seen when the fighting boys were falling to their death in scores; but he did return when it was known that the survivors had not only held the ground but also had pushed the attackers far back. His mission this time was to see for himself the amount of booty that had been captured. There were very many cartons of beer and rolls of cigarettes, and other things. Okenna ordered these to be conveyed to a given address in Oban.

So pleaded the private who in his rage had sent a bullet into Commandant Okenna's skull.

Both Biere and Professor Makamadu were in a state of terrible indignation. Which was funny! Just because Imperator had at long last come out openly to declare his stand, or to stand in for fate! The announcement said that he had declared his all-out support for the other side.

'You two surprise me,' I laughed, with a superior air. 'You ought to have sensed something like that all the time.'

'Frankly, I had believed he would be neutral all through,' the English master sighed.

'He never really was!' I pointed out. 'He claimed he was, and you credited him with good intentions.'

'The war continues all the same,' the professor swore, delivering a lively blow on his left palm.

'What can I offer you, Prof.?' Biere asked.

The professor requested mineral water, and I asked for beer.

We were in Biere's house, and it was evening. The sunset clouds dissolved and reappeared in a vast radiance of alternating colours.

'You may have heard,' he said.

'No? . . . What?' the professor and I replied together.

'It is still a secret, but they say we may have to evacuate Oban very soon.'

Nobody spoke.

Then, the sound of an exploding shell shattered the silence, and shook us in our seats. We exchanged glances in mutual sympathy.

'So close!' the professor exclaimed.

The bombs resumed. They fell again and again. And their flying vibrations re-echoed in the heavens.

The Plobe met at the usual place, which was a room in the offices of the Ministry of Information, at nine in the morning, but only to disperse soon after. The sounds of exploding shells had become unbearable and there was a lot of commotion all over the town. It was agreed that we should re-assemble in the afternoon at Yemuka Town Hall, which was three miles to the south of the town and therefore only one mile beyond Christ High School. Everybody should be there by three o'clock.

Biere arrived at my house by noon. He certainly was not in high spirits. I asked:

'The war situation, is it?'

He hesitated. 'It isn't just the reverses,' he said. 'No, not just the war situation.'

'Thou art then to be numbered among the brave of the nation,' I said in an attempt at good-humour.

He was disconsolate. 'You may have noticed that the generality of the fighting forces as well as of the civilian population feels the same way,' said he with difficulty. 'The reverses in the field do not upset one so much as the other failings.'

'Oh, that?' I exclaimed. 'It is very much around still?'

'It is,' and he nodded, sadly. 'And it seems even more powerful now. Look at us, fighting in order to establish an ideal society—just and honest and all, and what do you see instead, even while our boys are dying in hundreds?' He spread out both palms, signifying that I should complete the rest of the story in my mind.

'But has anything just happened?' I asked him. 'Anything that has put you in such a mood just now?'

'Some of those people who procure food for the Armed Forces should be arrested and shot in public.'

'Without trial?' I laughed.

'Trial? They will be tried, of course, but they should not be allowed to exist after that. Fancy collecting money for food not supplied, Roland. Did you know such a thing has been going on?'

'No. I imagine,' said I, 'that being the more experienced type of actors, they hide their tracks skilfully, so that you don't get to discover them until it is late.'

He rejected the theory with a ponderous shaking of the head. 'They are just hiding behind the war, that's all. And the war includes protection from relatives in authority.' He gave instances. 'Is that right? Those are well protected in high circles.'

'By no means right, Biere!' said I, with some levity. 'Gross abuse of office, that's certainly what it is.' Then I went on to rebuke him: 'But these things should not have upset you so much. There are happier things around, after all.'

His spirits had improved considerably by the time we were ready to leave the house.

The first taxi we hailed sped away without taking any notice of us.

We waved to another, sparing our breath this time. The driver pulled up grudgingly, and as we approached the door he complained: 'As much as two pounds for a single cup of salt!', before turning round to us. His face was cloudy, totally repulsive. 'Where to?' he demanded.

'Yemuka Town Hall,' I declared.

'Ten shillings for both of you,' he announced, adding, before I could say a word, that haggling was no use. All the same, I offered two shillings, which was the normal fare; then three. He replied with a string of recriminations. How much did salt cost? And fuel, and spare parts? Still grumbling, he started the engine and took off slowly. Then he halted again. 'It is the so-called big men,' he charged, 'who, after every bit of roguery, hide their faces behind a beard.' He went on, incoherently: 'A certain well-dressed villain who calls himself a Transport Controller took away this very car last week, telling me he would use it for the war, yet the seats still have a strong female odour on them.' The gear clanked and the engine zoomed.

Biere warned me that the beard would certainly lead me into trouble.

'Let's try this one. Taxi!'

The driver was more human than any of his predecessors. He pulled the car close by and flung the door open. And the fare was only five shillings.

But he kept looking into the driving mirror as the car moved.

'Let's hope we're not fighting what may in the end prove a futile war!' Biere whispered.

'Why?' and I pinched his thigh muscle. 'See how anxious the driver is about our identity.'

'Lest we should be enemy infiltrators, no doubt!'

'Oga, how is the war getting on?' the driver asked, turning an angle.

'Very tough,' said I.

'True, it doesn't seem things are so bright.'

I merely told him he was right. And just then, the artillery resumed. One bomb exploded close by, shattering a section of a building and causing a general stampede. The driver manoeuvred the car through the crowds, refusing to halt for the waving passengers, until we came

206

to the check-point midway between Christ High School and Yemuka Hall.

The crowd here was immense; confusion reigned. Old and young jostled and shouted while the armed civil guards on duty barred the exit. To add to the confusion, lorries and cars fully loaded with human beings and property began arriving. The horns blared, or honked, or hooted, in an infinite variety, and the passengers shouted, all calling down God's severe anger on the guards. But the latter held their ground, daring any to cross the bar. The instructions, said they, were that the inhabitants of Oban must not be allowed to desert.

We approached the guards all the same. Pushing his way through, Biere presented his card to the one who looked like the leader. A noisy conference followed. Then, they agreed to let us pass, provided it was not in the car.

'There is some explanation to it, isn't there?' Biere asked when we were some yards beyond the point.

'To what?'

'To keeping the civilians back even though it is definite the town is on the verge of falling.'

'Perhaps to provide cover for others to evacuate.'

'That's what I mean,' he affirmed. 'Others, including the army.'

'And the Plobe.'

'Frankly speaking, I do not feel unhappy about the new venue.'

'Nor do I,' I said.

We had done the greater part of the distance between the check-point and the hall.

'There is something I think I should tell you,' he said. 'We are likely to have a chairman soon for the Plobe.'

'How?'

'I was only acting. A substantive chairman has now been proposed.'

I was stunned. 'Why? What is the need for another appointment?'

'The question will probably answer itself when we know the details.'

A shell exploded while he was speaking.

'Let's hurry; I don't like these sounds.'

'Nobody does! They make one so nervous.'

Another shell fell, just a few yards away, shattering a woman's head and ripping her neck open. A hand grabbed me from behind and began to pull out my shirt, which was white-coloured: a war plane was in the air. We lay flat on our stomachs.

It was in the confusion that followed that the crowd broke through at the check-point, like a formidable flood, and the exit from Oban started.

For some days it seemed as if the situation had been contained. The soldiers had halted the attack, with many losses on either side. Morale began to rise once more. But this was short-lived. The other side poured in in still larger numbers, with more guns and ammunition and armoured cars. This soon became the pattern all through. It was to happen again weeks later at Alara, and then Ania and other places. . . .

And so, after the first day's meeting in Yemuka Town Hall, in which really we did not achieve much because of the confusion, we never met there again. As a matter of fact the building was wrecked by a bomb two days later. We moved further south, down to Owana, which was some thirty miles away.

Owana was situated between two hills and wrapped in green vegetation. A large school compound at the centre of the town accounted for the greater part of its fame. Who did not know about Owana Boys' High School, which lay ensconced between the hills, with tall gmelinas shading the roofs? What made the school famous was its academic standards; there was never a year in which the performances of its students in the school leaving examination did not resound throughout the State, and even beyond. The school had long closed down, of course, and now the site was being used for Government offices.

It was a transient arrangement. A good many of the offices evacuated from Oban first landed there and regained their breath, before thinking of the next move. Thousands of people streamed up and down, while many more continued to arrive, all of them full of good cheer in spite of what had just happened. Already, the local people, with sound commercial sense, had set up hotels in hastily-erected sheds, giving them the most topical names, like Refugees Inn, Hotel de Traveller, Wayside Paradise, and Victory is Ahead. In addition, scores of hawkers, with loads on their heads, paced up and down, shouting advertisements for groundnuts and oranges, bread and biscuits, and second-hand clothing. Their business sense had told them that many of those arriving from Oban had come with practically nothing in the way of food or clothing. Some had left with nothing at all, not even mats!

It was to the last category of refugees that Biere and Roland belonged. The whole thing had caught us completely unprepared. By the time we could get back into Oban after the meeting, most of the town was under heavy mortar fire. We had a bit of consolation, however. Those who had managed to rescue some part of their belongings and to bring them over to Owana were now being held virtual prisoners. Not knowing where to keep their property, they had to confine their movements to a few feet away from the spot. I had no such worry; I was completely free—free indeed from any form of belongings. Had I not lost my entire library, I would perhaps have been happy. Biere on the other hand felt positively sad. In particular, he could not bear the loss of his Milton's complete works.

He was getting more and more pensive, too. It was the trouble with him; he often took things too much to heart. How many times had I told him so? Biere, you really need to storm and burst from time to time. And you need, also, to try the funny side of life. Otherwise, you will get weighed down sooner and later. Take my example … Yes, I knew what it was that was eating him up just now. It was the new chairman proposed for the Plobe.

Biere had owed his position in the Plobe largely to Colonel Nzellia, who had nothing but admiration for every word from Biere's lips. Why he should admire, and even revere, Biere so much was difficult to guess, the more so considering that the colonel lived in style. Could it be explained away by the fact that, as a law student at London University, Nzellia had attended a series of lectures on English language and literature under the auspices of the British Council? That was long before he enlisted in the army. But now the colonel was no longer around. An altogether unwarlike soul, he had moved over to a para-military assignment immediately the war broke out, and currently he was known as Principal Co-ordinator of the Civilian Corps, a duty as nebulous in name as it was in its scope.

Why replace him with Doctor Anibado, of all the humans in creation? I could see Biere's point, but that was not sufficient reason for one to feel beaten and shattered. The best approach would be to give the new man, or devil, a fight. Let us pool our resources, of heart and mind and mouth, and give the man Anibado what he so much deserved.

One full week had passed before the Plobe was able to meet at Owana. 'Well, gentlemen,' the Doctor began, smoking his pipe.

He was dressed in a grey cotton shirt and brown khaki trousers, which seemed to suggest a self-advertising, or even mock, modesty. He looked extremely confident and composed. It was that air of guiltlessness, the total lack of conscience, which one found most annoying about the man.

'We'll do some introductions first,' and he declared, for everybody to take note, that he was the new chairman; and that he was resolved to serve the nation to the best of his ability. We began from his right—Okay Baby first; then, Joe Allison who had been in charge of trade unions; then Biere; and myself; and Obasi Ello, in charge of teachers; and Una Bressi of the Civil Service Union; and finally, Joe Anoke.

Biere spoke:

'Mr. Chairman, we all welcome you into the Plobe. I believe I am speaking for everybody when I say we'll serve conscientiously and to the best of our ability, just as you did.'

The other nodded extravagantly, and puffed out thick coils of smoke.

'A little question, Mr. Chairman,' I indicated.

'Yes, Mr. Medo? Feel free to ask,' he said.

'Would it be possible to give us some hint as to whether any more changes are likely to be made in the membership?'

'Oh, yes; yes.' He spread out in his seat. Eyes fixed at the ceiling, he puffed out coils of smoke. 'I can tell you one or two—no, just one—outright. Professor Makamadu is no longer with us: he has gone over to Production Services. There will almost certainly be some more changes, but that will be after the reorganisations I have in mind.'

Biere wanted to speak, but I pinched his thigh. 'Wouldn't it be advisable to get on first with such reorganisations, so as to know who and who are likely to continue in the Plobe?' I asked.

'I propose to put forward a paper on the matter at the next meeting or so,' he said, solemnly. 'We can afford to wait until then.'

'We may on that account have to adjourn in good time today?'

'If members want it so,' said he craftily, then he went on: 'But don't think we have nothing at all to discuss at today's meeting.' Then, he pulled out a packet of cigarettes, took one for himself, and passed the packet round. He was quite an extraordinary man, I thought. Firm and yet warm, and eloquent, with an insidious twist of the voice at the right time, accommodating both sarcasm and compliment.

'For example, we could discuss the war situation,' he suggested.

'Chief, may we know what will be the title of the paper you will present?' asked Anoke.

'Title? You can never tell until you have finished composing. Mr. Ekonte who studied literature will tell you better.'

Biere confirmed this, in spite of his mood; and that disposed of Anoke's dangerous curiosity.

'Weren't we going to discuss the war situation?' Okay Baby reminded members.

There the man seemed at his best. 'The boys are doing an excellent job, in spite of the super-human odds,' said he, jerking his body all the way from the head down to the waist. 'In their frustration at lack of progress, the enemy are now preparing frantically for Portcity.'

'Portcity!' voices exclaimed.

'Oh, yes. What else did you expect? They now want to either sink or swim. And sink they will! They can never make the journey. They probably know they cannot; it is the distant lord pushing them into it all.'

Biere glanced left, at me.

'Exactly!' I nearly shouted.

'He wants our money, nothing else, and is using the other side to get at it,' Anibado elaborated. 'But he will never succeed.'

'He can never,' came the involuntary chorus.

'Portcity will remain an elusive shadow to him.'

Biere then spoilt the music: 'I imagine it is only human.'

'Did you say—?' Anibado wondered.

'What I mean is that it's all part of human greed, this wanting our money,' said he. 'And the quality is traceable not only in the white adventurer but also in the local inhabitants.'

'The point is well taken. Gentlemen, isn't it so?' he asked, concentrating his attention, apparently, on the pipe which he now held in position in his mouth with his hand; and got the only reply that could have been expected. And then, he declared: 'The only thing one would want to say by way of amendment is that our main business at the moment is to deal with those who, after slaughtering our kith and kin in tens of thousands, are now descending upon us to finish off those who are still alive. Isn't it so, gentlemen?'

Some agreed outright; and one or two, besides Biere and I, held their tongues.

'If I may come in again, Chairman,' I said.

'Yes.'

'Remember that those people didn't get up one morning and begin to kill. There was a long chain of incidents leading to the troubles, and I believe that's what Biere was referring to.'

'Exactly!' Biere took over once again. 'Unless we seriously get down to the core of the disease, all the efforts that go into the present war, and all the losses in life and property will be wasted in the end. And assuming we will win the shooting war, the victory may prove to be a defeat after a short time.'

'Let's say, but for purposes of argument only, that you are right. Where then do we go from there?' Anibado asked.

'Where we mustn't go from there is to underestimate the moral aspect of the war.'

'Won't others say something? Or are you held spellbound by the standard of the debate?' Once again, he began laughing. But I could sense he had been nettled. What he did next was to manoeuvre the discussion to the less controversial issue of the gallantry and hardiness of the boys in the trenches. The news about Portcity was really disturbing, however.

Nobody seemed to have realised the actual strength of the forces being assembled for an attack on Portcity. There were reports of infiltrators trapped and dealt with, gun-boats sunk or captured, and large quantities of arms and ammunition seized. The stories raised the morale of the civilian population as well as of the fighting forces themselves; and in spite of the air-raids, which had now become both sustained and intense, the former refused to evacuate the city but rather went on ferreting for infiltrators.

To give a further boost to the morale of the population of the city, it was decided that the Plobe should move down to the area, and concentrate its activities there for some time. The next meeting would, therefore, be held on the first Saturday of the coming month, which was six days off, in the city; and the venue would be the Negro Inn situation close to the Government residential area. It was at that meeting that he would present the long-awaited memorandum, the chairman promised, having failed to keep his word for the third time. Biere and I travelled together, arriving on Friday afternoon. The whole town was on edge. It seemed as if fear had been injected into its bloodstream. There were subdued whispers and exclamations everywhere; and there were fewer cars on the city's streets than I had ever known. The story told was that many of the vehicles were being used to convey men and stores to the war front, for two warships, invulnerable to bombs or rockets, were fast advancing. The ships would not try to reach the port direct, for the channel had been effectively blocked; instead, they would land at a disused harbour some thirty miles to the east from where the soldiers on board would set out on a land invasion which would cut off the city, decisively, from the hinterland. But let them come along, some were boasting; they would meet their full deserts; they would fall into the lion's teeth. Many others in their trepidation began to pack their belongings, only to learn about the latest decree by the local civil defence organisation to the effect that none would be allowed to leave.

Rumours began to circulate a few hours later. The ships had actually landed . . . The troops had disembarked . . . Fighting was going on . . . The invading troops had been blotted out, to a man. As the speculations mounted, the booming of the guns became clearly audible, also the sound of bullets borne by the serene evening breeze.

'Biere, something is definitely happening,' I observed.

'Fighting is happening,' he amended. 'One begins to wonder if the Plobe will be able to meet tomorrow as planned.'

'May or may not.'

'Drinks for the two outcasts,' he proposed.

'Why outcasts?'

'Because the chairman has virtually cast us out. I have a feeling he has been busy organising the other members' support.'

'That may in fact be the case, Biere!' said I. 'And that must have kept him busy all these weeks at the expense of his much-promised bulletin.'

The waiter arrived, took the order . . .

'Scheming!' he murmured, lifting the glass. 'I believe there will, again, be no paper.'

'Then we'll tackle him, without waiting for the paper.'

'That is, if he convenes us.'

The night was dark; only that section of the town where the hotel was located seemed to have been lit with electricity, and even then, the bulbs had to be shaded against air-raids. Portcity was today like a huge grave over which loomed a terrible danger. One could sense that something had gone definitely wrong. And the guns continued to boom: castanets sounded continuously, with occasional drum-beats. The notes had a weird ring, like the incantation for a blood bath.

The sounds subsided in the early hours of the morning. Then rumours took over once more. But by ten o'clock the Ministry of Information vans came in to break the suspense.

'Go out to the stadium, everybody,' the man at the loudspeaker called as the van passed. 'Go and see some of the captured men.'

'We go?' Biere asked.

'I go—that at least I know,' I told him.

We were among the first to arrive, largely because of the nearness of the hotel to the stadium. We therefore had good viewing positions. And the captives, about fifty in number, were already on display, all of them young boys full of life, their hands tied behind their backs. They looked dishevelled and distraught, and had patches of blood on parts of their bodies. One of them, right in front, was weeping and screaming, calling upon his absent father to come to his rescue. As his

214

voice descended to a sad cadence, he held out both his palms at me. 'But why did you come here to fight?' I asked in a safely ambiguous tone.

'Please, sir, beg them on my behalf,' the boy pleaded hysterically, bending his trunk to the right and then to the left in a supplicatory gesture, and the tears rolled down from his eyes, streaking his cheeks.

'Answer him, why did you come here?' somebody else demanded from among the crowd. 'Not to kill, eh?'

'I was only a student,' another captive gibbered. 'They caught me ... They said I must follow ... Sir, please help me. I will fight on your side.'

I opened my mouth and closed it again. Biere signalled to me, and I moved out, just in time before the crowd pushed.

'How many people did your own father kill over there?' I heard, clearly.

The crowd surged. But the soldiers on duty drew their guns.

'Shoot me, soldiers,' sang a woman, berserk, a big club in hand. 'This is my only chance. They killed Willie, my only brother, over there.' Heedless of the guns, she dashed through the barrier. And some of the crowd followed. The soldiers now lost control.

The crowd surged and surged; they charged on the captives in a frenzy of mad hate. Their bitterly vengeful spirit could not now be satiated by seeing alone.

'What has that boy done, Biere?' I moaned as soon as we had extricated ourselves from the scene.

'Ask me! But lower your voice please,' said he in reply. 'Your view is certainly sound, but those who have organised such treatment for the captives will not be impressed if they hear you.'

We moved farther and farther away. He turned round.

'That is exactly what they ought to have done to that man Anibado and his type,' he said.

'And on both sides,' I agreed. 'Destroying our youth for nothing!'

'You can be sure Anibado had a hand in what has just happened.'

'Anibado? Yes.' I was busy tugging at my beard. A sensation of horror had gripped me, benumbing me to the point of inanity.

CHAPTER TWENTY-EIGHT

The immediate threat to Portcity was averted. Reports said the attempt cost the other side a whole brigade plus large quantities of stores and equipment. Two gunboats were captured almost intact. Both the soldiers and the civilians had combined in the operation, and now morale was very high once more.

But we had no illusions. That was what had happened at Oban; then at Alara; then at Ania. And indeed, shortly after, the air-raids resumed. The planes roared and the anti-aircraft guns boomed; then, doom ... doom ... doom ... doom! Smoke, shrieks, and wailings. People died in scores. Rising to the occasion, one of the more locally-based churches enjoined its members to pray to God to save the lives of the citizens, and got the radio to carry the appeal. But the message went much farther than the church could have intended. A very distant broadcasting station reported in its regular daily commentary on international affairs that the people were in their desperation commending themselves to God.

'That is extremely shabby and profane of them,' I ranted at the radio.

'You still have the energy for anger against inanimate objects have you?' Biere asked in reproach, watching as I stormed in my seat.

'Terribly inhuman too.'

'You have much more serious issues than that to occupy your mind, my friend. Did you know that your chairman had been here in Portcity all these days?'

'You mean it?' I asked in my surprise.

'Somebody saw him. He has been busy organising the rest of the members against the two of us, and also setting up what he calls the local branch of the Plobe.'

'When did you get to know about all that?'

'This morning,' he said. 'And they have been meeting without us. And also, it is now clear that it was Anibado, and no other, who got the crowd at the stadium worked up to that pitch.'

'Very upsetting! ... We may consider returning to Owana then, since they don't want us.'

His silence showed that he did not approve.

'There is this invitation for a meeting day after tomorrow though,' I reconsidered.

We discussed it for some time. Then we agreed we should attend. And we would tell Anibado what we thought about his chairmanship. I was to be the principal prosecutor, and Biere would call me to order if I should start on Imperator instead of facing the full-blooded miscreant right before my eyes.

'Well, gentlemen, shall we begin?' he began, leaning with his back against the chair, slightly turned, one leg crossed over the other, and holding the stem of the pipe in his mouth with his hand. 'We are happy that what we had feared has been averted, and that Portcity is still intact. I must apologise for delaying for so long before convening the meeting. We wanted the tension to go down first.'

Biere turned and our eyes met, and he started to bite his finger-nails. 'I am glad to inform you that I am now in a position to lay before you the memorandum on our future operations.' He opened his briefcase and took out a heap of pink-coloured papers which he pushed forward to the member sitting closest to him, for circulation.

The memorandum was a four-page document, single-spaced. The first page gave, in the author's own words, a brief review of the activities of the Plobe before his accession to office. The second page attempted, still in his own words, to give credit where credit was due. Then, in the rest of the memorandum, Anibado dealt with what he termed the Modus Operandi for the New Phase. There had been too much theorising, said he by way of an introduction; and too much idealisation which could not strike the heart of the masses in the way that was required. It was necessary to go for a more poignant note, concentrating on the issues which would appeal to people's sentiments, thereby generating the bitterest hate for the other side. 'Only in that way,' the learned man declared, 'can we prove our worth. We must leave moralising to the bishops.' What an idea! I told myself, still reading down. So that was how what had started off in an impressive style had now petered out! I looked up with scorn into the author's face—at the infidel, the abode of *id*. He was a typical one: relentless, conscienceless, ruthless; and yet likeable, provided of course you did not cross his path to wealth and glory; and very affable, a gift which he employed in winning the unwary over to his side. It was said too he was a generous man.

I folded the paper up. Biere was busy underlining particular sections in red.

'Interesting!' I sighed.

'Mr. Chairman, I suppose we have all read it through now. May we begin?' Una Bressi suggested.

'Has everybody read it through?' Anibado asked. 'If so, let's go ahead.'

'I do not know whether the chairman would prefer that we go home with the document so as to study it more thoroughly before we begin to discuss it,' Okay Baby proposed. Of late, he had been assuming the very safe role of an unbiased mediator.

'You can't!' Biere snapped, at which I fixed him with an intense glare which must have given us away as conspirators. 'This is war time, and in war, procrastination is dangerous,' he amended with considerable mellowness. 'So I suggest we go ahead.'

'No objection then,' Okay Baby withdrew.

'Here!' I raised my hand.

'Yes, Mr. Medo.'

I stood up, for greater effect. 'I want to draw members' attention to the fact that this matter has been delayed for many weeks now, and we would do well not to allow any more delay. And having said that, I want to proceed right away to my own observations on the paper.' I picked up the paper before me. 'Perhaps the best thing would be to take it page after page.'

'Sorry; hold on, Mr. Medo,' I heard; then: 'Come in, Doctor Sohabia.'

'Doctor who?' I asked, and turned round.

Sohabia was already inside. He was all smiles, full of confidence and dignity. Then he apologised, in a quiet way, for being so late, and for interrupting the discussion.

There was a brief flurry of greetings and introductions, and then Doctor Sohabia sat down between Okay Baby and Una Bressi, at the centre of the arc.

'Doctor Sohabia takes over intellectuals,' Anibado announced, and the latter nodded. 'But we'll come to that later. Go ahead, Mr. Medo.'

I cleared my throat, thereby speeding up the process of recovery from the shock. 'One may allow the first two pages to pass without much in the way of comment. We are not, perhaps, the ones who should appraise our work. I am more worried about the theme of the Modus Operandi, especially where it requires us to infuse in the masses a deep-rooted hatred for everything about the other side.

'Let's get it clear, Mr. Chairman. I am not saying that we should do anything that could be construed as treachery or sabotage. Far from that! We are all deeply committed to the struggle, although it seems now, most regrettably, from differing motives. My point is this: Why don't we find a positive and constructive, and noble, motive for our endeavours? Should we lose the lives of our youth just because we hate? Do you see my point?'

'Are you asking me?' he asked in reply, looking most unimpressed, and smoking his pipe diligently.

'Asking ourselves,' I said.

'Well then, why don't you, being one of us, suggest an answer?' he rejoined.

'Very well then. You see, Doctor Anibado, I feel very happy at the opportunity being offered to me now, although the offer has been made unconsciously. And I wish to utilise it to the full, if you don't mind. The root cause of this present struggle is greed and injustice. And much as it has been said that injustice and wrong will always remain the lot of man, it is equally true that man will ever continue to struggle for justice and fair play, not minding what it costs. I am sure most members would agree with me. Justice, justice, justice! Justice which, in the words of Aristotle, is a sovereign virtue, more wonderful than evening or morning star. We want a society where the ills of the past are not repeated.'

'Hold on!' he cut in. 'Aren't you saying in effect, Mr. Medo, that we should ask our soldiers to direct their bullets at what you call injustices of the past—whatever you mean by that—instead of at the enemy before our gates?'

'What I'm saying is that the former is even more dangerous, in that it possesses its victim's soul. The latter is both tangible and visible.'

He shook his head, then shrugged with derision. 'Do members agree with him, please? I personally don't see his point.'

Biere came in at once to save the situation for me. 'What I think Roland is saying is that we ought to be fighting both ills simultaneously, or at least not to do anything that would give the impression that in fighting one ill we are supporting the other. What is happening at the moment is that the enemy at home gets more and more entrenched as we fight the one from outside. One should of course admit that the same thing applies to the other side—may even be worse there! But we are not planning for their well-being; we are planning for that of our people.'

Doctor Anibado turned half away from Biere, in disgust. 'Any other views?' he asked.

'Yes, Mr. Chairman,' I charged on him with fury before any could give him the support he was canvassing for. 'I should be glad if you would allow members, including myself, adequate time to say out our minds on this most vital issue.'

'Me too!' Biere added.

'It does seem that the two of you have been thinking together.'

'Very much so,' I accepted, then went ahead: 'It is an altogether distressing situation that you should have made such a proposal in your memorandum. We have, on both sides of the conflict, innocent boys losing their lives every minute of the day. And the military leaders, still on both sides, are innocent of the root causes of the present war. If the boys are going to continue to make sacrifices, we should be able to hold out for them some definite hope for a cleaner future—a future in which one man does not monopolise the good things intended for many, or where one country does not impose upon another. You see my point?'

'Go on.'

'Good. The whole thing is in fact one colossal, bloody irony. Many of those who brought about the whole mess are now prodding the soldiers on, on both sides, to fight and destroy themselves—so that in fact the latter will not turn the guns on their persons. And the white works manager, or administrative officer, or commercial fellow, who did awful things in the land has now either gone home on glorious retirement or is inciting one side or the other, in his quiet but effective style, from his home; while the white missionary, on the other hand, is being exposed to all war perils, distributing food and clothing to the needy and attending to the soldiers on the battle fronts. These thoughts make one sick.'

'You seem rather inspired, Mr. Medo,' Doctor Sohabia observed. 'I mean no offence,' he added promptly, sensing my reaction.

'So then, the old practitioners are once again in control, inciting the soldiers and populace on both sides. We know them well. Their common factor—be they local or foreign—is love of lucre. So the philosopher put it. And they operate on a grand scale; they sack cities and plunder temples. . . .' I paused to regain my breath.

They all stared, Biere smiling, while the chairman looked bored or at the best indulgent.

'Are you spent now?' Anibado asked.

'Spent? Definitely no!' I replied. 'There is a story which you may know already. It is about a famous warrior in Greek mythology. He set out on an expedition of conquest and loot. And while he was on the sea, a mighty, terrible wind arose. Then he consulted an oracle. Do you know what the oracle advised?'

'Tell us.'

'He was to pacify the wind with a maiden's blood. Now, match your characters, gentlemen of the Plobe.'

'Splendid!' Biere Ekonte exploded. 'Most splendid!' he said again while the tension and silence continued.

'Plucking off of rose petals . . . Real red, fresh palm-oil spilling on the grassy fields.'

The silence was deep. The words seemed to have penetrated the man's heart, at long last. His brow wrinkled.

'I move we adjourn, Chairman!' Bressi interposed, and several voices echoed in support.

Then Sohabia spoke: 'Before the adjournment, Doc, let me say that Mr. Medo's point is very well appreciated. But frankly it would be a very risky affair taking up the issue now. We ought to have before us one overriding purpose, which is to win the war. Anyone, crook or saint, who could assist in that is welcome as far as I am concerned.'

'I'm afraid I don't agree,' said Biere, tartly. 'And by the way, what do you mean by winning?'

'Defeating the other side.'

'Who defeats? I am of the view that if things continue to go as at present, we may discover in the end that we have merely installed in power an enemy worse than those against whom we are now directing the guns.'

'There is a point there,' Okay Baby said, 'but all the same we must first finish with the enemy we see. Let the attention of our boys not be distracted.'

'Look, look, look!' Anibado cried with impatience. 'We are running round and round the same circle. Mr. Medo, it is you who led us into this type of thing.'

'It isn't he; it's the facts before us,' Biere answered him. 'Horrible, soul-shattering experiences. Take the common example of lorry owners demanding exorbitant fares from refugees escaping from enemy guns. Or the crime of purchasing the same consignment of food, for the army, several times, with the result that the vote buys only a small fraction of what is needed. The boys in the trenches suffer terribly as a result. And yet, we are fighting to win! There are even worse stories. Yesterday, it was something about bank officials discounting a thousand-pound cheque for eight hundred. Do such things really exist everywhere? Tell me, gentlemen! I suggest that we need to address our minds seriously to the problem if we really wish to survive as a nation. It is no use saying we'll deal with such issues after the war; such men would have entrenched themselves so strongly by then that they rather will deal with you.'

The chairman merely called him a pessimist.

There followed an interlude of jest and laughter, partly sardonic and partly genuine, but all the same uneasy. In the end it was agreed that further discussions on the memorandum should be postponed till the next meeting.

That was to have been our valedictory address, for we had resolved not to attend any more meetings after that day's. And now, we had compromised our resolution. It was because we had allowed ourselves to be drawn into chat and laughter towards the end. We had been assuaged; the edge was gone out of our feeling. It was to the chairman's credit, whatever might be said against him. He had accommodated our ranting, without losing his temper; without even looking stern. He was an extraordinary man, combining the most admirable with the most anti-social qualities.

So, we would continue to attend their meetings. Biere said it was the wisest thing to do, if only to embarrass Anibado with our presence. We would behave like that group of rascals at the university, the gad-flies, who joined most of the societies and attended all the meetings just to voice their extraordinary views.

The venue for the coming meeting would be Beka. We would both be there.

Beka, which was some forty miles from Portcity, was a large commercial town of very robust and loud inhabitants who once, at the onset of the war, had vowed to crush the other side with their fists alone. Two or three devastating air-raids had long since made them retract, and now they were as nervous as any other town. However, since the war fronts were still a considerable distance away, they had not yet begun to move out to their village homes in large numbers. Life there was therefore described as being still normal, and the claim was reinforced when several Government departments began to move in as part of the policy of evacuating the offices in Portcity. The Plobe was one of the bodies that would evacuate to Beka.

Three Peugeot station-wagon cars, all looking brand-new, pulled in at the office the next morning, with the chairman in one of them. Dismounting, Anibado began to explain, with a smile of triumph, how he had had to preach from one room to another before he could persuade the fellows of the Transport Control Department to commandeer as many as three dependable vehicles for the Plobe. He was glad to say that the three now before us were the best available anywhere, he added with exaggeration. And the drivers were the best too. 'So!—' He failed to complete.

'You are a go-getter,' Biere's tone had an edge of sarcasm.

'I will do everything to see to the comfort of my members,' he replied, flattered.

It was midnoon as we drove out of Portcity on our way to Beka. The weather was bright. On both sides of the road was farmland. The yam vines had snaked up the props, and the straying tendrils had been gathered neatly into line. Cocoyam plants, cutting across the yam plot in rows, spread out their leaves in graceful resignation. There followed, after these, acres and acres of maize plants with their deep-green leaves which looked like sword blades. The heart thrilled to his clear promise of an abundant harvest. Then as I put my head out of the car window, a warm midnoon draught struck the face. I inhaled lustily, and a sense of revival came into me. But the feeling was short-lived. . . .

The driver halted by the side of the road, a few yards from the bridge spanning the narrow river ahead; then he looked up, to the sky; then he said he thought a war plane was in the air. How had he come to the feeling? I asked; and he advised, like an expert, that we should watch the pedestrians—watch their eyes as well as their legs.

I soon found myself hugging a tall tree in the bush, some ten feet from the river.

The jet plane came roaring, silencing men and animals. Then it began to circle, searching for the bridge. And the water went on flowing down peacefully, undisturbed by the deadly pranks above. This tiny river must have travelled hundreds of miles before reaching here, I reflected; it had traversed regions inhabited by friends and regions inhabited by foes, fertilizing the soil all along and treating its beneficiaries impartially.

'Roland, Roland!'

'Yes, Biere!' I answered him from my crouching position. 'I'm coming.'

Over fifteen minutes had passed already. Probably the plane would not return. So we set off again.

Biere began looking out of the window.

'You are certainly heeding the driver's advice, aren't you?'

'Well, yes,' he muttered. Then, like a real eccentric, he began pointing into the bush as the car speeded and the green field rolled and the trees raced.

'Patches on the field!' he cried, beaming.

'What is that?'

He pulled out a sheet of paper from his file and handed it over to me. 'How is this?'

I read:

And now the fields sprawl—ravaged, lacerated,
Where the battle has raged for days on end,
Red stains on the green leaves and patches on the ground
Urging the groans from dark mother's heart.

'The first stanza of *Patches on the Field*. I wrote it just this morning.'
'So you have, at last, begun to write?' I was jealous.

The first thing I saw when I entered our new office at Beka was a letter from Mamma. She had sent it to Owana but somebody had brought it to Beka, ahead of me, and left it on the table. I was to visit home, at once and without fail, to see what could be done about Isaac, who had just joined the army. And in a postscript, Dorothy, writing in her own hand, wondered whether the war could not be won without Isaac.

CHAPTER TWENTY-NINE

The final assault on Portcity came a few weeks later, with a pincer drive from the southern creeks and the mainland to the north. In the latter case, the invading forces successfully landed at the very base from which they had been repulsed in the first instance, then marched through to the principal road leading out from the city, thus cutting off the city from the hinterland, from where they began marching south, towards the city itself. Resolved not to fail again, they pushed on and on, in spite of the heavy resistance from the other side and losses in men on both sides. And soon, the defenders began to weaken, and with that the morale of the civilians cracked. At long last, the attackers had, as it were, succeeded in letting holes into the bowels of the town, and now the population began to pour out in tens of thousands.

The drive had been incredibly fast and the collapse equally sudden. The population moved out in a continuous, sombre stream. There were cars and lorries and push-trucks and bicycles; but most people went on foot, including men and women, boys and girls, old and young. There were mothers hugging their children to the breast, yet still moving; and there were others dragging their infants by the hand, big loads on their heads. They all moved northward, towards the hinterland towns that were outside the reach of shell-bombs and rockets. To them, nothing could be worse than the flying fire which had kept exploding into the city in the last few days, shattering some of its victims to bits.

That was the report Okay Baby brought.

I had intended to visit Umuntianu that day in response to Mamma's letter, and had told Biere so. Biere too had meant to work on his poem. That would, he said, be an infinitely better service to the nation than attending the meeting fixed for that evening. We were certainly not wanted in the committee, and our performances, in our latest role of gad-flies, had not achieved much in the way of converting the Chairman, or he us, while Sohabia and most of the rest had not moved an inch from their ostensibly neutral and safe position.

'So, why continue?'

'No point really,' I had agreed, still thinking about the last meeting in which Anibado had referred to the theatricalities, as he put it, of two good friends in the Plobe. Anibado was replying to a remark from Biere about an inner circle in the Plobe. Then he had gone on to explain, in a very sober tone, that there was no inner, or outer, circle as such, but that he had left it free to members to regulate their individual enthusiasm for the activities. It was not his intention to deprive any of his membership, but those who felt they couldn't continue were free to withdraw. Did that answer the point raised by Mr. Ekonte? Then, cutting in, I pointed out that he had evaded the issue completely. Biere accused him of merely wanting to stage-manage matters. But he was not ruffled. He proceeded to read out his plans for setting up local units of the Plobe. . . .

So, after that meeting we resolved not to attend any future meetings.

Yet, today Okay Baby was making us change our minds once again!

Okay Baby's stories about people moving out of Portcity had been very touching. The situation was to be discussed by the Plobe. It was

226

necessary that both of us, and everybody, should attend, he went on to plead. And then, answering our objections, he made the most revealing remark. After all, nearly every one in the Plobe, including possibly the chairman, knew that we were right, he said; but everybody was fearing for his neck: nobody wanted the security men around. ... And besides, we were not attending to please the chairman; it was in the interest of the suffering who had had to abandon in a hurry what had been their homes for years and years. We submitted to his entreaties in the end.

The meeting was brief, or rather it was hardly a meeting as such. Okay Baby made a moving plea, and the chairman gave his assent: every member should go out and see the fleeing men, and do something to encourage them. It would not be fair to leave the task to one man alone just because the man had the misfortune to be in charge of refugees. We saw the point. We set out shortly after.

Some eight miles away, the road was almost full with the first batch of people who had left Portcity, mostly on foot. Cars and lorries had begun arriving in large numbers, collecting some of the travellers and their belongings. There was some order about it all, and some genuine sense of service.

'See that one!' Biere pointed at a moving car every part of which had now been converted into a carriage, with cartons and boxes protruding here and there, like a festoon, and not less than ten heads inside.

Our driver was skilful enough, meandering into the least space available. His patience, too, was admirable, only that he impaired it now by hooting his horn at the car in front of him. And the stream of pedestrians continued to move.

'Biere, this is an experience,' I said.

'Yes.' He spoke absently, then exclaimed: *The Trek.*

'What's that?' And I got the reply: it would be the next theme, a new movement, of his poems. Then he talked about other things, as if he was afraid I would ruin the inspiration for him by discussing the subject.

Two miles farther down, an immense crowd was gathered in the premises of a small school by the roadside.

'What's happening?' I wondered.

'Driver, halt and let's see,' Biere said.

Hundreds and hundreds of travellers had camped on the premises, under a good cover of tall gmelina trees. They had spread their mats and made fires and were now boiling yams or any other thing they had to boil. But not all of them: some lay tired and worn out, hoping for a ration from those that had, which they invariably got.

'Sir, let's collect these ones on the right and go back,' the driver suggested.

'Why? Don't you want us to go farther down?' Biere objected.

'Not that, sir,' he replied politely, smiling with guilt. 'They have no food to eat.'

'How do you know? Why don't you say you are afraid of an ambush?'

'True, sir!' he confessed. 'Nobody wants to die,' he philosophized.

'Let's move down a bit further.'

Another mile. The road was a bit clearer here, the main stream having moved ahead. But there was a small crowd by the side of the road, all of whom wore a mournful look.

The car pulled up at the opposite side. Then, from habit, the driver fetched some twigs with which to cover the chromium parts.

'What's that you're doing? Camouflaging?' someone demanded, fiercely, and added, without waiting for a reply: 'You are afraid of death. Why don't you deck everybody here?'

It was difficult to understand him, and we simply remained quiet. But the driver retorted:

'The forest is free; you can mask yourself from head to foot with the twigs if you like.'

'You big men are more interested in your cars than in us,' he accused, making himself clear at last. 'And yet it's you who caused this war for which we poor people are suffering.'

The driver seemed to have taken this last one in good part. 'Is anything wrong?' he asked.

'Everything, if you want to know,' he said, his tone low and sad. 'Go over there and you will see them burying a child.' He moved away.

The crowd was beginning to disperse. The shallow grave had been covered with a mound of earth less than four feet long, with two sticks tied in the form of a crucifix at one end. The mother still stood by, however, gazing closely at the earth that concealed the remains of her child. Then she crossed herself, and heaved, as if she had just emerged from a trance.

'Hei! He is gone. . . . Adieze is gone!' she wailed.

We followed behind her, to a nearby tree where her surviving son and daughter were waiting under the shade.

'Hunger—that was what took him,' she wailed. 'Nothing else!' The tears streamed down and she sobbed, from the depth of her being. Throwing herself down on the ground, she cried and cried, and then she converted her sorrow into a song: 'I have not seen their father. He went by a different route when we were leaving. I cannot see my own father or mother. They did not come out when Alara was captured. Who is there now to help?'

'Mamma, I am hungry!' whined the child by her right. And the crowd, having helped her to bury the dead, shouted their commiserations and continued to move.

We had nearly persuaded her to follow us to Beka with her surviving children. Then, a nun who happened to be passing, pulled up and made a similar offer; which she accepted instead.

Mamma pronounced, on hearing the story, that the white-robed nun was an angel of God in disguise. She shook her head in affirmation; then repeated the statement. Dora began to laugh.

'What is amusing this one?' she objected.

'Mamma, there are too many angels around these days,' Dora tried to tease. 'Yesterday, it was Alex and Sarah. And the day before, it was the priest who gave you a whole cup of salt.'

'And there is no mention of me, why?' I said. 'Mamma, am I not an angel too? And Biere also.'

She said nothing, as if she was still tabulating our scores in her mind.

'We did as many as six trips, conveying the refugees into Beka, and we provided the petrol ourselves and we bought food for some others.'

'Pharisee!' she laughed. 'You have money and all; the nun hasn't.' Then she changed: 'You may be one after all, my son. All my children are good; they are like their father and mother who bore them.'

'Good,' I prompted.

'Even Alex! He is now a most worthy son,' she continued. 'How could I have been managing for salt without him; or without Sarah, his wife? She's changed a lot—Sarah has, and for good. . . . Take your time, don't break the needle!'

Dora winced.

All this time, Dora was busy mending her Red Cross gown while Mamma sat behind her to ensure she did not turn the machine handle with uneven force.

'Mamma, Dom and Louis too are good,' Dora said soon after.

'Has your mother seen either of them for months?'

'Dom is working at Beka; I saw him with my own eyes,' I said.

'What about Louis? Is he working too?'

'I didn't see him.'

'You didn't . . . They say he's wanting to go and fight.'

'Let him, if it is true,' I rejoined. 'After all, you all agreed we should fight, though nobody appears to want his own child to do the fighting.'

In a very swift and very complicated mental process, she snapped at me: 'Don't you think you are old enough to have your own son too?'

Turning round, Dora stared at her with a smile of censure, then said with compassion:

'Rola, were there no Red Cross workers to help the people running away from Portcity?'

'Plenty of them,' I replied.

'They should have helped them.'

'Some did, but many others helped themselves rather—by running away.'

'That is not good,' she declared. 'We are taught to help others first.'

'That's exactly what you would have done, and then you would have got yourself killed,' Mamma said to her with a scowl.

'Mamma, what about Edoha and Ogidi?' I enquired.

'Edoha? I hardly see him. He has now built a temporary house at home but is hardly ever there to receive visitors; rather he goes from house to house complaining about what the war has done to him. Ogidi is the one who comes from time to time.'

'Rola, he is annoyed with you,' Dora cut in.

'Who?'

'Ogidi. With you and Alex.'

'What have we done?'

Mamma replied: 'He says that you asked Isaac to go and fight while Alex did nothing to prevent Isaac from going.'

'Oh, I see!' I said.

'It doesn't prevent him from playing on his calabash though.'

'The right persons to get annoyed with would be those who caused the war. In any case, I never discussed any such thing with Isaac and didn't know, until you wrote, about his joining the army.'

'Who else caused the war but those who massacred our people and are now coming down to massacre us too?' Dora recited, almost singing.

'Parrot!' Mamma remonstrated.

'It's what we learnt yesterday.'

'Where?' I asked.

'In the Red Cross. I hear it's you people of the Plobe who wrote it.'

'Most interesting.'

'I have it in my note-book. Shall I go and bring it?'

'Quickly.'

She rose from the floor with some effort. She had been growing fat of late in spite of the war—thanks to the special ration of stockfish and rice, and corn-meal, which the Red Cross provided for its workers.

The notebook contained little more than she had already recited.

Alex and Sarah, plus their two youngest children, came in a little after. Mamma called Alex's arrival the work of God. She would want to talk to me seriously in my elder brother's presence. I told her I was at her mercy. It was already evening, in any case, and I had decided to stay at Umuntianu for the night. Then she disclosed she was preparing some special meal for the two of us. And she was sending word to Anene, the wine-tapper, to send her a jar with which she would entertain her children.

Anene not only sent the wine across shortly after, he sent it free. He was only too glad to do that for the late friend's wife and children.

231

And that was not all. The wine had a tingling, sweet and bitter essence. As Mamma played host, in a noisy way, to the restless grandchildren, and Sarah and Dora cooked supper, Alex and I sat in the frontyard, drinking. Alex was well on his guard. I was not.

At last, Mamma managed to send the children over to Sarah, and came and sat with us.

'Let us discuss the matter now, before the two of you get totally drunk,' she said.

'Which matter?' Alex asked.

'Two of them in fact.' She then named them. One was Isaac, the other marriage.

She lost readily on the first. If the war had to be won, then it was people's children who must do the fighting, we pointed out. And although Isaac was just one person, in the same way every other soldier was just one person. I went on to remind her that it wasn't everybody fighting in the war that would lose his life, or even be wounded. She sighed with defeat, yielding ground so readily in order to proceed to her next point.

'Had you a child of your own, you would have been able to appreciate what I'm saying,' she said.

'But Alex has,' I refuted.

'None of Isaac's age.'

'I see!' and I stifled a yawn. 'That too is an offence, is it?'

'You cannot put me off with questions today, Roland my son.'

I filled another glass. But before I could lift it, Dora came and carried it away, for her personal use.

'Please, Alex, help your mother to talk to your younger brother,' Mamma spoke again. 'Talk to him before he disappears again.'

'What's the name of the girl?' I asked.

'If it has come to that, give me just a week,' she declared with mock exhilaration, and drew nearer. 'I should be able to find you a good girl from a good home. Say something, Alex.'

'What?' Alex laughed. 'I think he's told you he now wants to marry, hasn't he?'

'He has!' She sounded both sarcastic and offended.

'We will now begin to look for somebody.'

232

She opened her mouth, as if she was going to name a bride. Then, she closed it again.

'Marriage, marriage, marriage; every time!' I protested.

'Why not? You are nearly thirty now, don't forget,' she persisted.

I hiccupped. 'Even more, to be exact.'

She shrugged her shoulders. 'God forbid that I should allow my son to drift.'

'Who is drifting, Mamma?'

'You are—Roland, you!' she called, aloud. 'You and your friend Biere, headmaster's son.' She took a deep breath. 'Look at your head—it's like a wild forest. And look at your jaws!'

'I like it so.' I patted the hair and stroked the beard, with tenderness.

'You look like Pontius Pilate.'

How it came about that she thought Pilate had looked diabolical I could not guess. My reaction was to laugh just as Alex did; and to fill yet another glass.

She left us and returned to Sarah and Dora and the children.

I had begun to see through a haze. It was not because of the descending darkness of night; the drink had settled in and was now demolishing my brain and wrecking my nerves. I rose. I staggered to the right; then to the left. Finally, I went into the bedroom.

I flung myself heavily into the bed, and cried out lustily, and exhaled, freeing my respiratory system from the choking pressure of alcohol. . . .

Voices and voices, and voices still! Shrill, piercing. Yet there were only three persons involved. Chioma was arguing with Pius while Sarah, their mother, shouted fruitless orders.

'Chioma and Pius, please let us rest!'

'Small Mamma, go and sleep now.'

Even on the brink of sleep, I forced myself to laugh. With that, the headache returned, the reverberations reaching down to my eyelids this time.

'Sarah, have you some tablets for headache?' I called from the room.

She consulted with Alex, then announced she had some. But Mamma reminded me that there was yet another cup. I asked her to drink it herself.

'Mamma, I'll take the medicine to him,' Chioma said.

'No, I'll take it,' Pius whined. 'I'll take the medicine to Isaac's Papa....'

I knew when the children came, one with the medicine and the other carrying a cup of water. I was still conscious too when I drank the tablets down. Then the headache came in a fierce thrust, meaning, as it seemed, to overpower the tablets.

'Is he about to die?'

'Tah!' Chioma struck him, gently, and called him a thief.

A scuffle ensued. . . .

Came dawn. It was bright. The birds were calling, and a cool, healing breeze was blowing. I threw my limbs well apart, indecorously, in full relaxation. The drunkenness had worn away considerably, but there was this tedium which seemed pleasurable, and the nausea which I detested. And remorse too, except it had its counter-dose: the atmosphere was homely and relaxed and forgiving, with no sound of guns and rockets and fear of raids.

Voices and voices! It was the two children again. They were most entertaining this morning.

'Now, tell me, two plus twelve?'

'And you tell me, four plus four?'

'Four plus four. . . . Eight.'

'All right, you tell me now, nought plus nought?'

Chioma gave the correct answer but Pius insisted, with some logic, that it was two. They broke into my room for arbitration.

But they soon forgot what it was they had come for and began asking about practically everything that crossed their minds. And then, they invented a crawling game in which they crossed from one side of the bed to the other, with me as a centre barrier which must be scaled. Suddenly, I reached out my hands and caught the two of them together, and they laughed. I hugged them to my chest and they talked and talked, asking very many questions to which I replied in very few words. Their company thrilled me; and in the contact with their bodies, a current passed through my soul. Was this part of the joys of parenthood? Blissful—that was the word. But mark you, it did not come automatically with marriage. It depended on many other things, including whether you had the patience to keep the matrimonial vow for so long, until the children began to arrive. . . .

The mere thought was frightening. Roland Medo would be saddled with a woman for all that long! But others had done it, and some had succeeded. I would try, but God help her if she was the wrong type—loud, garrulous, lazy, and so on. I would rotate her round; then, a kick in the back; after which I would urge her to go straight to court. I would plead before the learned Judge that I simply couldn't manage her; and I would even suggest to him that he take over and marry her, if he should fail to agree with me.

What then were the specifications? Tall, elegant; smiling, winsome; decidedly beautiful. I could not compromise on any of these. Gentle in manners, sober, simple in taste, equable in disposition. They say all such prescriptions go to the winds when it comes to actual execution, like the plot of a novel before it is written. Not for me!—there would be no compromise. Now then, to the possibilities, the magnets. They were few. Ruth would have been fine. She had the looks, the bearing, and the manners. Never mind that the disaster called Lobe lured her away the way he did, only to start something most unfair, to her and me, about the paternity of her children. She certainly would have been happy to cross over, but I had stated before her, point-blank, that the thing she did with Lobe was marriage and that the man Lobe was very much alive. She was therefore completely out. . . . Maria? She too had the looks, and the femininity. But she was out! Or wasn't she? Think of the ringed neck and the luxuriant lips, big bluish eyes, delicate smile, her strength of will. Put it this way: not entirely out. . . .
Her sister? She was definitely eligible, this one. I could still see her, right before my mind's eyes: fresh, probably unadulterated; erect, dark-skinned, well-spoken. Could I discover her again? . . . But her temper! That could disappoint; she was irritable, from what I had seen of her. It was perhaps youth, nothing else. Consider more her clearly positive qualities. Her teeth were pure white, noticeably, which could, conceivably, be a reflection of her inner soul—the outward sign of her inward purity. Louisa was her name—I overheard her mother calling her on that day. Louisa sounds musical.

Where could one trace Louisa? The refugees in that camp must have moved several times since Oban fell. She at least must have moved farther down, into the heart of the country. Girls of her type usually did, so as to avoid any possible encounters with soldiers, on both sides,

235

who often won their brides with their guns. It was the same pattern all through the ages—soldiers of classical mythology won theirs at the point of the spear.

I wonder how she would be looking now, with all the things that went with the war. Probably emaciated, because of the privations, unless she was of the type that annexed themselves to men of influence. Who did not know that such things were happening in the land? I think I'm getting morbid. She doesn't look the type: her countenance was harsh and repulsive, suggesting strong determination—virginal austerity. Louisa Medo! That sounds well enough. But where are you? I will find out sooner or later. I'll find you out.

This thought had persisted for long. Perhaps that was how the more promising marriages were conceived. It would be in order if I mentioned it to Biere at this stage. Biere had promised to visit Umuntianu today, in the interest of his nerves. He would be arriving in a few hours' time. There were two things I had already listed in my mind for our discussion. One was his poems; the other, our final decision about Doctor Anibado's Plobe. Louisa would be the third.

'Rola, Rola!' Dorothy chimed.

'Dora, Dora!' Chioma retaliated on my behalf, while Pius barred the door to her with his very short hands.

'Rola, there's warm water for your bath.' As she was going away, the two ran after her demanding something for their mouths.

The clock by the bedside showed it was after eight o'clock. Two hours from now, Biere should be in the house, I told myself, yawning and smiling simultaneously.

CHAPTER THIRTY

I waited and waited.

The story reached me days later. Security men had arrived early in the morning and found him busy writing. They asked what it was all about and he replied in just two words: 'Some rubbish.' Then they gathered all the papers on the table, which threw him into a fit, which was understandable for his soul was in those sheets. But they told him that was only by the way; they were taking him away too: they would provide safe accommodation for him. 'Safe for the State, of course,' added one of the three. Biere would not resist either by word or action, but merely protested his loyalty to the State. They told him that was not the point. What then was? They drew his attention to the police Land-Rover waiting outside with a few armed men at the back.

The offence Biere was accused of could have been summarized as impairing the public zeal, and the informant, the principal accuser, was no other than Doctor Akunna Anibado.

And why had they left me out? Perhaps, I thought, because the route I plied had, until of late, been a popular one: I began to stray from the time Biere and I converged, when we discovered what Imperator and Anibado had in common. More likely, it was a deliberate plan to separate us and leave Biere companionless while they washed my brain. They would fail. It could be they had worse things than mere detention in store for me: they were letting me loose with the intention of taking me unawares and unsuspecting. Anibado could not have forgotten those forceful jabs from left and right which I delivered on behalf of Biere and myself. I believe the thing had penetrated his thick hide; and now, he would be wanting to get his own back. Anibado could start building up public anger against me, until, one day, a mob would rise and call me names, and strike at me, and finally tear me up, shouting 'Traitor!' Biere could in that case be considered fortunate. The Security men were keeping him away from any mob, probably in a prison cell. But for how long? Shouldn't I go to look for him?

Mamma ordered that I should stay quietly in Umuntianu, at least for some time. She did not expect anybody to come to unknown Umuntianu to look for me, provided I didn't attract their attention.

But she came to realize, only a few days later, that the Security men were very thorough indeed; that they knew Umuntianu almost as well as they did Beka. Four of them arrived in a Land-Rover.

'You are Mr. Medo?' asked the hefty, middle-aged one, the butt of a revolver projecting from his pocket.

'Which one? There are several of them,' I dodged.

'Roland Medo.' He added mercilessly: 'The bearded one.'

'Rola, who's that?' Mamma asked from the house.

'Visitors,' I simply told her, and then to the hefty one: 'Yes, I am.'

'What do they want?' she asked with some trepidation.

'It is all right now,' declared a small lean one among the four.

She had already arrived at the scene. 'What do you say is all right? And who are you?' she demanded, with a look of aggression, like a pullet guarding her chicks.

They were human enough. 'Mamma, nothing is wrong,' the lean one said. 'We only want to have a talk with your son,' the hefty one said. Another announced that they were in a bit of a hurry, and asked the driver to start the vehicle.

The tears had begun to flow from her eyes even before we boarded the vehicle.

'You and your friend Biere are such terrible hotheads, why?' the lean one asked.

The hefty one ordered the driver to go straight to Beka.

Their tone was by no means hostile, I thought; they were not so bad after all. They even seemed sympathetic, especially the hefty one who kept asking questions about the family—whether Mamma had me alone, and whether I was her favourite child, and so on. And then, he commented about the tears in Mamma's eyes. That, said he, had reminded him about the day he lost his first son, during the war that was still on, especially how tears had streamed down the boy's mother's eyes for hours on end. I looked at him with some compassion, while the others tried, mercifully, to change the topic. The Land-Rover rattled and bumped.

The office at Beka was sparsely furnished. There was an old wooden table, with drawers, and four chairs in all. There was at one corner a school writing desk, one of the many taken over from the nearby schools, which had long ceased to function. A police clerk was writing at the desk when I was marched in by another armed policeman. The two of them conferred. They were lucky that the superintendent came in when he did, for I had decided not to say a word in reply if they asked a question.

The superintendent had a file in his hand and a baton under his armpit; and three others of varying ranks followed behind him. He looked confused, or even baffled, scratching his head and biting his lips until eventually he sat down.

'Yes?' He looked up at me.

The others turned, looking at me also.

'Who is this man?' he asked with a frown.

The man behind the pupil's desk replied on my behalf.

'Oh, you are Roland Medo? I see.' He shook his big, balding head, importantly. 'You know why you have been brought here, don't you?'

I shook my own head.

I expected he would storm at me for my arrogance and all, which would have been an opportunity for me to tell him a few things I knew about police methods. But he did not. Instead, he adjusted in his seat and held up his hand, the fingers interlocked, poring into the page of the file open before him.

'I don't think I'll spend much time with you,' he said, his eyes still on the page, as if he was reading out a prepared speech. 'We just want to caution you.' Then, the man was transformed into a monster. A paroxysm of power had gripped him, and he seemed to have expanded to double his size; he sounded shrill and insufferable. His face was as taut as a bow string. 'You are known—you, Roland Medo, and your friend whom we don't want to mention here—you are known to have been making utterances which are bound to weaken morale. I warn you now, you must put a stop to them. Any more of it—' He pointed through a window into the air. 'You won't come here; you will go somewhere else.'

Not a word came from me.

'You must sign an undertaking.' He pressed the table bell.

And the man at the desk answered and saluted.

'What about the statement—have you got it typed?'

'Yes, sir!' He opened the locker and took out yet another file.

'May I now say a word, Superintendent?' I spoke at last.

'Yes?'

'What all this is about I cannot understand,' I said, choosing the words with care.

'You will sign first before we can begin to answer your logic,' the clerk answered.

I was peeved. I waved him aside, frowning.

'Superintendent, sir, I am not clear,' I said.

He stroked his shining, barren forehead, and laughed genially. At last, he had reverted to the status of a human, a fatherly one. 'Please sign, Mr. Medo,' he said. 'In your own interest.'

'Must I?'

He rose now and picked up his baton and his file. 'Make sure he signs before he goes away,' he ordered his subordinates. 'And before I leave, let me warn you again: you will get into very serious trouble next time.' He inserted the baton in his armpit.

I opened my mouth to reply, but he was already on his way out. One of the others beckoned at me and held a finger before his sealed lips.

'What?' I bawled, ungratefully.

'This war!' another exclaimed meaningfully, shaking his head. The wall clock was striking. I could not tell which hour, but it was well after midnoon, and we had left Umuntianu before breakfast time. I signed over the thickly-dotted line, then dated the document. The summary was that I should refrain from making any further utterances of the nature we had been used to of late. Was I really going to obey it? I should have refused to sign. I was both confused and angry.

Outside the building, I stood still for some time. I felt dazed, depleted, defeated; uprooted, abandoned, shattered.

Where was Biere, please?

There were subdued murmurs—hardly any more than that, mostly from young men, and men of the working classes, who had jammed Beka from other towns that had fallen into the invaders' hands. 'But you and Ekonte were saying the right things. ... Ekonte! He is a martyr. ... We like the things they were saying. ... That Anibado is not a good man. ...' And such other things. They were most annoying. 'Awful cowards!' I would retort. 'Why don't you have the courage of your convictions? ... Who wants your inarticulate compliments? ... You are after your salaries, and so you cling to your posts at any cost. ... You grumble in the dark and grovel in the day. ...'

'Medo, Medo!' Agaro hailed me one morning. His tone could not have been anything but ironical.

'Yes?'

'Nobody hears your voice these days,' he said with a malignant grin.

'Do you want to hear it?' I stung at him, forgetting the written undertaking to the police: 'Take it now: You are free to collect somebody's ten per cent in addition to your customary two-and-a-half. It doesn't matter that we are losing our boys by the thousands each month.'

He looked clearly nettled. Everybody knew what he had been doing as a Government Works Inspector, but the local contractors knew best. He called me blighter and bastard and other names and went on to threaten I would go the way of my friend. I requested, seriously, that he should show me if he knew the way.

It was time I removed this hair, and the beard too. The cause was lost. Or rather, it was lost only for a while. The hair would come up again in a fresh crop with the revival of the cause.

It had become a big weight on my head. I felt most uncomfortable, the way I had not done before. I could no longer bear the heat from the black and hard and kinky and oily growth, a bad conductor. What I had on my head was a woollen cap the tiny threads of whose fabric seemed to pierce through into my brain.

Or rather, I would mow the hair down as soon as I had found Biere. I would continue to search for him: no time to spare for the moment. Biere first. The hair could wait.

I enquired in nearly all the probable places, starting from the prisons around Beka. Some of the authorities were difficult to approach, but most were sympathetic. And everyone was on his guard. They were all afraid of the Security men, who had ears all over the land. You could not blame them really; it had to do with daily bread. Then, at last, I got a clue, from the very police station where I was recently cautioned and made to sign that I would keep my mouth shut. A police officer, Security Branch, asked whether I had tried the new detainees' camp at Odida, midway between Siaku and Umuntianu. I told him I hadn't. Glancing right and left, he muttered I should.

Now I was on my way to Odida. The sun was shining fiercely and my throat was dry. A long stretch of road still lay ahead. This was the same road Biere and I had used years back. But then it was narrow and winding, almost a footpath; now, thanks to the oil company, it was broad and had a hard, tarmac surface.

I went on foot. I had long ceased to have a car—in fact, from the moment I left Beka for Umuntianu and things began to happen. I would not use a bicycle either: what was the point taking one when you had to ascend and descend all the time? It would mean wheeling the bicycle most of the way. So I had decided to go on foot.

There were some four miles still to go. I was now at the middle of a long ascent which would terminate after another two miles. Maybe he was there! Would I see you alive and well, Biere Ekonte? And then I began to rehearse for the reception. 'Biere, did you know it would come to this? . . . When will they let you free? . . . Biere, how will it all end? . . .'

Suddenly, people began pouring into the road, from all directions.

'Has anything gone wrong?' I asked.

'Everything!' one of them gasped. 'The enemy is less than six miles away. I don't know what our own soldiers are doing!' he added with irrational bitterness.

The situation became very tense in a matter of minutes. The invaders had set out on a march which would cut off that fertile belt and eventually bring them into the very heart of what was now left of Bokenu, virtually ending our self-proclaimed independent state. Hardly firing a gun, they moved on with very little opposition. Some reports added that they treated the people of the areas through which they passed with extreme kindness, which made their passage all the more easy. However, very many of the inhabitants discountenanced the stories, while others held it was a trick to lure them into their doom. One day, perhaps, their soldiers would assemble everybody for a real carnage. Had not such a thing happened before in some places? It was people with such fears who were now flocking into the roads and escaping south.

The fleeing men also told stories about preparations for a confrontation by our side. Siaku would be the meeting-point and the troops had begun to assemble there. They had had the story from the officers themselves. 'True?' I exclaimed, and swallowed. I was anxious about

Uncle Ogidi. And then, a shell landed, right there in Siaku. After that, a plane began to roar. We took cover in the bush.

I proceeded from the bush straight to Ogidi's house.

He was playing on the calabash bowl when I arrived.

'What are you doing, Ogidi?' I asked in reproach.

'Old-with-beard, welcome,' came his reply, and he resumed playing, one leg over the other, his face expressionless.

'Why don't you move out of here?'

'Move out? Where to, my sister Rebecca's son?' he asked, to the rhythm of the music. 'Move to death or to life? How many days has your mother's elder brother in this world?'

'So you won't move?'

'No, my son; I'll stay in my house—stay and die where my spirit is.'
The prongs exploded into a maze of notes, sad and solemn and sustained. In the end, he slapped the bowl with his palm and he sighed in resignation.

'And what about you? What are you here for?' he now asked.

'On my way to Odida. I called to see you,' I informed him.

'You've done well, my son. But this Odida, what for?'

'Looking for somebody.'

'You? A woman to marry I hope,' he guessed.

'A man rather. And a friend.'

'Who?'

'Biere, with whom I visited you more than once.'

'I know him well. Is he in the army?'

'Not that; he was removed by the police and nobody has seen him again.'

He looked me over, from head to foot. 'You have a good heart, my son,' he remarked. 'The police at Odida?'

'Not that; I am just going to enquire whether they took him to Odida.'

'But you can't get there now, can you? Unless you went right round, avoiding the land between here and the first houses there; and even then, it would be very risky.'

'I would still try.' I rubbed my palm over the eyes in an effort to clear the haze.

'No word about Isaac? He didn't write to you?'

'No; they don't write,' I told him.

He resumed playing on the calabash. 'Dora called this morning.'

'Yes?'

'She said they are doing Red Cross.'

The road was an obscure, winding, foot-beaten track. I had done only a mile or less.

'Halt! Hands up! Who are you!'

Chills ran through my spine. I obeyed the order all the same.

The lieutenant who was commanding the company lying in ambush came up, looking fiercely into my face.

'Ah!' He hissed, flicking his fingers in disappointment, and his countenance thawed. He was looking like a human now, but for his attire.

'Good afternoon!' I dared.

'Afternoon, sir.' He smiled.

'I know you, don't I?'

He shook his head in affirmation. 'You were our Latin master in Umane School.'

'Name again?' I asked, and took in his ruffled but handsome form from head to foot. He must have been twenty years old, or less.

'Julius Ejide,' he said.

'Oh, yes; alias J—Ejid.'

He laughed. 'We didn't know the tutors took notice of such things.'

'We did. Julius, what's happening?' I asked him.

'About the war?'

'Yes, about it, and over this sector.'

'They've been advancing at a meteoric speed, but we are determined to wedge them there.'

'Your usual expression! Soon the wedge will be crushed!'

'No, sir!' Julius promised. 'The battalion is determined. My own company is based around here; that's why we decided that civilians should move out. When we are dug in, then we'll attack.'

'Good.'

'What about you?'

'How, Julius?'

'I mean, where are you going to?'

244

'Oh, I thought you meant some other thing. I am trying to get to Odida to see somebody.'

'Odida, through this way?'

He was beginning to sound suspicious. It was necessary to disabuse his mind. 'Through a bush path,' I said to him. 'This is my mother's town. We came here a lot when we were small and I know practically every footpath.'

'You are the man we need then. You will help to show us all the possible approaches.'

'You are so sure that I won't be a security risk, are you?'

'Sort of enemy agent? No, sir,' he said with candour, shaking his head. 'I know you well.'

'But that would be after I had gone to Odida and returned successfully,' I proposed.

He began to reply, then halted suddenly. 'Take cover! Quick!'

I dived behind a tree.

The plane was already directly overhead, pumping bullets and firing cannons all over the place. Some soldiers died while many were wounded. With compassion and efficiency, the colleagues began removing them to the casualty collection point on the rear. Still ahead, on the left flank, a fusillade started which was to cost each side hundreds of lives.

'You'd better hurry away and forget all about your trip to Odida,' the lieutenant advised. 'Or better still, you could help us to collect the dead and wounded. Look at that one there!' He pointed at a body still lying unremoved close by. 'They haven't picked him up yet.'

I went closer ... My heart was shrinking. 'My God! ... My God! Lieutenant, I know this one.'

'Yes?' He too came nearer.

'He is of my own blood.' I touched the body. It was cold. I lifted the arms. They were limp. The bullet had pierced through his heart. Isaac seemed to smile even in death.

'Isaac!' The lieutenant himself exclaimed. 'Pity indeed. He was one of the best in this company. May his soul rest in peace.'

I did not know when the Red Cross arrived at the scene. The casualties had been very many, it was said; it was therefore necessary for them to move down to the spot. And now they were scattered all over the bush, picking up dead bodies.

Then a Catholic priest came along.

'Officer, do you mind, I would like to administer the last sacrament to some of the wounded.'

'Go ahead, Father,' the lieutenant gave his consent, though adding that he personally did not believe in anything called sacrament.

He was just bending down to attend to the first, a heavily-built lad whose genitals the bullets had grazed. The plane came roaring across; then a second. We saw them bank. . . .

They got the lieutenant. They got the priest too. Terrible! . . .

And who was that? It had pierced her, side to side, as she was dashing—dashing towards me. Did I not hear her call my name? . . . Oh God! Dora! . . . Dorothy! . . .

And it got me too! Right on the forearm. The pain seared the heart. The earth was rotating. Everywhere was buzzing.

A shell bomb fell into the confusion, taking its own toll. But not me!

'You are lucky, man,' Doctor Nelo said. We had been contemporaries and sort of friends at the university.

'Yes?' I grunted, blankly.

'Indeed, and in every respect. No bone—just the tissue. And that in the left arm.'

'The irony of it all, Doctor Nelo!' I exclaimed. 'Those children mown down to death. And the priest!'

'Yes, we've seen the bodies in the mortuary.'

'Including the Red Cross girl?'

'Dorothy? I know her well. She worked with me for some days.'

'She's my sister.'

'Yes? Pity indeed! Are you Roland?'

'Roland Medo.'

'It didn't occur to me! She was always talking about you. Pity indeed.'

He wrote the prescriptions. And then he said to me: 'Injections and dressing and two or three days' hospitalisation, after which you should be able to go home. It is a pity about Dorothy.'

246

The nurse gave me a bed. She also gave me some tablets to drink down. In the awareness that I would continue to live, the mental pain, the chagrin of my all-round defeat, came back in an overpowering intensity. The infidel! I must concede your victory. You may even beat a drum; you no longer need to hide.

The tablet had begun to work. I had crossed over to the region of sleep, and dream, in so short a time.

'—Look at Anibado. What are you doing here?'

'Just finished my book. Very nice title: *The Wind Pacified.*'

'Very fitting. But mark my word; only pacified. A new phase will soon begin.'

'You think so?'

'Why not?' I point into his face. 'There will be no peace until you and your type, the infidels, have been run down.'

'What is our type?'

'Robbers and cheats; and latterly murderers too. You've been murdering our lads, and today you took Isaac; and Dorothy too.' I wail. 'The old woman once said that life resumes after a storm. When life resumes you will pay for your misdeeds.'

'You and your friend, Biere! You preach a gospel without followers. Tell me, who are your disciples? You don't even have any slogan. You are lucky you are still alive to talk all the rot. Left to me, you and that fellow Biere would have faced the firing squad.'

'But what is our offence?'

'Weakening the nation's morale in such a grave war.'

'What war? Look, all this shooting is now meaningless. What do we fight for again? To install men of your type?'

'Idiot!'

'You are in a mood for name-calling today? Murderer!'

He laughs. 'You know what amuses me?'

'Villain, tell me.'

'You remind me of two children I saw this morning.'

'And you killed them?'

He goes on: 'They were fighting and one held the other down on the ground, knee over belly and hand on the neck, and the one on the ground went on shouting: "If I get up it will be terrible for you!" '

'Have you finished?'

247

'Yes.'

'Villain! If I get up it will be terrible for you.'

'And when do you get up?' he laughs.

'When we begin to revolve, I will be up and you will be down, and I will be crushing an infidel's neck.'

I was awake once more. I was no longer thinking about Anibado; it was now the priest. His image floated before my eyes—the serene look, even in death, the resigned, forgiving attitude; the blood patches on his chest. He was a young man, perhaps my age. And an Englishman. Father Leo had been born in London, then reared in Liverpool. That morning, he had spent hours distributing salt and medicine to his fleeing parishioners; and then, when it was noon, he volunteered to go to the front to attend to the dying. So much was loaded into that brief account. Indeed one could expand it into a book. I could perhaps do it myself. Yes, I would try to fathom his inner self, tear open his heart and explore the nature of his calling, leading to the last and supreme act of his self-immolation. I could make it a fiction, changing the scenes and characters out of recognition and using a brisk and unsophisticated title. And Dorothy would have an important place in the story.

'Are you Mr. Medo?' asked a big female nurse in a low, secretive voice, tapping at the bed-head.

'Yes.'

'There's a note for you from a patient in the Security ward over there.'

'Is it Biere?' I shivered.

'I don't know.' She had delivered the note hurriedly to avoid notice.

Biere had been in the hospital for the past ten days, suffering from hypertension. It was Doctor Nelo who had just informed him I too was there.